UNDERCOVER

UNDERCOVER

A novel of a life

Keith Bulfin

KEITH BULFIN

BANTAM
SYDNEY AUCKLAND TORONTO NEW YORK LONDON

A Bantam book
Published by Random House Australia Pty Ltd
Level 3, 100 Pacific Highway, North Sydney NSW 2060
www.randomhouse.com.au

First published by Bantam in 2010

Addresses for companies within the Random House Group can be found at
www.randomhouse.com.au/offices

National Library of Australia
Cataloguing-in-Publication Entry

    Bulfin, Keith.
    Undercover.

    ISBN: 978 1 74166 950 3 (pbk.)

Cover photograph by Getty Images
Cover design by Adam Yazxhi/MAXCO
Internal design and typesetting by Midland Typesetters, Australia
Printed in Australia by Griffin Press, an accredited ISO AS/NZS 14001:2004
Environmental Management System printer

10 9 8 7 6 5 4 3 2 1

FSC
www.fsc.org
MIX
Paper from
responsible sources
FSC™ C009448

The paper this book is printed on is certified against the Forest
Stewardship Council® Standards. Griffin Press holds FSC chain
of custody certification SGS-COC-005088. FSC promotes
environmentally responsible, socially beneficial and economically
viable management of the world's forests

¿Se puede confiar en él? (Can he be trusted?)

Sí, se puede. (Yes, he can.)

Contents

Prologue

Mexico City

The curtains of my hotel room are drawn against the cloying warmth of this stultifying afternoon. The air-conditioning unit is on high, blasting cold air, but still my shirt is stained with telltale signs of perspiration. To try and calm my shattered nerves I take long, slow breaths, and fixate on the noiseless change of time on the electronic clock: 11.14, 12.10, 1.47, 1.59. I pace the room, ignoring Al as I talk quietly to myself. Steady, mate. Take it easy. Long, slow breaths.

The phone rings at precisely 2 pm. I look at the illuminated numbers on the bedside clock and shoot a nervous glance at Al before picking up the receiver with a shaky hand. 'Hello? Keith Wilson here.'

Miguel Díaz does not offer me a return greeting. 'My clients will be at the El Grande Hotel in half an hour,' he says, with reptilian coldness. 'They've got the cash: ten million. Come immediately.' Before I can reply, he hangs up.

Al, a giant of a man standing over two metres tall, with wide square shoulders and coal-dark eyes, leans in towards me from his chair on the other side of the room. 'Well? What's the plan?' His voice, heavily inflected with his native Colombian, has a casual tone, at odds with the occasion. He unnerves me. 'What's going down, Keith?'

I force myself to sound upbeat, though in truth I am shit-scared, my mouth parched and heart beating hard. 'The deal's going down, Al. It's time to hit the frog and toad.'

We walk out into the stifling heat of this Mexican summer. For the umpteenth time, I wonder how I – a conservative, middle-class banker well into middle age, a community-minded family man from country New Zealand – became an undercover agent for the United States Drug Enforcement Administration (DEA) infiltrating the money trail of the Mexican drug cartels. But more importantly, now that I'm in this nightmare, how the fuck am I going to get out of it?

Miguel Díaz – a slim, fit man in his early forties with slick black hair and an abrupt manner – is a well-educated former investment banker whose main client base is Mexican. He also deals with clients from Guatemala, El Salvador, Honduras and Nicaragua. Al has not met Miguel, which is disconcerting.

The DEA demanded that we not disclose Al is coming to the meeting until I introduce him at the handover of the cash. I am not keen on doing business this way: the meeting will be tense enough without throwing Al into the ring at the last minute. But I have no choice. I am way out of my depth here, a foreigner, a white person, a *gringo*; out of my depth in a country where I can neither speak the language nor understand the culture.

Miguel is sitting behind a vast desk which he has moved so that his back is to the window and he faces the entrance to the suite. I extend my hand to him and he stands to reciprocate the gesture, not once taking his eyes from Al. I introduce them and realise too late that there is a slight nervous stutter in my voice. 'This is one of m–my associates. His name is Al. He c–can be trusted.'

Miguel eyeballs Al without speaking, before gesturing for us to sit down. 'My clients will be here shortly,' he offers, waving in the general direction of two chairs. I grapple for something to say to break the tension. Miguel is obviously nervous, looking at his watch and rolling his thumbs in rapid succession.

He's nowhere near as nervous as I am. Al completely stuffed up the last operation we were on together, when a Mexican cartel banker asked him about a technical banking term. Instead of shutting up, Al tried to bluff his way through. It didn't wash.

'*¿Usted es un banquero, no?*' the banker demanded. You are a banker, aren't you? The meeting came to an abrupt end.

'I'll do all the talking about the banking,' I told him before we left to meet Miguel. 'Last time was a disaster. So shut up, for Christ's sake and just back me, okay?' He grunts agreement.

Miguel's cellphone rings. 'They're on their way up,' he says, leaning back in his chair and visibly relaxing. 'I should now tell you a little about them.' He pauses, a smile playing on his lips. 'They are brothers. Very, very wealthy brothers and very, very dangerous. They are in the sugar industry.' The sugar industry is code for the cocaine trade. Cocaine, that seductive, addictive white nose-candy, known in Spanish as *perico*, which creates intense euphoria in users and whose street market value in the United States exceeds the revenue of Starbucks. And these traders are from Colombia.

Cold fear envelops me. I don't dare look at Al, who is Colombian and well known in his native country as a DEA agent. His casual demeanour has disappeared now, his face the colour of chalk. Al excuses himself to use the bathroom, not looking at me as he crosses the room. Mexican drug cartels are ruthless, but they don't touch the Colombians for imagination with torture and murder.

Mexico City, built on the site of the Aztec capital Teno-chtitlan and pockmarked with archaeological sites, colonial buildings and museums, is steeped in history. But, on the flight down there, Al did not talk about the wonders of this ancient civilisation. Instead, he delighted in sharing gruesome stories with me about the punishment meted out to traitors by the Colombians. The Colombians have long been connected with Mexico, shipping much of their illegal produce through Central America. They are always doing deals with Mexican cartels who buy from them to move drugs into the US. But when things go wrong . . .

'Confidential informants, known as Charlies, are crucified, their hands nailed to the front door, and they are gang-raped before having their throats cut,' he said, in between gulping a bourbon and Coke and stuffing cashews in his mouth. 'Others have their penis and testicles cut off and stuffed in their mouths. You don't mess with Colombians.'

The DEA figures Al will be safe working in Mexico since Mexican drug cartel leaders, unlike the Colombians he's worked with before, won't know who he is. At this late stage, I can only pray they're right. The trouble is, I've got a horrible feeling they're not.

No one has warned us to expect Colombians and the DEA hasn't factored this in. My stomach churns as though filled with liquid and I place both hands on the chair seat to steady myself. There is a quiet knock on the door.

'It's open,' Miguel calls out. 'Come in.'

My legs feel rubbery, as if they will give way underneath me, but I force myself to stand as the brothers enter the room, one thin and tall, the other stout. They wear impeccably tailored Italian suits and share the same hard brown eyes.

'Mr Wilson?' They smile, putting their briefcases on the floor and shaking my hand. 'Our mutual contact speaks very highly of you.' Their backs are to the bathroom that Al is using and we are caught in the awkward moment between introduction and action. I wipe my palms on my suit trousers and grapple for something to say that doesn't give away the fact that I am shit-scared.

The toilet flushes. The Colombians swing round to face the bathroom, and then whip their heads back to us with an accusatory glare. 'Who is in there?' they demand. Before Miguel can answer, Al's huge bulk is framed in the doorway. He is smiling, confident, as though nothing is amiss. Within a split second, his smile breaks and they tense. The Colombians have recognised Al. And he has recognised them.

All hell breaks loose.

PART ONE

Love, Sport and Gaol

1

I was born in the deep of winter, August 1946, the result of my parents reuniting after a long separation during World War II. Milton, where we lived, was a deeply conservative town that lay fifty kilometres south of Dunedin, on New Zealand's South Island. It boasted just five hundred people, none of whom were Maoris. Founded as a milling town in the 1850s, it came to prominence during the gold rush era as a major staging post for prospectors seeking their fortunes.

My parents came from farming stock. My father Edward, a ground mechanic in the air force, was Protestant, but my mother, Cecilia, was an Irish Catholic. Their love affair, deemed a disgrace, scandalised their respectable farming families and, as is sometimes the way in small towns, they were thrown out to fend for themselves. Dad was only forgiven when he returned from active service in the Pacific Islands in the last year of the war, his mind completely shattered. Shell-shocked, this proud, quiet man spent twelve months in hospital, staring vacantly into space, lost in his own world.

My brother was five years older than me, my sister born ten years after my birth. Stranded in the middle, I felt like an only child. Quiet and shy by nature, I blended into the background.

By the time I was born, my parents were off the land. Father ran the bus service from the nearby town of Lawrence to Dunedin and drove me to school every day. Waitahuna Primary, where I went from prep until high school, was a small building of two rooms where the two teachers delivered a solid, basic education.

Mother had made arrangements for me to eat my lunch at a roadside café every day. No other students ate there and I cut a solitary figure in school pants and shirt, a tall skinny boy sitting alone at the Formica table. I couldn't play with the others after school either, because I had no way of getting home if I missed the bus. Full in the morning, the bus was empty in the afternoon when I returned home. I stared out the window at the hilly terrain as we made the long journey.

While I was used to my own company, I was never comfortable with it. I always felt a deep sense of loneliness, but there was no point telling my parents. Problems were to be endured with quiet dignity and a stiff upper lip. Whingers were told to shut up and get on with it. Reserved by nature, I did just that.

At the age of fifteen, I needed to extend my schooling beyond the confines of Waitahuna Primary. With my rudimentary education, the esteemed Christ College, where my brother was educated, did not accept me. The next option was a Gordonstoun-style boarding school, a tough Presbyterian bootcamp run by staunch Scots. If I had felt lonely at home, I was about to find out what real loneliness meant.

Bastardisation was rampant at the school, younger boys fresh meat for older bullies who preyed on the weak. I was a passive victim to these bullies, who forced me into cold showers and demanded I make their beds and clean their shoes. I was not strong enough to say no to them, copping many a bashing at their hands. But instead of crying out for revenge, the bruised and bloodied face that stared back at me in the mirror scorned my weaknesses. *Coward. Gutless wonder. You get what you deserve.*

I didn't like to see other boys bullied, either. But although I would comfort my fellow victims, I couldn't defend them. I couldn't even defend myself. After one monumental attack, where I had the daylights beaten out of me, I thought I might retaliate, but common sense prevailed. Fighting back or telling a teacher was not an option. It just invited another hiding with more attackers. The teachers, too, were free and easy with the use of the cane.

Academically, I wanted to excel but my ambition did not match my talents. Unused to Latin, French, biology and history, which were not taught in my two-room school at home, I instead channelled my energies into sport, particularly running, rugby and swimming. I was driven to prove I was as good as my brother, that I was not a failure. I could do that on the sporting field.

I played every game of rugby at boarding school for the first two years, but in the important games that counted for the school colours I was benched. When a player was injured, I finally got my chance. As I started to take off my jacket, another player demanded he should go on instead. I didn't argue and watched my chance to play a big game for the school slip by. I did not speak up, and I never forgave myself.

Blond-haired, with a slim build and 1.85 metres tall, I was pleasant-looking enough and, though shy by nature, did not lack charm. I left school at eighteen with an average pass and no education about life or sex. It was 1964, the height of the hippie movement, but the magic of flower power and free love had completely passed me by in the claustrophobic confines of that Presbyterian boarding school.

Much to my deep shame, I was still a virgin. Shortly after leaving school, I met a sandy-haired girl with grey eyes and a flirtatious pout at a party near where my parents lived. Reserved around women, I flailed for something to say to her but failed miserably. To my amazement, she wasn't particularly interested in conversation. I drove her home from the party and she lingered in the car outside her parents' home. 'They're away for the night,' she told me, taking my hand and indicating I should join her inside the house. Within five minutes, she had seduced me into bed. Afterwards, I lay awake all night, overwhelmed at how good it was to finally have sex and determined that, from now on, I would have it as often as I could. To my disappointment, I was to find out that not all women were as generous with their charms as that lass from Nelson.

2

It was 1968 and I was twenty-one years old when I moved to Australia after an invitation from the Power House Athletics Club in Melbourne. Mother had tears in her eyes as I said goodbye, and my father predicted I would only be gone for six months. That made me more determined to be away longer. The club had invited me to train with them to compete in the Australian Athletics Championships, where I went up against Peter Norman – who won the silver medal in the 1968 Olympics and stood next to Tommie Smith and John Carlos as they made their famous Black Power salute – and Greg Lewis, a top sprinter for Australia. It was a good experience, but I didn't make the finals. I also played rugby for the University of Melbourne and through coaching helped students realise their sporting ambitions.

I started work as a cost analyst in the financial department of the Ford Motor Company. Leaving the confines of country New Zealand and a harsh boarding school had a liberating effect. I was bitten by the travel bug and, after twelve months with Ford Australia, transferred to their company in South Africa, where I had been given a year's contract to play rugby with the Crusaders at Port Elizabeth.

I met Susan while travelling in London in 1971. This dark-haired, dark-eyed girl of Lebanese descent took my fancy so much that we became engaged in December 1972 on returning to her home town, Melbourne. Three months later, we married. I was twenty-six and Susan was twenty-five. We couldn't have been happier.

Papua New Guinea beckoned. I accepted a position at the University of Technology in Lae, working as an internal auditor in the administration department and lecturing in accountancy and business studies. Outside work, I was actively involved in the university's fundraising committee. I also worked for the Kellogg Foundation on internal auditing in developing countries and ironically, given later events, was assigned to the Papua New Guinea Ombudsman's Commission to investigate the collapse of its country's Savings and Loan Society in 1976. Hampered by my meagre educational results, I completed my Higher School Certificate by correspondence from Papua New Guinea and later gained a Bachelor of Arts with a double major in economics from the University of Queensland.

Rugby union and athletics occupied much of my spare time. I coached both at the University of Technology and was assistant coach of athletics for the national team when preparing for the 1974 New Zealand Commonwealth Games, the 1975 Guam South Pacific Games and the 1976 Montreal Olympic Games. I was the Papua New Guinean 800-metre athletics champion that same year.

In 1977, Susan and I returned to Australia where our first son, Sam, was born. I started with the Olympic Tyre Company as an internal auditor before moving to Randall & Co. to work as a mortgage broker two years later. In February 1982, and then in March 1983, Susan and I were delighted to announce two more births, Mark and Kate.

In 1984, with my career in full swing, I joined share-brokers McKinley, Wilson & Co., overseeing the department that managed more than five-hundred-million worth of institutional capital invested into privately controlled companies. Two years after starting there, I was made an associate partner of the firm at the age of forty. Voluntarily, I gave lectures for the Melbourne Stock Exchange on mortgages and interest rates and ran monthly investment meetings for our clients at our home.

The kids all went to a private school and we lived the good life in the upmarket seaside area of Brighton. When I wasn't working, I was coaching rugby at the University of Melbourne and private schools, helping the Life Saving Society of Victoria and teaching swimming. Life was sweet. I was a happily married man with a lovely wife, beautiful children, beautiful home, a successful career, money in the bank, respect and credibility. And this whole pack of cards was about to come crashing down.

In 1987, with interest rates going through the roof, I was asked to finance a theme park in Queensland and a casino in Alice Springs. The loans were sought by a property developer and his companies. A court later held that these loans were arranged fraudulently on the basis of inflated valuations on the properties. Overstretched from over-borrowing and unable to draw a crowd and turn a profit, a problem exacerbated by the 1989 Australian pilots' strike that crippled tourism, the owner went belly-up. Despite his fervent view that all would eventually come good, he couldn't pay the eighteen per cent interest rates.

I had borrowed money for the developer through Australia's longest-established friendly society. People were trying to withdraw cash and we bridged with an aim of refinancing the loans. But the media had begun to scrutinise the property developer and soon created widespread panic. They reported that the friendly society was overexposed because of the developer and that the shares would drop in value. The public lost all faith. The friendly society was taken over and the mortgage trusts were frozen. Investors were advised either to take a discount or to sit tight. Those who took the discount lost money, those who stayed firm got a windfall.

3

In 1993, the Victorian Fraud Squad raided our Brighton house at six o'clock in the morning, while my family watched on in mute horror. Afterwards, the Squad went to work at my office, in the middle of Collins Street, turning the place upside down to find the documents they were looking for. I stood back and watched, thunderstruck. They were going me for conspiracy to defraud. The charges were that I had conspired to defraud the friendly society by putting dodgy valuations on the casino and the theme park.

I was arrested in February 1995 and the Fraud Squad officers were blunt in their assessment of my future when they phoned my lawyer. 'He's going to be charged, and he'll be released on bail. But he'll go down for this.' They would make sure I did.

By the end of that year, I had declared myself bankrupt. When the trial started in September 1997, I was fifty-one years old and had handed over everything I owned, totalling millions of dollars, to the receivers: my house, two cars, shares and cash. This nightmare had now been hanging over my head for four years, but it was about to get a lot worse.

Although I believed myself to be innocent of all the charges brought against me, my poor faith in the justice system led to me making a guilty plea. I thought it would be better than losing in a prejudiced court and receiving a heavier sentence.

In a move I would live to regret, I pleaded guilty on four presentments containing counts of obtaining financial advantage by deception, making and using false documents and fraudulently inducing investments. I faced the onslaught. I knew I would have to go to gaol, and my world was crumbling around me. My confidence was shot and I developed a nervous tremor in my hands.

The Fraud Squad boys sat in the body of the court. All twenty of them in their cheap suits had come to ogle me in the dock. My lawyer, Bill Carmichael, rake-thin and tall, sneered at them: 'Is there anyone left in the fraud office, or are you boys all having a quiet day?'

Susan drove me in every day of the two-week trial and dropped me off at the court entrance. She never came in. On the last day, I said goodbye to the kids at the door. I couldn't speak for crying. An hour later, I walked into court with just the suit I was wearing, nothing more. Judge Williams pronounced sentence: five on the top, with a two-year minimum. I felt cold, as though it was happening to someone else and feared my knees would give way under me. I vaguely heard him pronounce that I was unlikely to re-offend, which gave me no comfort.

Bill Carmichael took a more pragmatic approach. 'We could have fought harder, mate,' he said, consoling me with a handshake, 'if only we had the dollars.'

The Director of Public Prosecutions appealed the sentence and I was re-sentenced, this time with six years on the top and three on the bottom. I would not see the outside world before September 2000, at the earliest.

I arrived at Beechworth prison, a four-hour van ride from Melbourne, on a bleak September day in 1997 with overcast skies and imminent rain. The walled fortress of the gloomy gaol loomed ahead of me like Colditz Castle, impenetrable and dank, and I instinctively shuddered. A line from Dante's *Inferno* repeated itself over and over in my brain: 'Abandon all hope, ye who enter here.'

I was classified as a C2 prisoner, the lowest rating in the prison system, which would allow me to work on a prison farm, attend university and take home leave.

I was in a daze and was placed on suicide watch for the first two days. After that, I was put in the remand area among the general prison population, where I stayed for four months. The old hangman's noose area remained at the centre of the cell block, a relic of the ghastly torment visited on those prisoners in the past who had been sentenced to death. It became my torment too, walking in the shadows of men who had swung by their necks for their crimes, often watched by other prisoners within the block who would give them a send-off, claps or jeers before they dropped.

Overwhelming panic engulfed me even before I was escorted to my cell, a small dark tomb of frugal light. I baulked at the doorway. 'I'm claustrophobic,' I whimpered to the guard. 'Please, can you tell them I'm claustrophobic?'

He had heard it all before and ignored me. 'In you go,' he barked. 'And welcome to Beechworth.'

A truck driver who had used drugs to stay awake and whose truck ran off the road, colliding with another vehicle and killing its occupant, was in the cell next to mine. We became friends, of sorts. Dark depression shadowed him and he couldn't lift his spirits. I spent a day talking to him, trying to console him with positive thoughts and encouraging him to remember that one day he would be free again, as they closed his cell door. But that night he found freedom his own way, ripping up the sheet from his bed and hanging himself from the cell window. He hung there all night before he was discovered.

I found out about his suicide in the most primal way, from the screams of the prison guard who opened his cell the next morning and discovered the dangling, limp body. I was called as a witness to his coronial inquiry and could add little of consequence to ease his family's anguish, beyond reiterating what was so bloody, painfully obvious: the man was depressed. He had tried to tell people that. He had needed help. The prison vicar carried out a service outside his cell, his parents and other family members in inconsolable grief as the stark reality that his life could have been saved sunk in. I sat on the edge of my bed, trying to stay calm. It didn't work.

Using my training, I taught swimming courses for SwimVic for other inmates. One young bloke, in for drug offences, set himself a target to swim one kilometre. In two weeks he was within striking distance of his goal, but one day he didn't turn up. The ready supply of drugs in prison proved too much for him to resist and swimming just fell away.

To preserve my sanity, I enrolled in a Master of Applied Science course at the University of Ballarat, which I was allowed to attend without supervision. I hoped to improve my skill base so that I could gain employment in that area on my release.

4

I was due to give evidence for the Crown in the trials of other individuals involved in the theme park and casino financing debacle. That's when the threats from a standover man, Malcolm Pearce, started. Pearce had funds invested with our company and, when his money went down the gurgler, he gunned for me. He wanted his original investment back, plus two million. There was no point paying, even if I had the money. He would just have demanded more.

Pearce had a short fuse and, when I didn't return his abusive phone calls or answer his letters, he began to violently threaten me. My family home would be set on fire. My family's cars would be bombed. My daughter and sons would be raped and shot. My daughter would have acid thrown in her face.

Prison officers, set up by Pearce, rushed my cell, delivering punches, dragging me out by my hair, screaming and kicking me. After each bashing, as they closed my cell door, they delivered the same message: 'Pay Pearce the two million.'

I came to learn the hard way that this vicious bastard meant business. From the time the verbal threats started, ugly mail arrived at our home. Susan received a bereavement card expressing sympathy for the fact that I had died, and a wreath warning that time had run out. Over the space of two months, from April 1998, three of our family cars were incinerated in our driveway in the middle of the night. Sam, calm and in control, ran outside to stop the fire with Susan and Kate frozen to the spot, screaming. Mark could do nothing, sitting inside the lounge room, stunned and mute.

All the vehicles were destroyed but the cost to the family was much higher. Mark and Kate, trying to settle into their VCE exams, were distracted and traumatised. Sam was mortified and Susan was a mental and physical mess. Our home was placed under twenty-four hour surveillance and virtually became their prison. I was denied home visits because my safety and that of the prison staff could not be guaranteed.

And then I was stabbed.

I was walking towards a group of prisoners who turned to me, smiling. Instinctively I sensed that something was wrong. Two inmates grabbed my arms and I felt the cold steel of a knife plunge into my back. I couldn't see who had done it and fell to the concrete floor as the knife was pulled out. I could hear the prisoners laughing and the heavy footfall of prison officers approaching before I passed out.

I woke up in the hospital, my knife wound clean and stitched. The nurse welcomed me back to consciousness with a jovial smile. 'You're a lucky man,' she told me. 'The blade didn't do any permanent damage. Other than some discomfort, you'll be fine.'

Prison security grilled me when I returned to my cell, but I stuck with the golden rule of saying nothing. 'I didn't see who stabbed me,' I asserted. That part was true. What was not true was my claim that I didn't know who was responsible. Shortly after arriving back at Beechworth, an inmate cornered me. 'Pay Pearce the money,' he said, leering. 'If you don't, next time we stab you, we'll make sure you die.'

Because of the stabbing, which the authorities euphemistically described as an 'incident', they moved me in early February 1999 to Port Phillip prison at Laverton in Melbourne. Behind the entrance gate someone had hastily scrawled an accusatory censure: *Jedem das Seine*. You get what you deserve. The same sign had appeared at the German Buchenwald concentration camp and it seemed, on this dank day of icy winds, that I too was being herded, like the Jews, into hell. 'Abandon all hope, ye who enter here.'

For my own safety, I was placed in the Marlborough unit, which was designed to accommodate mentally ill inmates. Being in Marlborough was like living in an asylum and I kept to myself as much as possible. Two prisoners ran the unit with standover tactics and threatening airs and I resolved to stay away from them. But I couldn't escape all the inmates.

One, a mountain of a man with a violent record who stood two metres tall in bare feet, would step in front of me as I walked around the unit, his eyes gleaming with madness and menace. 'You're not talking to me today,' he would announce as I struggled not to show him how petrified I was.

'Oh, just busy with my thoughts, mate, that's all,' I'd say lightly, praying that he would let me pass without ripping my throat out.

A Turkish inmate, incarcerated for drug trafficking and dead broke, often cornered me and asked my advice on financial matters. When he got out, he said, he was going to return home and build a house for himself. The next day, this had escalated to his building a school. By the time I realised he was a bullshit artist, he was building the whole bloody village.

A feisty little Irishman sought out my company and I enjoyed his, for a while. But his paranoia that the IRA were going to come to Australia and kill him became increasingly incessant, and nothing anyone could say would calm him down. Every day, he babbled that he was in 'terrible strife, indeed he was, and only the good Lord could save him from certain death'. The truth, I later found out, was that he had moved to Australia when he was fourteen years old. He had never met anyone in the IRA.

Marlborough was a protected area and prison guards would escort me to the library, where I got my weekly ration of books that kept me sane. Sometimes other inmates came with me, drooling or ranting, and I was humiliated to be amongst them. 'Here come the goons from the funny farm,' other prisoners taunted as we walked into the library.

I wanted to get out of Marlborough and constantly complained to the guards that I should not be in the unit. 'I'm a low-priority, low-risk, minimum-security prisoner!' I pleaded with them. 'I have no degree of mental illness and yet I'm locked up with violent madmen. For

Christ's sake, get me out of here!' I needn't have wasted my breath.

'Bad luck,' they shrugged. 'Tell someone who cares.'

The inmates were heavily sedated and many sat like empty chairs, wetting their pants. I should have felt some degree of sympathy, but I was too bloody depressed and self-absorbed. By my first Christmas in Marlborough, I had fallen into a deep hole, cutting off all contact with friends and refusing to answer letters. I feared I might end up like the others in there. I was becoming dehumanised, just a number thrown in with other numbers, an experiment gone wrong.

On one occasion, I heard yelling as I walked towards the library and sensed people behind me. I turned for an instant to see two prisoners brandishing broomsticks and walking towards me. My heart was thumping as they got closer but I had nowhere to run and no one to help me. I tried to protect my head as someone clouted me around my scalp and back, raining blows. Another inmate had moved to shield my attacker from the guards, who were momentarily distracted with another prisoner.

My assailants moved so fast and with such ferocious force that I was on the floor within seconds, cowering from the repeated blows, blood pouring from my nose. I could taste blood in my mouth and my clothing was covered in crimson stains. By the time the guards noticed something was wrong, the inmates had seemingly vaporised into thin air. No one had seen anything. No one had heard anything. Or so it appeared.

I knew that Pearce was behind this attack. I also knew instinctively that, like in boarding school, if I wanted to survive in here, I had to shut up. When prison security came to interview me about the assaults, I told them that I had no idea who was involved, that I didn't see it coming because it happened so fast, and that I had no idea why someone would try to do this to me. With no witnesses and no statement, the matter was closed and filed away. I had received my warning from Pearce, loud and clear.

Two nights after that attack, the head of security, a bull-headed man with a short fuse, arrived at my cell and announced he was moving me to Charlotte, a secure unit that houses protected prisoners. I didn't want to go, and started gibbering a protest.

He stood with arms crossed and waited for me to draw breath. 'You finished?' he said, when I stopped talking. 'We have to send you there for your own safety. We've uncovered plans for extortion and also threats to kill you. You won't survive if you stay in here. There is a contract on your life, for between a hundred thousand and a quarter of a million. We found it when we intercepted the mail. These blokes aren't mucking about. We're moving you. Pack your stuff. Now.'

5

Charlotte was – and probably still is – a prison unit where God stayed outside, the inmates joked. Trouble is, they were right. Protected from the seething mass of other inmates, it had little sunlight, tiny cells, no open windows and no fresh air. In there, you ceased to exist, reduced to a zombie state and drained of any emotion, either joy or sadness. Washing, phone calls to family and walks for fresh air all had to take place within the thirty-minute daily break allowed the prisoners.

The rest of the time – twenty-three and a half hours a day – I would be locked up. My claustrophobia in Charlotte was overwhelming and I tried to settle into a routine that would break the terrible panic constantly threatening to steal my sanity. While most of the guys in the unit were content to watch television all day, I got up at 7.30 am, kick-started the day with a coffee and was working on my Masters degree by 8 am. I studied until 2 pm, which was when I knew I could no longer cope in my dingy cell.

There was a forty-millimetre gap under the cell door and every day I used to lie on the floor, my hands crossed on my chest, trying to still my rising hysteria. My breathing was laboured and erratic and I talked to myself, quietly. You're all right, mate, you're going to be fine. I'd concentrate on the positive moments in my life and fight hard to control my fear, but it never worked.

Every day at two o'clock, the panic started again. And every day, for the entire time I was locked in that hellhole, I lay like an animal for four hours on the stinking cold floor. The guards didn't care. They shrugged, totally uninterested, when I beseeched them to show some humanity. 'We've all got our problems, cock,' they replied. 'Get over it.' But I couldn't.

Like a child who needs a nightlight to allay their nocturnal demons, I needed light and air to keep me sane. Some days were worse than others. Some days, all I could do as I lay on that floor was weep. On those occasions, I prayed that I wouldn't mentally unravel before I got out of there. Every day was groundhog day, same as the day before.

I knew that I was deteriorating, mentally and physically. I found it difficult to hold onto cohesive thoughts and frequently broke down, crying uncontrollably. I felt weak, ashamed of myself, humiliated that I was not stronger than this. The ghost of the boy from boarding school, who wore the kicks and punches from the schoolyard bullies without retaliation, returned to leer at me in the mirror. *Coward. Gutless wonder. You get what you deserve.*

My face was pale, parchment-white from fear and lack of light. I resembled an old man with Parkinson's disease, trembling uncontrollably, unable to hold a paper or a coffee cup without dropping it. I was allowed one phone call per day and used it to talk to my family. I asked Susan to ensure that the line was free at the time I planned to call, but often it was engaged and I had to hang up. 'I haven't got through,' I would tell the inmates waiting to use the phone. They elbowed me out of the way to make their own calls. It was dog-eat-dog in there.

Prisoners were separated from any visitors they might have by a thick pane of glass, and inmates would loiter in the area behind the room, waiting for their turn to see friends and relatives. Susan hated visiting, humiliated at having to come into a prison and wait among the wives, girlfriends and children of people she wouldn't share the time of day with outside. Her distaste for the visits was palpable, reflected in her pursed lips and the angry flash of her dark Lebanese eyes.

I felt like a dead man walking when I entered the visitor centre in the monkey suit we were forced to wear, hands cuffed behind my back. The visits were always the same: the guard standing outside as we moved through perfunctory greetings and awkward silences until Susan again vented her disgust at what I had forced the family to endure. She didn't ask how I was getting on and I wouldn't have told her if she had. My shame and guilt were overwhelming. When I returned to the cell, I would be so emotionally depleted that I could only stare blankly at the walls.

I couldn't sleep. Constant fear of being beaten or stabbed gave me shocking nightmares and I panicked that my family was being targeted as well. I would wake up to my own screams, drenched in sweat and shaking. I listened for footsteps, the sound of a cell door being opened, and waited for the next beating. Despite being moved to this special unit for my own protection, I knew Pearce could still get to me. I was constantly tormented and couldn't tell a soul, because Pearce had told me that if police ever visited him, I would suffer. Worse, now that he had carried out some of his threats against my family, they lived in terror.

Don Granger, a police officer in the Fraud Squad who was the first to push me into acting as a Crown witness against others involved in the financing collapse, was concerned that I was losing my marbles. 'Stay here any longer, mate, and you'll go nuts,' he told me. 'I'm going to try and get you out of here.'

I nodded, bleakly. The brutality of the unit and the sudden eruptions of flashpoint violence that I could hear from my cell were so terrifying that I withdrew further into myself daily. I would prefer Pearce's threats to the reality of being locked up here with my claustrophobic demons. And it was starting to dawn on me that perhaps there were other reasons why I had been sent to Marlborough and now Charlotte. It was as though the system was determined to break me. But if that were the case, why? It didn't make any sense.

Granger visited me regularly and supported my increasingly desperate calls for clemency, giving me a laptop on which I could write letters to anyone I thought would listen to my story. Searchlights swept intermittently past my cell window throughout the night, the eerie silence broken only by the heavy footfalls of the prison guards or echoing violent outbursts of the other inmates.

6

Shortly after the first visit by Granger, I was handcuffed behind my back for a move. I had spent only a month in Charlotte and was desperate to get out of there, little knowing that where I was going was even worse.

Sirius East is a Supermax unit in Port Phillip prison, home to intractable bastards with serious, violent form who need to be isolated from others. I complained bitterly to authorities that there must have been a mistake, that I was a C2 prisoner in for a white-collar crime and I should be serving my time in a minimum-security prison. The complaint fell on deaf ears. The authorities had decided I should be moved to Sirius East for my own safety. I didn't want to go. Everywhere I turned, I saw reinforcement of the reality that I was on the wrong side of the ledger, that I was a sinner who should wear horsehair shirts, fit only to keep company with other sinners.

Sirius West was our companion Supermax unit, designed to house paedophiles, transvestites, Crown witnesses and rogue police. Monitored around the clock, the unit was home to twenty of the worst type of prisoners: evil bastard men you wouldn't want to be associated with. Their crimes horrified me and I flailed for any explanation as to why I had been thrown in amongst them. I shrank from them.

Security was extreme. In most units there were two officers for every forty-five inmates; in Sirius East there were two for the twenty. I had a single cell, two-by-three metres with no natural light, which had a small bed, desk, chair, shower, toilet and hand basin. The cell was locked at 7.30 pm and re-opened the next morning at 8.30 am. Inmates passed through double electronically-controlled doors to their cells, which had dead-bolted and key-locked steel-reinforced doors. Each cell had an inspection trap which required two keys to open, as well as a switch in the security office. The cells ran along the perimeter of a room which was the common area of the unit. When they were unlocked, prisoners could walk in a yard only six-by-five metres large. No chances were taken with those who tried to commit suicide. They were put in a cell, naked, with the so-called suicide blanket, designed so that it couldn't be taken apart and used as a noose. Prisoners did paid work once a week: screwing nuts on bolts.

One of my neighbours was a convicted rapist and double murderer who plied his nasty trade in Victoria for twenty years from the mid-1980s. He had an extremely offensive body odour, a nauseating mix of manure, milk and chemicals, a result of his work on dairy farms. His poor eighteen-year-old male victim was shot through the head and his sixteen-year-old girlfriend was raped before being bludgeoned to death. Solidly built and bald, sporting a bushy beard, the criminal was polite and calculating. You wouldn't trust him, and wouldn't want to cross him. He moved quietly around the unit, mostly keeping to himself, but was in charge of cutting inmates' hair. I wouldn't let him near me, let alone with scissors. He disgusted me.

So too did one psychopath, a former New Zealander who, with a criminal accomplice, subjected two teenagers to repeated rapes over a terrifying twelve-hour period as they drove them on a nightmare journey from New South Wales to Victoria. Finally, at an isolated creek bed, my fellow prisoner, a man of low IQ who had fallen under the influence of the older accomplice, gagged, tied and finally stabbed the girls to death with serrated-blade knives. When one refused to die, he put his foot on her body to keep her still. 'Upon the demon within you being let loose, it was not to be controlled until its lust and anger were exhausted,' the judge noted at his 1998 trial. As he was led away from court, having received a record thirty-five-year non-parole period, one of the teenagers' mothers screamed at him, 'I hope you rot in hell!' I have no doubt that he will. He could never stand still and he loved to be the focus of attention. He always seemed nervous, shifty, as though he thought something was about to happen.

A serial arsonist, a skinny runt with intense staring eyes and an aggressive personality, was in there too, serving an eighteen-year maximum sentence for manslaughter over a backpacker hostel fire. He was a nut case. He obsequiously sought protection from other prisoners but most turned away from him. Moody and overtly feminine, he exploded at a moment's notice. Acquitted of the six backpacker murders on the grounds of diminished responsibility and instead convicted of manslaughter, he later confessed to police his involvement in starting some of the 1983

Ash Wednesday fires, in which forty-six people perished. He also admitted to more than two hundred blazes in other arson sprees. When he was released from prison in mid-2009, he showed little remorse.

A homicidal bomber also lived in the unit while I was there. In his early sixties, he was a solidly built man who had the full respect of the other prisoners. You would make way for him in the food line, give your seat to him at a table and wait until he had decided whether he wanted to take seconds of sweets. I realised very quickly that I needed to watch what I said and did in his presence.

The daily routine of degradation and abuse left me broken. We lived in there like a primitive tribe, but without the communal bonding. The first siren was an ear-shattering blast at 6.30 am for the kitchen workers. By 7 am the nightmare would begin all over again. I listened for the heavy thump of boots, keys jangling from officers' belts and the sharp metal-on-metal clang of the trapdoor opening as they began their head count. It was only a few minutes before my trapdoor would open and the familiar rap of, 'Stand by your door with your hands on the trap!' was barked at me. I was just glad there weren't eight days in a week.

I befriended a young man sentenced to twelve months for minor drug offences. He had been placed in the unit for his own protection, because he had witnessed a murder. Unlike most of the inmates, he stood apart from the herd mentality and had dreams of what he would do when he left prison. Two days before he was due for release, his parents brought him a suit and tie, a homecoming gift for their prodigal son. He didn't know how to knot the tie and I taught him over several hours. Proud as punch, he grinned broadly when he finally mastered it. He said goodbye to me the following day, resplendent in his suit and gesturing proudly to the tie he had knotted himself. He was jubilant to be walking out of that hellhole. Three days later, he was dead from a drug overdose. I wept for him and for a system that failed to support all the young men like him, gentle men some of them, whose lives are ruined by time spent in gaol among people they should never have had to mix with, and who are then sent home with so little back-up.

I craved good company in prison, and helped the vicar run the church services. Most of the congregation dribbled and fell asleep, using the chapel as a place to hide from routine. For me, it offered a wonderful opportunity to spend an hour in civilised company, talking opera, wine and food. I had taken to writing letters to anyone whose attention I thought I could corner. Driven by anger and despair, I lobbied politicians to improve conditions in the gaol, to do something, anything, to help. It made me feel that my time inside was not utterly futile, that I could make people gain some understanding, some insight into what went on behind the high stone walls.

Inside, we lose our identity, becoming instead a number, a ration, a beast to be herded in the morning and penned again at night. Emotional expression – laughter, tears, sorrow, joy – is discouraged. Talking about pain is also discouraged. Prison is not for the faint-hearted. I learned fast to be ever-vigilant, ever-watchful; to trust no one, especially the authorities.

The prison governor had assured the public that Port Phillip prison was undergoing a period of rejuvenation, that the inmates were more relaxed and active than they had been before. It was nonsense. In reality, there was no morale-building and no cheering comrades, just security cameras, guards, metal detectors, dogs and flashlights. Sirius East prisoners spent most of their time indoors and did little exercise. They ate fatty meals and only the occasional vegetables. The poor diet exacerbated their restless anxiety and agitation: out of the blue they might try to kill themselves or someone else, using extreme violence.

Many Australian criminal lawyers expressed concern that being in lockdown for twenty-two hours a day was tantamount to torture, an inhumane way of dealing with human beings. One, who represented clients housed in Sirius East, commented that prisoners, fed up with pacing the twenty-metre-by-three-metre corridor, had asked him to visit them so they could walk from their unit to the interview area and get some fresh air. The lawyer's appeal, which sought a reduction in his client's sentence, failed. However, the judge did note that the Prison Act allowed only twenty-eight days' confinement, even when a prisoner had seriously misbehaved.

Over Christmas and New Year, Sirius East was dark and silent, the inmates slipping in and out of their cells like ghosts. They huddled like homeless men beside a dumpster in our small yard, making inane conversation and kicking the ground desultorily. No one remembered how to smile. When security raided the unit, they moved like a counter-terrorist group, clad in black. Over several hours they slowly, systematically, took the place apart, ensuring they missed nothing. Afterwards, they marched a few inmates down to the interview room for interrogation.

My library visits had been taken from me. Initially the library was locked when I went there with a prison guard, but the staff could no longer guarantee my safety there, given the persistent rumours that I was to be murdered. With nothing to read, I withered.

New inmates unused to the system would arrive frightened, like deer caught in the headlights. The first 'tour of duty', a recce of the unit in which they were to be housed, was a blur of fear and shame. You can't choose your neighbours and in there you wouldn't want to. The noise was chaotic at times, the cries of caged men echoing up and down the corridors. One, a raving psychopath, would stand in his cell and taunt the guards as they walked past. 'Ring the sperm bank! I should be donating so there'll be a lot more people like me around!' he'd yell.

I shuddered at the thought. These blokes, cunning and paranoid about their own security, would not shrink from a confrontation. Most of the prison officers were also truculent and aggressive, humourless in the extreme. One unwise word and they would tear your cell apart, so I restrained myself, never giving in to the temptation of showing annoyance at being treated like a naughty child. I would stand before them, mute and impassive.

I was sitting at the desk in my cell when I heard a man suddenly cry, 'Christ! Help me!' I looked out to see a fellow inmate fall to his knees, brought down by a brutal sucker punch, his scalp and face drenched in blood. Ruthless spectators swanned in to see the hapless man stagger to his feet, weaving like a boxer stunned by a knock-out blow. Bloody and disorientated, the contender raised his fists, desperately trying to block an incoming slug. Stumbling backwards, he fell unconscious and the guards took him away. 'Come on, back to your cells,' an officer snarled, herding the inmates from the scene. 'The show's over!'

7

In the gloom of a wintry, late afternoon two months into my incarceration at Sirius East, there was a commotion in the unit. I was used to the racket of angry men, the screams and cries of disaffected prisoners emasculated by the system. But this was different: this guy was ballistic, screaming dementedly in half-English, half-Spanish that he wanted to see the governor. I knew who he was even before he announced himself: Daniel Gómez.

At just thirty-seven years old, Gómez was the board-room face of the new Mexico, and at the height of his powers. Hailing from Chiapas, an impoverished, though oil-rich, Mexican state, he had organised the takeover of the Campo Nuevo Corporation, one of the world's biggest traders in pineapples. He had also, with the help of the then-president of Mexico, put together a syndicate of 'businessmen' and purchased two major public banks which the government had recently privatised. His personal connection with the president sealed the deal and gave Daniel access to the huge amounts of money in the banks' care.

Gómez, at 1.9 metres tall, exceptionally fit and immaculately groomed, was always in control and demanded the best from those around him. A creative genius, he was not a blue-blood from Mexico's old, connected aristocracy, but neither was he a peasant. His grandfather was a chemist, his father built a pharmacy chain and young Daniel – brash, brilliant and ambitious – attended the most prestigious university in the country to study business administration.

Later, he furthered his education in Spain and the US, and was fluent in Spanish, English, French and Italian. He had started working on a banana plantation and rose to become head of the co-op, before moving to shrimp boats in the Gulf. But in reality, Gómez was in the sugar industry. Cocaine was embedded under the trays of shrimps.

Gómez was a major banker for the Mexican and Colombian cartel families, and it was they who were the 'businessmen' that funded his acquisition of the government banks. He not only managed these banks for the cartels, but also oversaw their secret donations to the Mexican ruling party and to certain politicians, a total in excess of one hundred million. These banks were the washing machines for the cartels. When cash was banked, the funds were transferred to secret accounts around the world.

In 1994, the US dollar was devalued against the peso, causing significant problems for the Mexican financial system, which had borrowed heavily in US currency. The American government came to the rescue, pumping several billions into the country and, in turn, the Mexican government handed $1.2 billion to Daniel's banks to restore liquidity and help dissolve the loans the banks had taken out.

There was one problem with the bail-out plan. The money never reached the banks. Instead, the $1.2 billion was wired to Gómez's personal account in Switzerland and then simply disappeared.

So did Gómez.

He fled with the cash. First to Germany, then to Denmark, Austria and the impoverished Caribbean nation of Haiti, where he secured a fake passport, then on to Uruguay and finally to Melbourne, Australia.

Furious, Mexico's head of Interpol vented his spleen at a press conference about Gómez. 'He is the most-wanted man in recent Mexican history,' he told a room packed with reporters. 'Not only because of the crimes he committed, but because those crimes brought about an economic crisis in Mexico. He has damaged the whole Mexican society, ninety million people.'

While in hiding, Gómez turned on the news in his hotel room and saw footage from Mexico of government agents raiding the Estrella Bank, of which he was chairman. His employees were hustled away for questioning and he later learned that he had been charged with a number of counts relating to fraud, money laundering and tax evasion.

Gómez maintained that the whole case was a set-up to make him the scapegoat for Mexico's economic meltdown, which in 1994 brought the country to the brink of collapse and cost its taxpayers a hundred billion. The truth, he said, was far uglier. He argued that the economic crisis in Mexico was brought on by bad political deals, corruption, murder, double-crossing and international politics. His country's history was steeped in blood, but never so much as it is today.

Mexico is a land of varied textures and traditions, two million square kilometres of majestic mountains and fertile valleys, lush tropical forests and unforgiving deserts, teeming cities and breathtaking coastline. Resorts such as Cancún, Los Cabos, Mazatlan, Puerto Vallarta and Acapulco cater to the wealthy, while dirt-poor rural folk eke out an existence and millions huddle in city slums. Before the arrival of Europeans, the Maya, Aztec and others built enormous masonry structures. The Maya developed the most sophisticated system of writing in the Western world, which traced the path of the planet Venus and marked the passage of time with an elaborate calendar system. Their cities were on a par with those of the Romans.

Spain invaded Mexico in 1519, destroying the Aztec empire and subjugating native groups, ruling until 1821 when a revolution brought independence to Mexico. The three-hundred-year colonisation left behind a legacy of ninety-seven per cent of the population speaking Spanish.

In 1846, the US invaded Mexico as part of the Texas Revolution. American soldiers wore green uniforms, and the chants of the native Mexicans against their white invaders could be heard all over the cities: 'Green Go Home'. The term *gringo*, referring specifically to Americans but covering all white persons, was born.

France gained a stronghold in 1864, and established Maximilian, an Austrian archduke, as Emperor. Occupation ended three years later after opposition forces pressured France to withdraw. Within weeks, Maximilian was executed.

The armed phase of the bloody Mexican revolution ended in 1920, and was followed by the rule of the Institutional Revolutionary Party, known in Spanish as PRI, the *Partido Revolucionario Institucional*. This centre-left party, which resulted from the power struggle to stop revolutionary faction fighting, was known for four decades as the Mexican Miracle, but it came to symbolise fraud and corruption and was characterised by violence against voters. It was later termed a perfect dictatorship.

The PRI forged a corrupt union with the drug cartels as they grew in power throughout the 1970s and 1980s. They offered protection and turned a blind eye to their illegal activities in exchange for kickbacks. It worked. While appeasement to the United States with a show of open warfare on the drug trade was clearly faked, on the streets there was far less violence and chaos than there is today.

However, by 2000 the party was over, and a democratic election saw the end of authoritarian rule and an overthrow of the system that had shown such generosity towards the cartels. But it proved a double-edged sword: with the benign munificence now gone, the violence and turf wars escalated. Mexico degenerated into chaos.

The Mexican cartels supply more than ninety per cent of America's cocaine, as well as the majority of its heroin, marijuana and methamphetamine. On average, trafficking boosts the Mexican economy by up to eighty-two billion a year. That's a lot of dope. And there is a massive demand for it. Mexico's border runs for more than three thousand kilometres, meandering from the Gulf of Mexico to the North Pacific Ocean. There, on the US border, the lights of San Diego wink like an old whore, seducing those in the illicit drug trade to cross over and feed the inexhaustible market for corporate cocaine users, emaciated junkies and a tragic number of young people increasingly hooked on speed and its dirty sidekick, ice.

The effects of the Mexican drug war are devastating. Cocaine or marijuana may cost about the same as they always have, but the human cost cannot be measured. The body count in Mexico exceeds that of Iraq, the violence so commonplace that deaths are reported in the media with a yawning sense of objectivity. But in the city's cafeterias and bars, murder is the main topic of conversation.

Mexico's economy is not only fuelled by drugs and a spiralling anarchy but also by insatiable greed and fear. Everyone – prosecutors, law enforcement officers, politicians, military top brass and judges – is on the take. In Mexico, they call it 'snatching the silver', and the choices are limited. Take silver, or take lead. Do what the cartels want, or start planning your own funeral.

There's an overwhelming sense of unreality and disorder in Mexican cities that are ravaged by the ruthless power of the drug cartels. The fear, the chaos and the anarchy are palpable. Cartel leaders are the untouchables. Guarded around the clock, remote from the mainstream, they are surrounded by the intense loyalty that only illicit money can buy.

The street dealers, on the lowest rung of the food chain, are the most vulnerable, easy targets in a war that claims increasing numbers of casualties a day. Honest police fight a seemingly unwinnable war on two fronts: the narcos and the bent officials. The border town of Tijuana, opposite San Diego, festers with so much corruption that officials stop just short of admitting it has descended into lawless chaos.

Life is cheap here: on average one hundred and twenty people a month are slaughtered, often in broad daylight.

Throughout Mexico, the drug-related industry claims more than three thousand deaths a year and this brutal business is never more shocking than in the beheading of children. This has become one of the most sickening aspects of the turf war and no one, it appears, knows how to stop it. People are snatched from public places with little or no attempt at disguising their captors. Headless corpses, their faces reflecting the horror of the torture they endured before they died, are strewn around the city, dangling from buildings or dumped in the street. The cartels have access to explosive devices, which they attach to vehicles and can activate at their chosen time. These devices kill civilians as well as the cartels' targets. No one is immune.

What the Mexican government wanted from Gómez was information. They wanted to know where the bodies were buried, and the location of secret European bank accounts used to funnel millions of dollars to finance the PRI. The PRI indignantly denied Gómez's claims that his reluctance to help bankroll the defeated president was the real reason the authorities had moved on his banks. In a dramatic show of power, the party placed a full-page advertisement in the national newspaper, with the headline 'Daniel Gómez Lies', to rebut his accusations.

The cartels were not concerned that Gómez had vanished. They recovered their original investment from the profits of the banks, which had collapsed, as well as a percentage of the $1.2 billion, and received reduced bank fees for banking their cash. They also had the guar-antee of no direct link back to their secret donations to the Mexican government and politicians. But if the cartels weren't concerned about Gómez, the US government was. It was their money that he had stolen. They wanted it back.

In 1998, Daniel's time ran out. Arrested in a joint sting by Mexican and Australian Federal Police in Melbourne, the agents pounced on him as he returned from a jog along the beach to his palatial home in an upmarket seaside Melbourne suburb, where he paid more than four thousand dollars a week in rent. Mexican officials took several photographs, which showed him to be overweight and unshaven, photos they delighted in splashing over the front pages of their newspapers the following day.

8

Daniel Gómez's brother-in law, business partner and co-accused, Luis Sánchez, was also an inmate of the unit. Authorities had given him and Gómez the same story they gave me: they were moved into the unit for their own protection against serving and former prisoners trying to extort money. But the Mexicans did not take their incarceration at Sirius East lying down. Gómez had the services of one of the best lawyers money can buy, a ball-breaking QC who publicly admonished the Justice Department for incarcerating Gómez with the worst criminals in the state. Present company excluded, I thought, indignant at the slight.

In an effort to improve their situation or be granted bail, they took their gripes against Port Phillip prison to court. To their delight, a Federal Court justice agreed that the operators of Port Phillip had unfairly housed them and that the two men were ill-suited to the unit's harsh conditions.

'Sirius East,' he opined, 'cannot be considered to be stimulating and is not conducive to intellectual activities.

Instead, it is deadening and dampening. The applicants,' he continued, 'are ill-suited to be kept in Sirius East and have not, by their behaviour or attitude, brought upon themselves the need to be incarcerated in these difficult conditions.'

He concluded that the two men had been in the unit since August 1999 and that if their conditions did not improve, he would seriously consider releasing them on bail by late March 2000. I smiled at that one. I'd been there since March 1999. No one was considering releasing me on bail.

Living in Sirius East was like being on a bad acid trip inside a hall of mirrors. Everyone watched everyone else. And Daniel Gómez watched my back. In this sunless, violent hellhole, surrounded by a perverted rapist, a serial arsonist, mass murderers and sadistic sexual psychopaths, Gómez and I – both prisoners, both bankers and both at our wits' end – became firm friends.

From the time Gómez arrived at Sirius East, the language changed. *Muchas gracias* and *Viva el México!* became commonly used expressions by the inmates in the unit. Daniel placed a sign outside his cell door: *Favor de no molestar.* Do not disturb. He also immediately engaged several inmates to help him: one to clean his cell, one to wash his clothes, one as his full-time fitness trainer, and me. I was his financial economist who gave him the daily run-down on the stock markets and world economies. A rumour started that when everyone was locked down at 7.30 pm each night, prison officers would smuggle in food, wine and perhaps a woman or two for Gómez. Daniel had money and plenty of it: $1.2 billion could buy a lot of favours. As our friendship grew, I slowly came under his protection. I still suffered beatings when the cell door was closed, but I wasn't stabbed again. During the day I was left alone. By the inmates, at least.

Sirius East had its own brutal lieutenant who regularly resorted to violence to sort out differences or to make a point. My brush with him came without warning when he suddenly reached across and seized me violently by the shirt front. Buttons on my shirt popped open and my coffee cup slid across the table. My nose was bleeding and I ached with pain. But there was no point in complaining.

In February 2000, a neo-Nazi prisoner was investigated by prison authorities over the theft of a confidential file from the Sirius East security office. The missing file contained information on Gómez's Mexican visitors, his privileges, internal intelligence and transcripts of private telephone conversations. The investigation tried to determine how the file was removed from a locked security room and a locked filing cabinet, with the room and the unit under constant surveillance.

During raids, prisoners were kept in a holding cell with only a toilet. On one terrible occasion, I was locked down with another inmate who suddenly pulled a plastic safety razor from his pocket and started slashing it across his wrists. Blood was spraying on the floor before I grabbed the razor and urgently wrapped toilet paper around his arms. He was hysterical, tears dripping from his chin and his head shaking convulsively. It was his first time in prison. When he arrived he had colour in his cheeks and bright eyes. Now, just three months into his sentence, his eyes, shadowed by dark moons, were hollows in a skeletal face. He was nineteen. He stared at the wall, unblinking, for what seemed an eternity, his only movement a slight rocking of his head to and fro.

Port Phillip prison security forces had stormed Sirius East in the early hours of the morning, their clear intention to find the missing files and those involved in their theft. They had made us wait, and the kid was scared. They came for me first. Security rushed into the cell, shouting and screaming, and hauled me to my feet. They yanked my arms back and handcuffed me from behind before roughly and impatiently pushing me down the corridor and stairs. My head was pushed down to my chest, the handcuffs pulled up my back as far as was agonisingly possible.

The noise in the unit was deafening. Inmates screamed as security wielded their batons indiscriminately at targets. Two security guards dragged an inmate across the floor by his hair, the grimace on his face proof that he was not enjoying it. I was pushed into the security room where the missing files were supposed to be. This room at Sirius East was where you were photographed and documented as high-security inmates. Prisoners' mug shots lined the wall. Our faces haunted the place.

Security banged my head against the door and I was shoved into a chair. The guards took their time before they spoke. One of them came over to me and hit me over the head, yelling that because I was a close friend of the Mexicans, I would know all about the missing files. They slammed their fists on the desk and roared as though on cue. One of the other guards slapped me around the head. Reeling in my chair, my ears ringing, I looked up and tried to smile. Inmates become immune to bashings in the interrogation room. Generally, the assault is an open hand or closed fist, first to one side of the face, then back the other way. The gross indignity of the attacks and the cowardice of the attackers tasted worse than blood.

A guard was leaning into my face, the veins standing out on his neck. 'Where are the missing files?' he yelled. 'We don't mind if you rummage your conscience. Go right ahead.' I tried my utmost to stay calm. The room was stifling, the fluorescent light burning a hole in the back of my neck. I kept shaking my head to all the questions. He could see I wasn't going to give in easily. 'Nothing you want to tell us, is there, while we have you here?'

This seemed to be my cue. 'No, except . . .' I deliberately faltered. 'Um . . .'

'Go on!' he barked. 'What have you got to tell me?'

'Well,' I started, 'it's the man in the cell next to mine. I think he might be Lord Lucan.'

He was not impressed. 'Fuck off, you smartarse,' he spluttered.

Silence is the best rule in prison. If anyone had known anything about those missing files, their information simply melted away like ice-cream left out in the sun. The files were never found and the nineteen-year-old inmate was not the first to slash his wrists waiting for an interrogation. Nor will he be the last.

9

Port Phillip management decided that, as I was housed in Sirius East and therefore classified as High Risk, I would not be granted any further home leaves, despite being entitled to monthly home visits.

The one visit that I'd had was dreadful. My heart was pounding as I entered the house. I had spent less than twelve hours with my precious children over two years and did not know what to say to them. The leave time expired and I was driven back to gaol. I would not be given leave again.

My request to the head of operations at Port Phillip prison that I receive Custodial Community Leave received a curt and quick response. He reminded me that I had been placed in Charlotte and Sirius East for my own protection, based on the threat of at least six prisoners to extort money and eventually kill me, no doubt on Pearce's instructions. For this reason, under its duty of care to all prisoners, Port Phillip would not be offering me community leave even though I was eligible. And, he warned, my repeated writing and communicating to various agencies to complain that another agency was hindering my progress was not helpful to anyone. 'Leave to your family home to visit your wife is not approved, as the home is under surveillance after threats made to the family,' he concluded. 'Staff safety cannot be guaranteed and consequently the application is denied.'

'I guess that's a "no", then,' I said out loud to myself as I placed the letter back in its envelope.

In early January 2000, my brother phoned the prison with a message for me about our eighty-four-year-old father, who had been rushed to hospital, gravely ill. The message was delivered to me by a guard in a gruff voice. 'Your father is unwell. You need to seek permission to phone the hospital.'

I couldn't sleep. Anxious to find out Dad's condition, I restlessly prowled the perimeters of my cell as I waited for permission to use the phone. Three days later, it was finally granted and a guard idly watched me as I picked up the receiver.

My brother greeted me in a voice hoarse with grief. 'Hello, Keith,' he started and I knew immediately that I had called too late. I couldn't speak, the phone clamped to my ear in this godforsaken place as I swallowed hard to stop my tears. Acutely aware that my time was limited, I suddenly felt an urgent need to say everything that I wanted to say.

'I'm sorry,' I gibbered. 'I couldn't get permission to use the phone. I'm so sorry.' I could no longer stop the tears and no longer tried. My time ended and the guard was walking towards me, gesturing for me to hang up.

I felt an ache in my guts, deep and hard, and I tried not to heave as I staggered back to my cell. It was the midday count, and Sánchez and Daniel were in animated conversation until I drew close to them. I half-fell into Daniel and he steadied me with a firm but gentle hand. 'Stand straight, my friend,' he said, 'and tell me what is wrong.'

Within three hours, management notified me that special leave to attend my father's funeral would be refused. I am Protestant, but they sent me a Catholic layperson to offer me solace. Obese, with a hard mouth and false teeth that didn't fit, she flopped into a chair next to Daniel and started talking without preamble. 'What are we gonna do with you?' she said, waving her podgy hands through the air. 'You'd better understand straight up that you won't be getting any leave to go back to New Zealand for your father's funeral.' She started laughing as though it was funny and I shrank behind my hands, lost in grief.

Daniel broke the silence. 'Get out!' he ordered, standing. 'Get out of here!'

She hauled herself out of the chair, snarling. 'You don't want my help? Fine! I'll go!'

In the weeks and months that followed in this godless environment, hollow months when I deeply mourned the loss of my father and the fact that we had not been close, he came to me frequently: the way he held himself strong and proud, his quiet but determined demeanour and his hands weathered from farming. I talked to him, softly in the dead of night when the prison was still, whispering to him to forgive me for disgracing the family name, forgive me for my failures and for not attending his funeral. Sometimes I even imagined he could hear me.

Eight weeks before I was due for release, I had my first parole board hearing. I requested my suit from storage and stood nervously before the seven-man board headed by its chairman, Justice Kingshott. I was heartened to see them smiling: most prisoners turn up in their gaol garb and I thought my sartorial splendour pleased them. Justice Kingshott was the only person to speak. 'The board is impressed with the effort you have made with your studies,' he said, 'particularly in view of the fact you have spent your time in solitary confinement. How have you coped?' I told him that reading and knowing I would soon be back with my family helped me get through.

To my amazement, Kingshott acknowledged that it was very unusual for a prisoner with my low classification to be locked up in a maximum-security prison. 'The board accepts that you have done hard time,' he said. 'I recommend you contact your lawyers and ask them to put in a submission for a pardon.' I wanted to shake his hand, but instead bowed to the board as one does in court and walked out, grinning fit to burst.

10

The commencement of the trial, at which I was to give evidence for the Crown against the others involved in the theme park and casino investment disaster, was looming.

As the day came nearer, Pearce's threats increased. It had taken six years to get these directors to court, their lawyers playing, and winning, the game of dragging out the trial date. Now it had finally arrived, but I didn't even have time to get into my suit for court. The case against them was dismissed on the first day.

Ewan O'Donohue represented me in my petition for a Royal Prerogative of Mercy, which was supported by Fraud Squad Officer Don Granger. And I had a financial saviour. Daniel Gómez, incensed at what I had endured in prison, gave me eight thousand dollars to help with legal costs. The grounds for the petition were numerous: actual and threatened violence against me and my family, damage to our family property, my importance as a Crown witness and the fact that the sentence I had served was manifestly different from that which the court had anticipated.

In the submission, my lawyer argued that 'it is reasonable to suggest that the Court of Appeal would not have anticipated that my client's term of imprisonment would be so difficult and so terrifying'. He continued that the only safe place for me and my family was the witness protection program and that the prison could not guarantee my safety unless I was placed in solitary confinement, twenty-four hours a day. He added that, typically, a prisoner serving time for the offences for which I had been convicted would spend a large proportion of that time on a prison farm. However, as a consequence of my decision to give evidence for the Crown, I lived in constant fear and in oppressive conditions with dangerous criminals.

One deposition, from the deputy headmaster at one of the schools I had taught rugby, particularly touched me: 'I also believe that, notwithstanding the wrongdoing that Keith has done, he has been treated abominably by the authorities and is a shadow of his former self . . . Keith now requires gentle handling and assistance if he is to have a meaningful life in the future. He still has much to offer the troubled youth of our state, hopefully he still has sufficient drive left to take on the challenge.' I did too. I desperately wanted to continue to mentor young people in rugby and athletics when I regained my freedom. The question was: would their parents want me to?

The last thing I wanted was to have to go into witness protection with my family. It would completely change our lives. But the alternative, not going, was also terrifying. If things didn't change, either I, or one of the family, would be harmed or killed.

I had lost ten kilograms in the past six months. I refused to eat meat because the chefs indiscriminately urinated on food served in our unit, hoping a paedophile, otherwise known as a rock spider, would eat it. I longed for a healthy meal of uncontaminated food. And I also longed to make sense of my situation. Since November 1999, I attended twenty individual counselling sessions to try and understand my circumstances. Nothing helped.

Locked in that shoebox of a cell, I closed my eyes and listened to the sounds of the night, dreaming of my freedom. I missed the cuddles of my daughter, Kate, the playful banter from my sons and the easy affection between Susan and me as she draped her legs over mine while we watched television, or leaned over my shoulder reading the newspaper headlines. I had spent one thousand and ninety-five days in prison, nine hundred and forty of them in solitary confinement. It was September 2000 and I was fifty-four years old. Tomorrow, I was going home.

Susan visited me the day before my release. In all the years since my arrest, I had never seen her look so jubilant, overjoyed, for the children's sake, that we would be a family again. Our marital relationship was going to take longer to heal. 'See you tomorrow,' she smiled, as she picked up her handbag to leave.

Half an hour before lockdown, I was called to the administration. 'Take a seat, Keith.' The governor was shuffling paperwork and I was smiling widely. 'Tomorrow morning at 8 am . . .' he started.

I interrupted him. 'I know. I'm going home.'

'I'm afraid not. Immigration authorities will be here

to pick you up and you are to be detained before being deported forthwith to New Zealand.' I couldn't comprehend what he was saying. 'I think I have made myself abundantly clear,' he said, when I asked him to repeat himself. 'Now, if you will excuse me?' He walked out.

I sat in the chair, devastated, not caring that the prison officers could see me sobbing. As I walked back into my cell, Daniel was waiting to say goodbye. 'I'm not going home,' I told him. 'I'm being deported.'

The same fighting spirit I witnessed in him the day I was told my father had died came to the surface. 'You must fight these pricks, Keith,' he said, as we were herded into our respective cells. 'You must stand and fight.'

I didn't have time to reply. 'Someone ring my wife,' I said, before they closed the cell door.

PART TWO

Cartel Confederate

11

I call my lawyer, O'Donohue, the next morning. 'They can't do this,' he seethes. 'We'll move bloody heaven and earth to ensure you stay here.'

Terry Houseman is a retired Australian Police Commander for the Federal Bureau of Narcotics who has worked for the FBI. He and some security officers escort me by van to Maribyrnong detention centre, near Carlton. I have essentially been in isolation for three years and find the people huddled in groups in the common room extremely intimidating. Everyone here is either from the Middle East or Asia. I am the only white man in the room. My request to be put into a quiet place, away from the crowds, is ignored and I wander around aimlessly.

I have two visitors at the centre. One is Terry, who wants to know which inmates I mixed with at Port Phillip prison.

The other visitor is Malcolm Pearce. 'Leave Australia,' he snarls, 'and your family will get more of the same.' I know he means business, his long history of criminal convictions for gun possession and violence proves as much. I wish I had the guts to punch him.

Instead, I tell him what I am doing so that he doesn't return, find me gone and take it out on my family. 'I've got to go to Brisbane to act as a witness in a civil matter for a financial institution, nothing related to me. Leave my family alone.'

My lawyer writes a lengthy letter appealing to the judge against my deportation and stressing that my offences were of dishonesty, and did not involve drugs or violence. 'The victims of the crimes have been repaid the money they invested,' he writes. 'Further, my client received $1.864 million in commissions, all of which has been repaid. He has no prior criminal history and is fully rehabilitated. He has been a model prisoner.'

Numerous colleagues and friends from work, school and sporting activities also support my application to stay in Australia, describing me as a decent family man with a loving wife and children. This is almost true, but for the fact that Susan's love for me has worn very, very thin.

I arrive at Brisbane's Arthur Gorrie prison in the early afternoon of 9 September 2000. The heat is oppressive and the place reeks with the same stench as all the other gaols I've been in: despair, discontent and disinfectant. It is as though the smell clings to the walls, the rancid stench of sweat, blood and stale piss.

Straightaway, I realise that they are going to process me as a prisoner, not as an Immigration detainee. 'Strip!' an officer barks and I'm standing naked in front of two officers as they body-search me before forcing me to shower as they watch. I wither in front of them, trying to cover my genitals, grateful when they hand me a prison uniform to wear.

The Immigration detention wing is full so, for lack of a better option, they dispatch me to the medical wing. The male nurse is agitated, annoyed that I am there and taking up his time. He fires off a series of medical questions before shoving a stick, used to test urine samples, in my hand. 'Piss on that,' he snarls, pointing in the direction of the toilet.

The rooms in the medical unit are small and my old fears resurface instantly. 'I'm claustrophobic,' I tell him, my hands becoming clammy just at the thought of being locked in a tiny cell. 'I'm an Immigration detainee, not a prisoner. Can you find somewhere where I can stay that isn't so confining?'

He looks at me, flint-eyed. 'Are you kidding, cock? You're having a lend of me, right? This is a prison. You've got Buckley's chance.' He grins at me before he collars an officer. 'Where can we put this girl? He reckons he gets claustrophobia.'

Before the officer can answer, the nurse offers a solution. 'How about the detox cell? That'll sort out his claustrophobia quick smart.'

They frogmarch me to the cell, pushing me ahead of them and shoving me in. The key turns in the lock and I warily survey my new surroundings. No window to the outside world, only artificial light and a room big enough to step out five paces before hitting the wall. There is no TV or radio, nothing to do but wait for the hour I'm allowed out into the small concrete yard to get some fresh air. I know that by late afternoon I'll be lying on the floor, gasping for oxygen to try and calm my nerves.

The nurse is still on duty at tea time. I've gathered by now there is little point appealing to this sadist's better nature, but I have a go, anyway. 'I'm a vegetarian,' I remind him for the second time that day, trying not to look at the grey pile of meat mixed with mushy potatoes that has been unceremoniously presented to me.

'Claustrophobic *and* a vegetarian,' he scoffs. 'You've sure got some problems, mate. Are you gonna eat that?' I'm not keen, and tell him so.

He stands over the plate of food and eyeballs me. 'Well, you've got two choices. You can shut up and get on with it, or you can refuse to eat it and we'll throw you in the observation unit as a hunger striker. When you're in there, we'll put you in a straitjacket and force-feed you.' He pauses for dramatic effect. 'What's your decision?'

I avoid eye contact with him – always the best policy with any bully in prison – and mumble my response. 'I'll eat the vegetable.'

They refuse to let me make a phone call to Susan and by 6 pm, when they turn off the lights in my cell, I feel the horribly familiar signs of a full-on panic attack take hold. The only light in the cell is through a small window in the door to the corridor and I'm pacing back and forth, back and forth, as chest pains threaten to floor me.

I don't know where I am. Dazed and disorientated, I am lying on the ground with three people, including a female nurse, standing over me, screaming for me to get up and kicking at my legs. I can't move and they are dragging me by my hair and shoulders over to a wall and propping me up against it. I'm so weak that I fall sideways, like a rag doll, and an officer continually knees me in the side of the head to keep me upright.

'What's he in for?' one person asks.

'Immigration. He's being deported tomorrow. This is just a bloody act. He doesn't want to leave.'

Right now, I'd like to go anywhere but here. The nurse is screaming at me while she applies elastic on my upper arm to take my blood pressure. It's tighter than a tourniquet and I wince with the pressure. Now another bloke has entered the room and is speaking to his colleagues.

'He's not being deported, he's giving evidence in a trial tomorrow,' he corrects them, casting a dismissive glance in my direction.

'Obviously he doesn't want to go to court,' someone else offers. 'This is just a ruse.'

The officer knees me in the head again, to remind me that he's there. Waves of nausea are washing over me and I think I'm going to throw up with the pain in my chest.

'His blood pressure is right up,' the nurse announces, shoving aspirin in my hand.

Obviously tired of holding me up with his knee, the officer demands that they get me on a bed, picking me up bodily and tossing me onto the mattress. My body is twitching in spasms and alarm bells are finally starting to ring with them. 'Shit,' one of them mutters. 'This guy really is sick! It might be his heart! We'd better check him.'

The heart equipment doesn't work. They put me in a wheelchair and head towards the observation cell, the male nurse delighting in pretending to push the wheelchair through a door that's too narrow, and stopping just at the last moment. Lying on a mattress on the cell floor, a wag suggests that they give me a tablet to divest my body of all its fluids. 'You can lie in it, all night,' he smirks. I don't smirk back.

It's a long night in the cell, sprawled on the floor mattress and staring up at the ceiling. Perhaps I am slightly delirious, but faces from my childhood – people from the small town where I grew up, mates at boarding school, my mother's face when I said goodbye to her in New Zealand – crowd my thoughts. I feel tormented: powerless against the system, powerless against the people who administer it, powerless to do anything to help myself. Deep introspection is not my forte: I would rather swim or run to throw off my worries than think too much about them. Bitterness, I know, is threatening to overwhelm me but worse than that, the sobering, dark torment of self-pity. My alter ego, that lonely boy from boarding school who did not stand up to the bullies, chants at me incessantly. *This is your own fault, you brought this on yourself. Coward, coward, coward.*

The sobs start deep within me, my face burrowing into the mattress to muffle the sounds that I cannot stop. And it is in this moment that I understand, with frightening clarity, why shackled men so often take their own lives, how despair can lead them to calmly, quietly, knot a bedsheet around their necks and hang themselves. Stripped of dignity, of humanity, it must seem the quickest and easiest way out of their pain.

The male nurse is back on duty the next morning, delivering me a breakfast of bacon and eggs. He watches while I eye the bacon. 'Oh, that's right,' he laughs. 'You're a vegetarian.'

Dishevelled and distressed, I try to appeal to some

decency in him. 'I've had a rough night. I had an anxiety attack. I haven't slept at all.'

'Good one,' he says.

12

I've got to be in court in three hours but it's such an ordeal to get a shower that I choose not to have one at all. Humiliated at how unkempt I look, I am escorted to the holding cells at the Supreme Court, where the same ritual of strip-searching is repeated.

I feel miserable, dehumanised and impotent against the system, but at least the lawyers seem to understand. One look at me and they know something is horribly wrong. They huddle with the judge, like rugby players in a scrum. I am not privy to their conversation but the gist of it is clear: that I'm in no emotional state to give evidence. The judge nods, gravely. If I am okay to appear three days later, he will expect me back at court.

My escorts – one of them Terry Houseman, who originally accompanied me from gaol to the Immigration Detention Centre in Maribyrnong and who I now consider to be a friend – assure me that I will be returned to Arthur Gorrie as a detainee, not a prisoner. One even offers to bunk down with me in the cell for the night to ensure my safety. But back at the prison,

I am told that I will be spending the night in the hospital wing.

My reaction is instantaneous. 'No way. No fucking way.' The words spew out of my mouth before I can catch them, and I've started to shake. 'I'm not going back there.'

'Settle down, Keith,' Houseman consoles me. 'We've spoken to the judge, who has ordered a full inquiry into your treatment here. In the meantime, we're putting you on your own in an eight-bed ward and making sure you get a decent vegetarian meal. Then you can phone your wife.'

Susan is at breaking point when we finally speak. 'I've tried you several times over the past few days and the New Zealand High Commission has also made calls,' she says. Her voice is trembling, as much with helplessness as fury. 'They refused to put any calls through to you.' She pauses, exhaling a shaky breath. 'God, Keith, what a mess! What the hell are we going to do?'

The night passes uneventfully, and I speak to the head of security the following morning. He wants a statement from me about my treatment here, but instead I tell him I'll organise one when I return to Melbourne. I just want to get back home to my family.

The guard at reception, where I am to exit the prison, stands a few centimetres from my face. 'I understand that you saw the head of security this morning. Is that right?' He has the face of a punch-drunk boxer, eyes slightly glazed and I wonder, briefly, if he is mad. 'I also understand that you will not be making complaints against any of the staff at this facility. Is that correct?'

Before I can answer him, he beckons me to follow him to a cell near the reception area. 'Get in there,' he says, locking the door. He peers through the narrow slot in the door to speak to me. 'You're claustrophobic aren't you?' I nod. 'What a shame. What a terrible shame.' He has made his point.

Back at reception, he gloats that he has good news and bad news. 'The good news is that you're going back to Melbourne. The bad news is that the clothes you have to wear are soaking wet.' Again my escorts come to my rescue, fetching me a change of clothes.

Horrified at my treatment, Terry Houseman encourages me to agree to make a statement. 'I have never, ever witnessed anything like this before,' he tells me. Right now, all I want is out. I step from the reception area into the blazing Brisbane sunshine. I don't look back.

Ten weeks after being taken into Immigration, I have my day in the Administration Tribunal, backed by witnesses testifying to my good character. The retired headmaster of a college where I coached rugby speaks on my behalf. 'Keith is a decent man who helps the community,' he says, passionately. 'What are we trying to do, destroy him and his family? I don't understand.'

My son Sam, twenty-two, tells the judge he loves me and my younger son, Mark, cries. So do I. My past is regurgitated and I stand before the judge, wondering when it will all end.

The judge is solemn, but kind. 'I've heard your case,' he says. 'You have made mistakes. You've done your time; you're a decent man and a good family man. My decision is you stay in Australia. You should not suffer anymore.'

I am so relieved I want to shout out in the courtroom. But I maintain decorum, nod my head in thanks and return to the detention centre, where I bundle up my possessions and leave. All I need now is for the Immigration Minister, to make his final decision. But after what I've been through, I have little hope that the system will support me and the threat of deportation continues to hang over my head.

I should feel elated to be out of prison. Instead, I feel angry, embarrassed and ashamed. Suddenly I have the perception that people are talking about me, whether they are or not. Some former friends and people I had swum with refuse to acknowledge me. I decide not to go to that swim club anymore, and join another one. But my inner voice is becoming louder, my confidence broken. *Loser.*

Life at home is worse than ordinary. Susan and I bicker constantly but there is no love there, just a perfunctory, cold kiss on the cheek. 'Give us time,' I beg her, but she turns away, a dark cloud crossing her face. Guilt and admonishments are served daily with derisive looks and outright verbal explosions.

'Look at the mess you've got us into! I can't look anyone in the eye!' I have brought scorn and shame on my family and she will not forgive me.

The phone threats continue, veiled and overt. 'You're dead meat, Keith. Your family are gonna get it, Keith.' The phone rings in the middle of the night and I answer it. There is never anyone there.

Pearce contacts me with a threat that if I refuse to meet him he will blow up the family car. He orders me out of the house and drives me down to a nearby beach, holding a gun to the small of my back. There is no conversation as I march ahead of him to the low tide mark and kneel in front of him like an obedient Japanese soldier facing the samurai sword. The beach is deserted, clouds gather ferocity and there is a sprinkle of rain. I shiver in the chill, cold and in shock. Pearce points the gun to my head, screaming at me to pay him the two million.

When I don't answer, he becomes hysterical. 'Fuck it! Fuck you!' he yells as he pulls the trigger. I hear the click, and then nothing more. The gun is empty. He kicks me up from the kneeling position and puts his nose close to mine. 'It won't be empty next time. Find your own way home.'

Not long after this incident, I open the front door to find Pearce standing there with two of his heavies. This coward rarely attacks me when he is on his own. They belt me around the head and throw me on the floor with the usual warning to pay the money. Pearce is convinced I must have hidden bank accounts flowing with cash, but that simply isn't true. He and his heavies follow me when I leave the house, but the police warn me not to cave in to Pearce's demands, saying that if I give him any money, he will only want more.

Susan constantly reminds me of the terror she and the children felt when the car bombs detonated, the terrible 'whooshing' sound as the vehicles incinerated and the sickening stench of petrol. She huddled with the kids in the bedroom in the middle of the night, wondering who was stalking the house, wondering whether they could get past police surveillance, video or street patrols. A car door closing brought on a panic attack and she would hold her breath, waiting for a knock on the door.

She took the precautions advised by the Brighton Criminal Investigation Branch, keeping the curtains drawn at all times to absorb any flying glass from Molotov cocktails that might be thrown through the windows. But nothing stopped her terror.

13

In January 2001, Terry Houseman calls me. A former drug enforcement commander with the Australian Federal Police, Terry spent fourteen years with the US Justice Department, based in San Francisco, from where he frequently travelled to Mexico and South America. Returning to Australia in the late 1990s, he continued to carry out the odd assignment for the Drug Enforcement Administration, a division of the US Justice Department.

Created by President Richard Nixon in July 1973, the DEA's task was to combat the drug menace by providing a unified front of almost fifteen hundred special agents with a budget of seventy-five million dollars. As the drug scourge increased, so too did the DEA: by 1974, it boasted forty-three offices in thirty-one countries around the globe. Today, the initial taskforce has been expanded to more than five thousand, two hundred special agents with a budget of more than $2.3 billion. It has eighty-seven agencies in sixty-three countries. The mission of the DEA is to enforce the controlled substances laws and regulations of the United States and to bring to court any person or organisation involved in the growing, manufacture, or distribution of illicit drugs. It also supports programs aimed at reducing the availability of illicit substances on the domestic and international markets.

Houseman's phone call is to the point. 'Keith, I've got an employment proposal for you to consider, based in America,' he starts. 'Are you interested in meeting to discuss it?' I am very interested: jobs for international bankers who have done time for fraud aren't exactly thick on the ground. I need to return to work, for my family's sake, and for my own.

'Absolutely,' I reply. 'Where and when?'

We agree to meet the following day at a small café in the city. I am intrigued to hear his offer. Terry is in his mid-sixties, tall, grey-haired, with gentle eyes and a kind smile. He knows my background. 'Mate, I've been asked to arrange an interview with you and two officials from the US embassy in Canberra,' he ventures. 'I think it's in your interests to hear what they've got to say. It could work very well for you with your Immigration issue. If you're okay with this, I'll call them now.'

'Shit, this is moving fast! What does the job entail?'

'It's best I leave it to the agents to tell you that,' he says, gesturing to the waiter to bring some coffee. 'We've got an interview with them tomorrow afternoon.'

American DEA agents Kevin Takahashi and Craig Palmer have booked a conference room in a Chinatown boutique hotel. They are meticulously organised, tape-recording devices and notebooks at the ready. We move quickly through the preliminary niceties before they get down to business.

'Okay, Keith. We want to make you an offer to work for the Drug Enforcement Administration, which falls under the umbrella of the US Justice Department. What are your initial thoughts?'

'The DEA? Sounds interesting, but it's not my background. What would I be doing?'

'We need you to track the movement of funds from Mexico into the USA.'

'Why would I be the right person to do that?'

'Because you have the connections we need.'

'A lot of people have.' My antennae have gone up, but Takahashi doesn't seem concerned.

'Our interest is in Daniel Gómez, who was CEO of two banks in Mexico and who has the contacts we need within Mexico City's banking system. You've got the key to open the door to the drug cartels in Mexico.'

My hands have suddenly gone clammy. 'Okay, so you want me to trade on my friendship with Daniel so he will introduce me to bankers. Is that it?'

'In short, yes. And other contacts as well.'

'What sort of "other contacts"?' I am openly suspicious now, my mouth set in a firm, thin line. 'What sort of "other contacts" are you referring to?'

'Cartel bankers. Their lawyers. Their accountants. Perhaps the cartel leaders themselves.'

'You want me to betray my friend?' My voice has an icy edge, and I fail to disguise my anger. I stand up. 'Let me get this clear: you want me to infiltrate drug cartels in order for you to be able to track dirty money?'

Takahashi returns my stare. 'Correct.'

I am stunned, mute. 'Just hang on,' I splutter when I find my voice. 'You want someone to act as a go-between for the DEA and the cartels? You need someone who will be readily accepted by cartel families, who has an inside track to drug trade finances? And that "someone" is me?'

'Correct. We would like to recruit you to work for us. You have great experience with international banking and know Gómez.'

'Recruit me? That's a generous description. What you mean is you want me to play Judas.'

'Not exactly. I wouldn't put it like that, no.'

'I would! What's more, you're expecting me to construct a life of deception, to deal with people whose language I neither speak nor understand and at the same time maintain a detailed, albeit fabricated, business life?'

'That is correct. Yes.'

'Do you understand what you're asking me to do? If Daniel introduces me to cartel people then there is a risk – a fucking big risk – that they will think he has betrayed them. He won't get any change out of that. They'll execute him. And me.'

'We would never put you at risk, Keith.' Craig Palmer has entered the conversation, trying to water down the tension. 'You simply need to meet with these people and then leave the rest to us. With regard to Gómez, he has no association with any DEA activity. All he has done is made some introductions; that's all.'

His attempt to placate me hasn't worked. 'Maybe I didn't make myself clear the first time.' I repeat, 'Daniel has told me that if he introduces anyone to cartel families and something goes wrong, then he will suffer the worst possible reprisals. If he puts me in touch with cartel people and you arrest them, we will both be killed. That is one hell of a fucking risk, from where I'm sitting.'

'Keith, you've got some problems at the moment.' Takahashi has taken charge of the conversation again, but his voice is less placatory. 'There's the issue with Immigration, and with Malcolm Pearce. You work for us, and both matters will be resolved.'

'Resolved how?'

'You don't need to know the details of that. Secondly, we can help you become financially secure again, give you back your credibility and arrange future employment for you. We can organise a Green Card so that you and your family can live and work in the US. We will report back to the parole board and the chairman about the excellent work you are doing for us.'

'The parole board?' My mind is racing. 'Are they of the opinion that accepting this offer is in my interests, also?'

I refrain from adding what I'm now wondering, whether the US Justice Department has done some sort of deal with Australian justice authorities in order to nail Gómez through me. Was my incarceration in Sirius East, apparently for my own protection, in actual fact a set-up so that I could meet Gómez?

Palmer has rejoined the conversation. 'We will make sure that neither Gómez nor you are ever at risk. We promise you that.'

'I understand. But when it all comes down to it, I'm still betraying Daniel. And I'm not prepared to do it.'

'We will protect you both, Keith. You've got to trust us on that. Consider what is going to happen to you with Immigration. The minister has the final say and any recommendation from us about the work you are doing will go a long way towards allowing you to remain in Australia. The work will, in fact, convince the minister to approve your Australian citizenship. And the Pearce matter will simply disappear.'

'No risk at all to either of us?'

'None.'

'No risk for my family?'

'None.' Takahashi looks at his watch. 'Have a coffee and think about it. You'll be working in San Diego. You'll be safe. We'll come back in ten minutes.'

He is back in time, as promised. 'We'd like you to phone Gómez at Port Phillip prison, via his lawyer,' Takahashi suggests. 'Ask for him to return your call.'

I know how the system works. The lawyers phone the prison requesting that their client phones them immediately. The message is passed to the prisoner, who in turn phones them back. These calls are not monitored. The lawyer then transfers the call to my mobile phone. The agents want to electronically monitor the telephone conversation between myself and Daniel, to determine the relationship I have with him. Within the hour, he calls me back.

'Keith! How are you, my friend?' We make idle conversation for a moment. 'I wonder, Keith, if you could do some company work for me regarding my house?' he asks. 'I will arrange for my lawyer to pay you.'

'Of course. Get your lawyer to give me the details.'

Before he hangs up, Daniel gives me a word of advice. 'You should make your way to Mexico, my friend. Maybe I can organise some work for you. Think about it.'

'Perfect. Couldn't be better even if we'd written the script for him,' Takahashi grins when I hang up. 'Consider our offer, Keith. You'll be protected, Gómez will be safe, and your problems will be over.' He pauses for a moment. 'I commend your loyalty to this bloke. I really do. But it's misplaced. Remember this: he is a vital link in a chain in the dirtiest war there is. Just ask the thousands of people who have died across Mexico at the hands of the drug cartels, and the junkies whose lives are ruined by cocaine and smack. Your Daniel is no hero.'

I barely sleep, wrestling with the enormity of what they are asking me to do. I know with my prison record that it is impossible for me to return to the industry as a mortgage broker, but I desperately need, somehow, to gain an opportunity to redeem myself in employment and, more importantly, to regain the respect of my family. But I can't betray a friendship, which is my only entry into this opportunity. I need to think smart, think clever. I need to work out a way that I can protect Gómez and still do the work.

The next morning, I call Takahashi. 'Okay, I'll do it. But I do it on my terms. You protect Daniel. You protect my family. And you protect me.'

'Done deal, Keith. You've made a wise decision. When do you want to start work?'

14

I sometimes wonder whether Susan hears everything I say. Three years of raising the children on her own and dealing with the humiliation of me going to prison has hardened her and she is preoccupied, justifiably, with her own problems. Her elderly parents live with us. Her mother, eighty-one years old, has Alzheimer's and her father, almost ninety, is partially blind and hearing-impaired. Susan has had to resort to borrowing money from her sister and her parents to cope financially and she has her own health problems to deal with. On top of it all, she is exhausted from working full-time.

Now I have to break the news to her, and I sense she will be less than impressed. I'm right. I wait until we are on our own. 'Susan, I need to talk to you about something important,' I start. Her back stiffens immediately. 'I've been offered a position with the US Department of Justice and the offer is backed by the Immigration Department and the parole board.'

'Doing what?'

She is not taking this well and I am deliberately vague

in my answer. 'To track the flow of funds into the US. But I don't know much more than that at present. Look,' I add, too hastily, 'it's been strongly suggested to me that I take the overseas position, as it will help with my rehabilitation and in seeking employment back here in Australia.'

'You've already been away for the last three years, and this isn't fair on the family!' I can see her temper rising. 'Where will you be posted to, and for how long?'

'San Diego. I think it's for twelve months.'

'Twelve months! You know we can't come with you? I can't leave my parents, and the kids are at uni!'

'They've told me they will fly me home every few months. I'm required to report to the parole board and they will fly you and the kids to the States twice a year. It is an excellent salary.'

'How much?'

'Around twenty thousand dollars a month.'

'Do you have a choice?'

'Not really.'

She stares hard at me. 'This is insane, Keith, leaving the family again so soon. The kids need you.'

'Yes, I know. And what about you? Do you need me, Susan?' She glares at me and turns her back.

The US Justice Department flies me to the States for a brief interview. Before I leave, I do a little homework on the DEA. Mike Workman, the Director of the DEA, was previously an attorney in western Arkansas before becoming a US congressman. Though his work with the DEA was significant, he is more famous as being one of the House managers who conducted the impeachment trial of President Clinton in the Senate.

Workman's commitment was to indict high-ranking cartel leaders and to extradite them from Mexico, as well as freezing their assets and prohibiting Americans from doing business with them. Workman was only too aware of the obstacles facing his goals. In a wide-ranging speech to Congress he warned that one of the major issues for the US agencies is getting the Mexican government to allow extradition of high-level drug defendants to the US. The Mexican government has taken a very strong stance over the death penalty and life in prison is still viewed by the Mexican Supreme Court as a violation of their constitution.

The DEA has always seen Tijuana as a war zone, and has particularly targeted a large pharmacy and resort hotel near Rosarito, in Baja California, only a few hundred kilometres from the US border where thousands of Americans flock to acquire inexpensive medical drugs. US customs have clamped down on products coming from certain pharmacies in Rosarito because they are owned by the cartels. The more I read, the more I realise that half of Mexico seems like a war zone. And if I get this job, one way or another I'm going to be in the middle of it.

The interview outlining my position appears to be a done deal. 'We want you to start as quickly as possible,' Morgan Taylor says. Morgan is a woman with a tough face and a kind heart. She will be my first point of call and the go-between when I need anything done.

They confirm my salary and conditions, including flying me home to see my family every eight weeks and paying for them to visit. The deal sounds like heaven, with the downside of leaving my family again. I've been bankrupt since 1995 and on the bones of my arse ever since. Susan has never forgiven me for bringing disgrace on our family and it was a bitter financial struggle for her when I was in gaol. I'm desperate to regain respect, and to make a quid again to support my family.

It takes another eight weeks to tie up the paperwork before I can return to the States. The State Department in Washington is given my detailed history, but issues a waiver, allowing me a B1 and B2 visa to enable me to live and work there.

The Immigration issue is still hanging over my head, but just days before I am due to go to the States, I receive a letter from the department, advising me that, following a recent High Court decision, the Minister for Immigration and Multicultural Affairs does not have the power to deport or remove certain British subjects who arrived in Australia prior to 19 October 1973. 'As you fall within this category,' the letter continues, 'the Department will no longer be considering your liability for visa cancellation.'

It has taken them nine months to give me this advice. Tellingly, it has come from the High Court of Australia, rather than the Minister for Immigration. It seems curious: why would the parole board have told me the decision to work for the US Justice Department would help me in my fight against deportation, if legally they could not deport me anyway?

15

From the moment I arrive in the US, the Department of Justice bestows me with my working moniker, Agent Greece. From now on, all DEA and FBI agents will address me as Greece, and all cartel people will know me as Keith Wilson. My transformation is now complete, my former spotless reputation restored.

I will be stationed at San Diego. It is no coincidence that this agency, the biggest DEA station in America, sits opposite Mexico.

Daniel has talked to his people about me, using my first name, and the DEA writes up a file, placed onto the US Customs and Immigration database, so that the drug cartels can cross-reference my details via their paid informers. As soon as I start actively working, those checks will be done.

The room is crowded with people: Morgan Taylor; her supervisor, Jim; the regional director and two field agents; a special investigator from the Internal Revenue Service seconded to the DEA; and a senior DEA agent who is in charge of Charlies – confidential informers in Mexico.

Jim, who has the demeanour of a preacher from Bible-belt country, leads the conversation. 'The Bush Administration, this Justice Department and the DEA are extremely focused on fighting this war against drugs,' he says. 'We cannot stress enough to you, Greece, the damage drug cartels cause. It has therefore become necessary to enforce indictments and hit money-laundering activities much harder than we have in the past.'

So far, he has told me nothing I don't already know. 'The government has approved an aid package for the Colombian government to help fight the drug cartels,' he continues. 'The Colombians have managed to eradicate thousands of hectares of coca fields, but the supply is still there. The ongoing issue with Colombia is the paramilitary groups who are funded by the drug trade and involved in drug trafficking as well. The American government is determined to work with the Colombians and train their national police in going after the drug organisations.'

Morgan steps into the conversation. It's hard not to like her: a hard-nosed copper transferred to the DEA, she has a motherly approach, and a down-to-earth attitude. 'Greece,' she starts, 'Colombian drug cartel leaders are mainly based in Cali or Medellin, but most police services and the US government refer to Colombian drug people as "Cali" people.' I nod. 'What we'd like to invite you to do, please, is to go over your relationship with Daniel Gómez for us. His bank set-ups, personal history, anything you can tell us that may be of help. We are interested in tracking cartel money and identifying major distributors in the United States.'

I wave my hands, vaguely. 'I know nothing of his history, really,' I say. 'To be frank, I'm a bit mystified as to what you actually want me to do.'

'These people need a banker, a broker and an investment manager, all rolled into one,' she tells me. 'They need someone in whom they can place absolute trust, who can wash, rinse and spin-dry their money. You're that man: you come with Daniel Gómez's recommendation. But always remember who it is you're dealing with. They're totally ruthless. Cartel groups are known as octopuses, because they have tentacles spread all over the world. The only place for them is in a Supermax prison, a concrete tomb.'

'What sort of back-up do I get from the DEA?'

'Plenty. We'll be behind you all the way in every deal. But we don't have emotional relationships with our informants and, because of the nature of the work, you don't exist as far as we're concerned. It has to be like that.'

'So I'm persona non grata? Just like I was in prison?'

'Afraid so. But the difference is, we're behind you. You will be protected and inaccessible, under deep-cover security.'

In the afternoon, they bring in fresh blood: DEA agents who deal with Mexican cartel informants. They give me an exhaustive run-down on cartel families, who controls what and the innovative ways in which they smuggle drugs into the States.

The Arellano Félix family is one of the top drug cartel families based in Tijuana. Spanning the northwest of Mexico, they are less powerful than their major rivals in the Gulf and Sinaloa, who control much of the country's smuggling routes, but no cartel matches them for their extreme violence and criminality.

'This cartel features in the movie *Traffic*,' an agent explains.

'But they have descended into unprecedented violence in the years since that movie's release.'

Founded by Miguel Ángel Félix Gallardo, the cartel monopolised the drug routes from Tijuana to the United States for more than two decades, coming to power after Colombian cocaine leaders, deprived of their traditional means of trafficking across the Caribbean into Florida, teamed up with Mexican criminal elements. Arrested in 1989 for his part in the murder of DEA Special Agent Enrique Camarena, Gallardo continued to run his operation in prison from a mobile phone, until his transfer in 1990 to a Supermax prison.

This move loosened his power base and signalled a dangerous shift within the organisation: his nephews, the Arellano Félix brothers, gained power over the Tijuana cartel, with cells in fifteen Mexican states. Furthermore, a new faction, the Sinaloa cartel, was started by Gallardo's former henchmen, including the feared Joaquín Guzmán, known as El Chapo, meaning 'Shorty.'

The Arellano Félix family leader Ramón – a hulking 1.88 metres tall and known to his rivals as the Chief Enforcer because no one escaped his vengeful wrath – was on the DEA's most-wanted list, not only for his interests in the drug trade but because he was responsible for the vicious torture and murder in 2000 of three Mexican DEA agents who were building a case against the family. The agents' heads were crushed and their bodies found at the bottom of a ravine next to their wrecked car. In September 1998 alone, Ramón ordered the execution of eighteen people in Baja California.

Since the 1990s, using a crossing from Mexicali, tonnes of cocaine that would convert to millions of lines of the white powder have been smuggled into the States for its users, the biggest consumers of coke in the world. The brothers take no prisoners, killing anyone who stands in their way, including government officials, traffickers and bystanders. Marijuana, heroin and methamphetamine are also smuggled using sophisticated covert operations: a combination of employing corrupt police and intricate communications systems.

The family employs guns for hire, Hispanic gang members who live in the United States and who operate as assassins, and wealthy sons of Mexican families, known as Narco Juniors, who cross on dual passports between the two countries. The currency the cartel trades in is money, drugs and guns. Their tactics are intimidation, violence, bribery and corruption.

The agent, a stout man with red hair and freckled hands, continues with his briefing. In what prosecutors later believed was a spectacular bungle, the Roman Catholic Cardinal, Juan Jesús Posadas Ocampo, died in a fusillade of bullets at the Guadalajara Airport in 1993. His murder created an outcry in Mexico, a deeply religious country whose people are known for their pious obedience to Jesus Christ. The brothers had confused the cardinal's car with that of rival drug gang leader, 'El Chapo' Guzmán.

That did not stop their human carnage. In a chilling warning to authorities in 1996 not to mess with them, they fired more than a hundred bullets into a Mexican state prosecutor outside his home, before driving their van back and forth a dozen times over his broken body. To capture the brothers and break into their financial operations would be a major coup for the US government.

In 1996, a bodyguard for the Arellano family was arrested and interviewed by DEA agents. He described in detail the paramilitary precision which Ramón brought to the task of coordinating the cartel's security. One of his responsibilities was to plan the murders of rivals, officials they could not corrupt and cartel members who fell from grace. 'If Ramón was bored, he would instruct us to find someone to kill,' the bodyguard said. 'The person nominated would be dead within a week.'

'The drug trafficking corridor through Baja California was, and remains, one of the most lucrative routes on the US–Mexico border,' the agent tells me. 'Together, the DEA and the Mexican government are working to try and reduce the flow of drugs and to break the violent grip the Arellano family holds on the area. You are one of the tools we will use to help break that hold.'

By the time they finish, I feel like I've swum a hundred laps.

The next morning, we run through the complex web of how cartels operate. The red-haired agent is in charge again. 'A lot of these people are well organised and invest in real estate, private and public companies, resorts, hotels and shopping centres,' he says, pointing to a whiteboard that outlines what he is telling me. 'This is their front of being successful businessmen, while others, like Pablo Escobar, start off as small-time criminals and then move up into the drug trade.' Pablo Escobar. The name is familiar to me from my conversations with Gómez. 'With their sudden wealth, they buy mansions, airplanes and zoos, and invest in private armies to protect their markets and their own skins.'

By the 1980s, Colombian drug cartels controlled more than eighty per cent of the world's cocaine trade. In response to the international and domestic crackdown, the powerful Medellin cartel stepped up its terrorist attacks, including car bombings and political assassinations. With American government assistance, the Colombians managed to track down the main cartel leader, Pablo Escobar, the biggest cocaine drug lord in the history of that country and the United States. Escobar ruled Medellin with an iron fist, murdering police officers, judges and Colombian presidential candidates who were pro-extradition to the US. In November 1989, his cartel group planted a bomb on a flight believed to be carrying a candidate, killing over a hundred people. His target wasn't on board.

When Colombia banned extradition in their constitution, Escobar handed himself in to the Department of Justice. But there was a twist: he would serve his time in a prison that he himself built. When it was completed, it was more like a resort hotel. Daniel Gómez had proposed a similar arrangement with Australian authorities, but they weren't keen to take him up on the idea.

Escobar had it all, but blew it when he assassinated two people within his own prison. He escaped and both the US and Colombian governments, and the Calis, had him on their most-wanted list.

When the DEA and Colombian police went through his prison, they found confidential files bursting with information on the DEA, their investigations, informers and contacts. This information had provided Escobar with the names of people he needed to murder in order to survive. He killed thousands, using his infamous deal, *plata o plomo* – silver or lead. Bribery or bullets. He was killed in early December 1993 after a prolonged gunfight, his death paving the way for the Calis and Mexicans to take control over the drug industry in Colombia.

In the afternoon, Morgan grills me on how I would set up a bank and control the flow of funds. 'You need to establish an investment bank that has a licence to carry out financial transactions,' I explain. 'But since you're owned by the government, that shouldn't be too hard.'

Morgan trains me on how to transfer the essentials of a meeting onto my laptop and how to email data from a camera through to DEA headquarters. 'Your brief,' she says, 'is to operate a private bank, Essex Finance Limited, based in San Diego. We need to draft a standard letter outlining our services that will be sent to each of the cartel families in Mexico.' It takes us hours to set out.

> We deal primarily with clients from Mexico and various South American countries. We are not a public company, therefore we do not advertise. We operate solely on referrals. Daniel Gómez has referred us to you. Most of our clients have a need for discretion and confidentiality. We have a British corporation with corporate bank accounts as well as established banks in London, England. If necessary, we are able to provide offshore corporations in order to form a new foreign company on your behalf. The majority of our clients have utilised Panama to set up their foreign accounts. However, these accounts can be set up in a country of your choosing.
>
> These documents can be prepared in a variety of formats and once they are justified, the funds can then be transferred from the foreign account to the account of your choosing. We prefer that our clients maintain considerable funds in their numbered accounts at the London bank in order to show that the British corporation has the ability to provide the loans in question. Another advantage is that Essex Finance Limited can make purchases as your agent, again providing you with discretion and confidentiality.

The commission we charge for the movement of your funds will be negotiated prior to conducting any transactions. We guarantee the security of your funds during the transaction phases involving any of our accounts. Our business is based on discretion and we would appreciate it if you would treat this information with the same level of confidentiality.

Though it presented a sober, conservative face to the world, in reality Essex Finance was a banking facility that could accept large amounts of cash from anywhere around the globe, cash stained with the blood of thousands of victims of the ruthless drug wars which would then be laundered clean for cartel families. Essex would provide the US government with an opportunity to track the movement of funds from the drug cartel families to international bank accounts in Europe, the US, the Caribbean and Asia. It would also enable them to obtain records of their assets, bonds and stocks, property, art and offshore trusts as well as a list of their contacts in the US drug trade.

It costs the American government fifty billion a year to fight the war on drugs. They have increased their expenditure to buy weapons, fighter jets and submarines. But for all their firepower, success against the might of these cartels is extremely limited. It is operations like Essex Finance that can have a far greater impact in breaking the cartels' crushing hold, by taking their cash and assets and destabilising their power bases.

16

The DEA has arranged for me to stay at the Holiday Inn in El Cajon, close to their headquarters. I head to the swimming pool when I arrive and watch a woman in her mid-thirties frolicking in the water with her three young children. She is blonde and beautiful. We start chatting as she dries off the children.

'Claudia,' she smiles, extending a slender manicured hand. 'And these are my children, Martina, Klaus and Anja.' Though she speaks English well, her accent is German. 'I am here to start work in the Medical school at the University of Southern California and am busy trying to find a house to rent,' she tells me. 'The university has only agreed to accommodate us for one week at the hotel and I am in a hurry to settle.' I know nobody here and invite them to join me for dinner, an invitation Claudia readily accepts. From that moment, we become virtually inseparable, despite our eighteen-year age difference.

After I secure an office for the bank, I help the family look for a house to rent. The first one comes with a view overlooking a public park, which the kids love. But there is a catch: the agent needs a bond of four thousand dollars and a month's rent of sixteen hundred dollars. Claudia does not have enough money to cover the costs until she is paid. 'I'll fix it up for you and you can pay me back later,' I say, signing a cheque. She hugs me.

'Keith, you need to find somewhere to live as well,' she says as we walk towards the car. 'You get on well with the children; why don't you move in with us?'

'I'm married, Claudia. I have a wife and family in Australia.'

'Why are they not with you?'

I start to answer, and think better of it. 'Okay,' I say. 'You're right, I do need to live somewhere.' I don't kid myself that it will be platonic. Susan and I are now married in name only and, after three lonely years in prison, our relationship wasn't any better on my release.

That night at the hotel, Claudia and I sleep together for the first time. I haven't been with someone I feel passionate about for years, and it is special to be intimate again. I should feel guilty, but I don't. I have fallen into the arms of a wonderful woman. It is a whole new lease of life for me. Within a week of meeting Claudia, I have fallen in love.

I tell Morgan Taylor that I am going to move in with Claudia, and to my surprise she encourages the situation. 'This is perfect cover for you, Greece, and will also help to protect your own family in Australia. It makes them far less of a target for anyone. We will pay your share of the rent, as agreed.'

Within twenty-four hours, the deal is done. The children are enrolled in the local schools and Claudia buys a bicycle to get to university every day. The DEA comes around as soon as we move in. They fit some devices to the telephone line, put up security lights and an alarm and fix security doors on the front and back of the house. They check the front gates to the driveway, spend a few hours making sure the house is secure and leave.

Claudia often speaks to Morgan, who transfers the call to me. Claudia thinks Morgan is my secretary and we agree on that strategy. Susan also has no knowledge of what I am doing. She thinks Claudia is a friend who shares the rent and I work for the US Department of Justice in a clerical position. If she has any doubts, she never lets on.

The cartels send their own security personnel to check my office and home and to photograph me. The DEA record all their movements, knowing they would do their research on me before handing over millions of dollars in cash for me to bank. They had their lawyers check everything surrounding Essex Finance, from incorporation, to tax returns and company directors. All documentation is held at the registered office in the British Virgin Islands, which has a plaque outside announcing its name. Tortola, the largest of the three main islands in the group, has its own cartel people on the island, so a plaque had to be there otherwise the Mexicans and the Colombians would become suspicious. Daniel told me several times: 'You must have everything in order, otherwise they will not use your services. It is all about trust.'

Daniel Gómez has a cousin, Juan, living in San Diego, who invites Claudia, the children and me for dinner at a beautiful restaurant in the city's Gas Lamp Quarter. A photographer walks around taking snapshots of diners, and approaches our table, smiling and gesturing for us to sit close to have our picture taken. Juan enthusiastically agrees, slinging his arms around the backs of our chairs.

He wants memories of this occasion to send to Daniel, he says. But it isn't as innocent as it sounds: Morgan tells me later that they suspect Mexican cartel people were in the restaurant, observing us, and that the cartel arranged the photographer.

17

It is time to make my first test run, to meet Daniel on his home turf. I prepare for the trip with great care, ensuring I have all the documentation I need, that my suits and shirts are pressed and my shoes shine. This comes naturally to me: boarding school taught me to be meticulous in my personal grooming and to fold my clothes with military precision. The DEA hands over ten thousand dollars cash and a booking at the prestigious J.W. Marriott Hotel in Mexico City, in the wealthiest part of town that caters to the elite. This area is a world away from the poorer parts of the city populated by indigenous Mexicans. Here, private security firms guard the streets, the shops stock designer clothing and the restaurants are alive with the scents of lilies and roses.

The DEA also gives me explicit instructions not to wander out of the hotel and to contact the US embassy if anything goes wrong. Their instructions are clear: I am to tell Daniel that I am coming down to Mexico and would like to see him, and that I have started a bank with funds from an old friend in San Diego. 'Tell him you want to be introduced to some of his clients, who might like to have a "creative" banker,' Morgan instructs me.

Daniel fought against his extradition to Mexico for several years in Australia until a satisfactory deal was struck with the Mexican authorities. A satisfactory deal for Daniel, that is. Upon his return to his native country, he was immediately released and, after several months, all charges against him were dropped. Like nothing ever happened. Rumour has it this freedom cost him thirty million.

Daniel greets me like an old friend when I call him. 'It will be lovely to see you, Keith,' he tells me warmly. 'I look forward to it very much.' I give him my prepared spiel about the bank. 'I am pleased you are doing something after prison. I have a client in mind for you, but be warned: don't fuck him around. Just do the transaction and, if it is successful, you will have more business than you can handle.'

It is my first trip to Mexico. Millions of city lights blink at dusk and not for the first time I wonder what the hell I am getting myself into, and how dangerous this assignment may turn out to be. This is a country whose morgues serve as a grim reminder of the ruthless and indiscriminate violence of the drug cartels. Mexico City teems with twenty-seven million people and I am overwhelmed at the clamour and chaos before I even leave the airport.

Two Mexican men in suits, hair slicked back, hold a cardboard placard with my name on it. I walk over to them. 'You are looking for Keith Wilson?' I ask. They do not speak English and do not respond. Instead, one grabs my briefcase and the other my elbow, pushing me ahead of them to an upstairs carpark. The Mexican with my brief-case is speaking in rapid Spanish into a two-way radio, and I have no comprehension of what he is saying. I also have no idea who they are: if they are Daniel's men or members of another cartel. They usher me into a waiting black van with a driver and bodyguards, all carrying weapons. The van, followed by two others, roars out of the airport into mainstream traffic, the streets thick with dust and pollution and the cloying stench of a pitifully overcrowded city.

Smog hangs low and the sickening smell of exhaust fumes permeates the air. The traffic is bumper to bumper, grindingly slow, and I peer out into the darkness at the unfamiliar surroundings. The French and Spanish influ-ences on the city's architecture lend it an old-world air, a sense of stepping back in time. Older women, wide of girth, favouring the traditional brown and dark russet colours of the Mexican plains, mingle outside shops, gossiping, while younger women in Western clothing – short skirts, high heels and large, cheap gold loop earrings – sashay down the street. Women in their thirties in riotous coloured clothing, vivid yellows and bright greens, break the monotony, standing out from the crowd like some exotic peacocks and their partners, urban *charros*, wear their traditional *sarapes* draped like a blanket around their shoulders, their feet encased in ornate, pointy-toed boots.

A bodyguard hands me a cellphone, indicating I should speak. To my enormous relief, it is Daniel. 'Welcome to Mexico, my friend,' he says, in the confident tone I came to know so well in prison. 'You are being taken now to your hotel. The same people who picked you up will meet you in the morning at ten o'clock and bring you to our meeting. It will be good to see you again.'

At the hotel, another of Daniel's men is waiting for me, and hands me an envelope containing thirty thousand pesos. 'Enjoy your evening,' he says, pressing the envelope into my hands. 'But under no circumstances leave the hotel.'

I meet Daniel as arranged the next morning. Several bodyguards stand sentinel, demanding I leave my brief-case, watch and cellphone outside his office and checking my belt and shoes for weapons. It is, I come to under-stand, a normal routine. Everyone who visits the office goes through the same procedure.

It is good to see Daniel. He has lost the unhealthy pallor of prison and regained a robust complexion and is, as always, warm and inviting. 'The man you will be doing this for is Rommel Santiago,' he tells me after we make small talk. I recognise the name immediately from the list of cartel families written on the DEA control room whiteboard. I am frightened by his reputation, let alone the fact I will have to work with him.

Daniel grills me over the details of Essex Finance and his eyes harden. 'Keith, if you fuck this deal, we are both fucked. Do you understand?'

I am not to meet his client on this occasion, and the first transaction is seamless. 'I need you to move nine hundred thousand for him today,' Daniel says. 'Let us see if your system works.' I move through the motions, so familiar to me, transferring the funds from Chile to the Royal Bank of Scotland in Glasgow, through to the National Westminster Bank in London and then organ-ising Essex Finance to lend the funds back to the client in Mexico City.

When it is done, Daniel pumps my hand and beams. 'Welcome Keith. It will be nice working with you.'

I have passed muster, but suddenly realise the gravity of my situation. Anyone who betrays the drug cartels pays the ultimate price. Their life.

I continue making small transactions with the DEA watching. In the first few months, they are always under a million dollars, as are the purchase of shares on the London and New York stock exchanges. I want it that way, as I am dealing with selected investment houses and because small transactions attract fewer questions.

Slowly, the transactions get bigger: a fourteen-million-dollar transfer from a Tijuana holding company in the Bahamas to a hotel development in Spain; switching eight million from a Berlin account to our bank account in London before bringing the money back into Mexico as a loan from Essex Finance Limited to a trading company in Monterrey; moving sixteen million dollars from Argentina to the Royal Bank of Scotland in Edinburgh, through Essex then back to our client as a loan for his resort development in Cancún; and purchasing a house in Puerto Vallarta, on the Pacific coast of Mexico, for $3.8 million, switched from a drug cartel's account in Curaçao to our London account.

I make several loans, totalling around one hundred and thirty-five million, to a pharmaceutical factory in Santiago, Chile. The funds come from accounts in the Caribbean, Switzerland and the British Channel Islands, and are transferred to Essex Finance. We establish a trust company in The Hague, made up of several different family members of the one cartel group, which in turn makes a loan to a Mexican holding company, based in Mexico City. This company purchases eighty per cent of the pharmaceutical company.

Most of the transactions are cut and dried, but there are lighter moments. Standing in a hotel lobby preparing to meet a feared Gulf cartel member, I turn on my tape-recorder. I am petrified, and talking to myself. 'I'm scared, I'm scared,' I say, forgetting that the tape is on. A high-class call girl approaches, tottering over on killer heels and flashing an indecent amount of cleavage. She wants to come to my room and seduce me, she says. To allay any suspicions from the cartel bodyguards who must be watching, I ask her what her prices are, and for what services. She answers me explicitly, very explicitly: all recorded on the tape for DEA entertainment.

The most exciting transaction I am involved in is the acquisition of paintings at Christie's auction house in New York. A cartel family viewed several paintings that they want to buy, including those by Mexican artists Frida Kahlo and Diego Rivera, and Spanish artists Salvador Dalí and Pablo Picasso. Their funds are on deposit in Switzerland and thirty million dollars is wired into Essex's account. I am given instructions to purchase, within limits, and to have the paintings shipped to the Essex office in San Diego, where they will be collected.

Once the funds are in our account, I fly first class to New York and stay at the Waldorf-Astoria. I have notified Christie's that Essex Finance will be at the auction and that I will be bidding for several paintings on behalf of a European client.

Christie's collect me from the airport in their limousine and take me to lunch. An extremely attractive DEA agent, Sally, accompanies me. She is based in New York, and advises me that other agents will also be at the auction. I am given a white board with the number 9 in black that I hold in the air for the auctioneer to see.

Sally and I look the part. She wears a flattering black Armani business suit purchased by the DEA, jewellery from Dior which she has to return to the shop on Fifth Avenue, and reading glasses from Dolce & Gabbana, also to be returned. She is stunning. I successfully bid for the paintings and sit with a Christie's director to arrange for our Wells Fargo Bank to transfer the funds, a total of twenty-six and a half million, to the Christie's account at Chase Manhattan. Afterwards, I return my perfectly-cut pinstriped Armani suit to the store.

18

My first meeting with Miguel Díaz, shortly after starting with the DEA, takes place over a meal at the traditional Mexican El Bajio in Polanco. I explain the advantages of building a wall around our British corporations, which will wire the funds directly to an account when the client requests it.

'The account cannot be in Mexico,' I tell him. 'The funds can be parked in one of our London accounts, and your client gives us their shopping list. We then purchase anything they require on their behalf. We have the ownership, registered in an offshore entity, with no trace back to the client. It is the perfect cover.'

Miguel raises his concerns about the money coming back into Mexico. 'The bank documents would explain in detail that it is a loan from our bank to your client,' I say, casually piling a leafy salad onto my plate and refreshing our wines. 'And we can handle any questions the Mexican authorities will raise.' He seems satisfied.

Miguel boasts many high-end clients and is having difficulty moving money for one of them. 'Maybe you can help me with this problem?' he asks.

'I can, yes. What sort of banking method do you have in mind?' He has seen the letter from Essex Finance and we go through the contents in detail. He asks the odd question, but understands the procedure well. No one is aware of Miguel's connection to Colombia: not the DEA, not Al (the DEA agent assigned to my case), and certainly not me. The only information to which we are privy is that he has a client who needs to bank, urgently.

This, he explains, is my opportunity to prove to the cartel families that my system works and that I can be trusted. *Trust.* It is a commodity in short supply in Mexico. Miguel and I have nothing at all in common, except a banking background and our shared contact, Daniel Gómez.

'You know Daniel well?' I ask him.

'Very well, yes,' he nods, unsmiling. 'And you? You also are well acquainted with him, I believe?'

'Very well acquainted.'

He swirls the wine in his glass before speaking. 'One of my clients has funds in a Swiss bank, and they want to bring some of those funds back into Mexico without detection.'

'No problem. That's achievable.'

'Good. Then I will recommend we proceed.' He pauses, eyeballing me with a hard stare. 'You will have to meet them before they agree that you can work for them. They will need to ask a few questions.'

'What sort of questions?' The conversation has taken a malevolent turn and I hope my face doesn't betray what I'm thinking. *What sort of questions do drug cartel leaders ask? What do they do to you if you give the wrong answer?* My hands are sweating. This is totally outside my experience. I am way out of my depth.

'They need to smell you.' Miguel suddenly guffaws, a guttural laugh that reeks of menace. Just as quickly, his face is deadpan again. 'It's true. They will only deal with you when they can smell your fear, when they know you won't fuck with them.'

'Do I know who these people are?' I haven't touched my food but take a gulp of wine to try and calm my rising panic.

Miguel ignores my question. 'I will try and arrange a meeting in the next forty-eight hours. If they are satisfied they can trust you, then you will have more business than you can handle. And that,' he says, rising and extending his hand, 'will be good for both of us. *Adios.*'

Good for both of us. I can't see how I can benefit from any involvement in the sordid drug world. All I want is to regain some credibility and go home to my family.

Morgan doesn't hide her excitement at the possibility of a meeting with a leading cartel member. She has worked out a code based on a rugby game when we are speaking on the telephone. I am the 'coach' and she is the 'secretary'. 'Always remember that phones can't be trusted,' she warned me. 'Use them only in an emergency.'

'Hi, Morgan, it's the coach here,' I start when I call her. I feel foolish, as though I am playing a silly game from a Boy's Own adventure. But this is no game. 'I had dinner with one of the rugby agents in Mexico City, who has recommended me to one of his star players.'

I have piqued her interest. 'Fantastic news! Well done! What are the chances they will play for us?'

'Pretty good, I reckon. We're hoping for a meeting within forty-eight hours. I'll keep you posted.'

'Thanks, Greece. And good luck.' I grimace. Good luck? I'll need more than fucking good luck.

Soon enough, Miguel arranges to pick me up at the hotel entrance. We barely speak as he spins into the melee of traffic and races along the crowded streets, overtaking cars and running red lights. Some fifteen minutes later, when we reach the hotel where we are meeting, beads of sweat are clearly visible on my forehead. He brings the car to a halt under the portico and hands the bellboy the keys. We stride into the hotel towards the lifts and he pushes the button down to the carpark. This is not what I had expected.

'Where are we going?' I ask him, my voice strangled with fear.

He ignores me. We alight at the first level of the carpark where a black Mercedes with tinted windows is waiting. A driver nods a wordless greeting and holds the door open for me. I hesitate. 'Get in,' Miguel demands in a cold, flat tone. He has lost his guise of genial banker, his voice threatening and sharp-edged. The driver races out of the carpark back into the streets, returning in the direction we have just come. I try and memorise what part of the city we are in, but it is completely foreign to me.

We enter an old part of town. The car stops and I follow Miguel down a narrow, winding street paved with large flagstones. Washing hangs from overhead balconies and the street is abuzz with sounds of music, television, laughter and conversation.

'Hello, Miguel!' The maître d' bustles over, shaking his hand and patting him on the back before he ushers us to our table at the rear of the restaurant. '¿Café, agua o vino?'

he inquires, grabbing a notebook from his apron pocket while frantically gesticulating to another waiter to check for patrons at the door.

'*Agua y café, por favor,*' I reply in broken Spanish, backing it up in English in case I got it wrong. 'Coffee and water, thanks.' I don't fancy an alcoholic drink. I feel terrified and overwhelmed, exhausted from batting out of my league in a foreign country with strangers who, I know, will not hesitate to kill me.

Time drags. My coffee is cold and untouched and I obsessively check the door for the cartel's arrival. Miguel now decides to tell me who to expect. 'These are two leaders from the Tijuana cartel,' he says. 'They are very powerful.' I know exactly who he is talking about: Ramón and Benjamín Arellano Félix. My stomach lurches.

Their arrival is heralded by ten bodyguards who sweep into the restaurant, carrying semi-automatic weapons. Outside, I know, will be the same number of men. The guards dress in suits, complete with tie and cufflinks, and are generally better educated than others from the same village or extended family from where they are drawn. Some are former military, seduced to work for the cartels by the lure of big money and reflected power. All will kill on demand. They are street-smart and utterly ruthless.

Ramón, with a flat nose that indicates it has been broken more than once, immediately senses my fear, looking at me with undisguised contempt. Benjamín, the financial brains of the operation and more refined than his thuggish younger brother, does the talking. 'We have one million dollars to bring back from Switzerland,' he tells me in a voice so low I strain to hear him. 'We will see how your system works. If it is okay, then we will pump more through your bank.'

I collect myself to answer him. 'Good. Miguel will give you all the details.' I start to spruik my Essex Finance proposal, but he raises a hand to silence me, indicating our meeting is over. The conversation has lasted no more than three minutes. Like a colony of worker ants, his body-guards move perceptibly closer as he gestures for me to remain seated, first shaking my hand, then Miguel's.

Ramón, following his cue, stands and takes both my hands. I can smell his breath, an acrid mix of strong cigar-ettes and last night's tequila, and can see thick gold chains through his shirt. He leans towards me, conspiratorially. 'It is very nice to meet you, Mr Wilson. But don't fuck with us. If you do, we will find you. We always find people we are looking for. *¿Comprende?*'

I stammer to find my voice. 'I understand,' I say. 'I under-stand perfectly.'

19

'They've got the cash: ten million dollars, US. Come immediately.'

Miguel hangs up. I pick up my briefcase while Al makes a quick phone call to Morgan. His buoyant flippancy makes me even more nervous. 'It's Al here,' he says to her. 'It's on. And we're off.' Al checks the tape-recording device — a benign-looking keyring that tapes when the light is off — to ensure it is recording. 'Okay, *amigo*,' he grins at me. '*Vámanos.*'

I don't grin back. I'm not comfortable with Al at all. For a start, he is a DEA agent, not a banker. He has been in the DEA for twenty-seven years and has the arrogance of someone who thinks they know it all. Secondly, he's Colombian and has been involved in a number of DEA stings both in Colombia and the US with Colombian drug dealers. That makes him an easy target for someone to recognise him.

He has also been shot at a few times, and carries the scars to prove it. But the DEA controllers in Washington, DC have insisted he come with me to provide some form of protection, despite his not being licensed to carry a weapon in Mexico. That doesn't bother him. He is carrying two guns: one around his ankle and the other in a shoulder holster. He struts like he has just got off a horse after three days herding cattle.

Al knows he screwed up last time. DEA management left him in no doubt about that, giving him a hammering when we returned from our meeting with a drug cartel banker. After listening to the tapes, Morgan and Jim swore and cursed and Al was instructed to let me handle the banking in future.

Now they are sending this bloke in with me again. 'After the last stuff-up, why are we bringing him along this time?' I ask Morgan. 'He's more a bloody hindrance than a help. It doesn't make any sense to me at all.'

'You need him for protection,' she replies, apparently not recognising the irony of what she has said.

'Protection? After the way he bungled the last operation? Surely you're having a lend of me?' I reckon the truth is that these fuckwits are scared I'll do a runner with their ten million in cash.

Al and I are both wearing impeccably-cut dark suits to look like conservative bankers. His cellphone rings a couple of times, the DEA control room in San Diego making sure that the line of communication is open.

He is still treating this like a joke. 'As soon as we have the cash we'll book a table at a nightclub and invite a dozen girls, compliments of the DEA,' he winks.

'Great idea, Al. But we're more likely to be given enough money for a meal at the golden arches, not a few thousand to blow at a nightclub. In the meantime, we need to concentrate on what we're doing here.'

I know that cartel members will have their bodyguards

everywhere around the hotel, near their vehicles and on the eighteenth floor where the meeting is to take place. The guards will be well dressed, making it difficult to pick them out in a crowd. Their own people back at the office will be waiting for confirmation that the meeting was successful and, afterwards, we will be followed until the transactions have been made and the money is safely in their account. I am under no illusions about the potential dangers: one slip and we are fucked. The Mexicans are not just handing over ten million in cash and hoping for the best. They will be watching us like hawks. I'm also disadvantaged by a complete lack of DEA training and not understanding a word of Spanish.

Our instructions are simple: walk towards the lift and don't look around. Look and act as though we are just a couple of American businessmen heading to our rooms. Don't talk openly, as Al has a Colombian American accent and I'm Australian. I survey the scene as we enter the hotel. The lifts are situated directly inside the hotel doors, past reception and the concierge, and I quickly assess how to get out. I hunch into my shirt collar and repeat my mantra to calm myself down. *Steady, mate. Take it easy. Long, slow breaths.* The lift is descending swiftly between floors: 27, 19, 12, 5 and now its bell announces 'Ground' and the doors spring open. We step in, and I take a shaky breath before pressing the number on the gold button. floor 18.

The elevator doors slide open, revealing a deep-blue patterned carpet in the hallway, muted lighting and an elegant timber table with a vase of magnificent oriental lilies. The numbers on the wall indicate we need to turn left. Our black leather shoes, shone to perfection, make no sound on the plush carpet. Al towers over me as we fall into wordless, synchronised step. The corridor is empty and silent, save for a cleaner's trolley parked at the far end of the hallway. I nervously adjust my tie outside Suite 1816, suddenly feeling as though my shirt collar is too tight. Arms folded across his massive chest, Al gives me the nod to knock.

Miguel's gruff voice echoes through the door. 'Come in!' he calls. 'Come in!' Al and I exchange a quick glance as we turn the handle. The door closes behind us.

Miguel's cellphone rings. 'They're on their way up,' he says, leaning back in his chair and visibly relaxing. 'I should now tell you a little about them. They are brothers. Very, very wealthy brothers and very, very dangerous. They are in the sugar industry.'

Al, pale and sweating, excuses himself to use the bathroom.

The Colombians enter, and the nightmare unfolds.

20

Al emerges and, realising he has been recognised by the gun-toting Colombians, takes out the nine-millimetre semi-automatic handgun hidden behind his back. Al fires first, taking aim at the shorter brother, hitting him twice in the shoulder and stomach. The return fire is deadly accurate, flooring Al with a single bullet. Miguel, still seated, has drawn a weapon, opening fire on the taller brother. From his position on the floor, the brother returns fire, hitting Miguel in the side of the face and killing him outright.

Smoke from the pistols fills the hotel room before a terrible silence descends. It is far more menacing than the chaotic noise of the gunshots. In the mayhem, the bedside furniture has crashed to the floor and I stand stock-still, my mouth parched and legs shaking. Al is slumped over the bed, blood seeping from the wound to his neck. The Colombians are sprawled on the floor, their bodies a bloodied mess. Miguel is on the chair, his head back and part of his face missing. I don't know how long I stand rooted to the spot before I become aware that I have pissed my pants, my jocks sodden.

I move cautiously towards Al and turn him over. His mouth and eyes are open, his face frozen in a shocked expression. The bullet has entered his neck and left a hole so large I can see through to the bed. Miguel, too, is clearly dead and I cautiously move to check the two Colombians. The tall one is dead, the other just breathing, shallow and erratic. I kick the dead man's gun to the other side of the room and then check the living man for weapons but find only his cellphone. I slip it into my pocket.

Al's cellphone has fallen onto the carpet. I grab it and call Morgan in the DEA control room in San Diego, realising too late that the phone is sticky with Al's blood.

'Al?' she answers the call.

I can't find my voice. I struggle to think straight with the cloying smell of blood and gunshot residue that permeates the room. 'It's not Al, Morgan,' I finally say. 'Al's dead.'

'Oh, Christ,' she yells. 'Hold!' I wait while she switches the call to the loudspeaker in the control room where Jim and other agents are waiting for confirmation of the cash pick-up. Morgan is clearly shaken. 'Jesus, Greece, what the hell happened?'

I am tripping over my words now, gibbering and close to tears. Urine has seeped through to my trousers and my body feels clammy with shock. 'The clients were Colombians. They . . . they recognised Al the second they saw him. He knew them, too. Miguel and Al are dead – and one of the Colombians. The other brother has been shot, but he's alive.' I am watching the Colombian as I speak. He is curled in a foetal position and mumbling incoherently in Spanish. 'This bloke needs help. He's going to fucking die if I don't do something . . . I think they thought this was a set-up by Al and Miguel to steal their money . . . or they thought it was a DEA sting. Either way, the Colombians have their people on this floor and downstairs. I've got to get out of here!'

Jim has taken charge of the conversation. He speaks calmly. 'Greece, do you have your digital camera, the one we bought you?'

'Yes.'

'I want you to take photos of the scene: the bodies, the hotel room, the whole box and dice. Download them onto your laptop and send them to us while we work out how to get you out of there.' I know why he needs them: the DEA have a detailed list of drug cartel people in Mexico and Colombia. He wants to see whether the people in the room match anyone on that list.

I am screaming at him. 'I don't have time for this! There's a fucking bloke dying in front of me and I have to leave before their bodyguards arrive.' I'm going to be killed.

'You won't,' Jim rejoins, his tone calm and firm. 'You have an hour before anyone comes, so get moving. First, ring room service and order lunch: wine, steaks, the lot. Place the order now, and tell them to knock on the door. Lock the door so no one can get in. Got that?'

'Yes.'

'Good. Do you have a speaker on the hotel phone?'

'Yes.'

'We'll phone you back on that. Walk around the room, tell us what you can see. Morgan is working with another team to figure out how to get you out of the hotel.' He hangs up.

I dial room service and order the food and wine. The order will be delivered within thirty minutes. Perspiration is pouring down my face, despite the airconditioning, and stomach acid seeps into my mouth. I open my briefcase and pull out the camera while I wait for the control room to call again.

'Have you placed the order for lunch?' Jim asks when he calls back.

'Yes, I have. Look, for Christ's sake, this bloke here . . .'

He ignores me. 'Do you have the camera? Is it charged?'

'Of course it's charged!'

'Look around the room. Take photos of it and three of Al from where you are standing. Move closer to him and take a close-up of his head and neck and then one of his whole body. Quickly.'

I do as he instructs, but dry-retch as I look at Al. 'I can't do this!'

'Yes, you can. And you must. Take a breath and get on with it.'

I raise the camera again and shoot. I have no training for dealing with any of this and the camera shakes wildly. Any minute now I'm going to pass out. The room is spinning but Jim is still barking questions. 'Did you do it?'

'Yes. Done.'

'Where are the Colombians?'

'One is dead as a maggot on the floor. He hasn't moved. The other has crawled to the side of the wall between the lounge and the bedroom. I've collected all the weapons so there's no worry there. He's moaning but not moving anymore.'

'Take some photos of them. At least four.' The injured Colombian moves slightly as I get closer to him. 'Where are his wounds?' Jim demands.

'In the shoulder and stomach.'

'Take some close-ups. Get his top off, so you have a clear view of them.'

'Fuck me, Jim! I'm a banker, not a DEA agent!' I'm petrified and repulsed at the thought of having to get any closer to the blood-soaked Colombian. He needs medical help, urgently. 'I work with money, Jim, not bodies. I'm not trained for this shit!'

'Maybe not, but you don't have a choice. Just do it, Greece. Now.'

I take several photos of the dead Colombian before I move over to his brother. He is mumbling to me in Spanish, words I can't understand. '*Si, si, si,*' I repeat, over and over. For all I know, I could be confirming to him that he is going to die any minute.

'Easy now, take it slowly,' I say to him as I lift his arms and manage to drag his coat off. I loosen his tie and remove his shirt, half-stuck with blood, peeling it from his body. The movement makes him whimper and he groans with pain. Little wonder: the wound on his shoulder and stomach is a gaping mass of coagulated blood. I'm at least relieved to see that the blood is bright red; as I know from the first-aid sports courses I have done, this is a good sign as dark crimson designates major internal haemorrhage and imminent death.

'He's in bad shape, Jim.'

'Okay, we know that. Have you taken photos of him yet? Also, empty his pockets and check for ID. Check the other guy as well.'

I rifle through their pockets but they are carrying only a small amount of cash, nothing to identify them to the DEA. 'There's nothing here to tell us who they are. Look, Jim, I'm going to have to try and clean him up a bit.' I rip up a bed sheet into two strips. I strap his shoulder tight, and then do the same on his stomach wound. 'Sorry, mate,' I tell him as he grimaces in pain. 'Sorry, mate.'

Jim is waiting on the phone. 'Is that done? Right. Now go and check Miguel.'

He is a pitiful sight. His head is back and part of his face is missing. One arm is dangling uselessly, the other still holding his gun. His mouth is wide open and his eyes frozen. All I can see is blood and bone tissue. I vomit.

'He's carrying four thousand dollars, credit cards, his driving licence and about two thousand in pesos,' I tell Jim. I'm crying openly and don't care. 'Look, I need to get out of here while I still can.'

'Not long now, Greece. Take some photos of Miguel and set up your computer. Plug in your camera and download the photos.'

There is a knock on the door and I jump in fright. 'Room service!'

'Check through the keyhole,' Jim demands. 'Open the door, but keep the chain on and tell them you can't be disturbed. They'll leave the trolley there and when they go, roll in the food and lock the door. Got that?'

'Yep.' I follow his orders and give the two young waiters a large tip. '*Muchas gracias*,' they grin, doing as they are asked and leaving the trolley outside the room. When I am satisfied they have gone, I pull the trolley in and lock the door.

'The photos are downloaded now and on their way to you,' I tell Jim. 'I've got to get out of here now.'

'Morgan's working on your exit,' he says. 'Try to be patient.'

'Patient! You've got to be joking!' Time is running out. It has been more than forty minutes since the Colombians arrived and it won't be long before their bodyguards show up, wondering where the hell they are.

'The photos are coming through now, Greece. Well done. We're almost there. I want you to tip some food on the trays. Pour a bottle of wine down the sink and leave some food on a couple of plates. Then put all that outside the door.' I'm leery about opening the door again unless I can make a run for it, but I do as I'm told. 'Now, check the cash,' Jim demands. 'Where is it?'

'I don't know, maybe in the briefcase.'

'Open the briefcase.'

I flick open the brass locks and look inside. In all my years of banking, I have never seen so much money at one time, piled high like small bricks. 'Fuck me,' I whistle.

'How much is there?' Jim asks.

'Hard to say without counting, but from the looks of this, I'd guess all ten million of it.'

'Okay,' he says. 'Stand by.'

PART THREE

On the Run

21

At the other end of the line, I can hear people yelling out orders and instructions being barked. I'm in a hotel room with a time bomb ticking, and these people don't seem to have a clue what they're doing. They don't even seem to give a shit that they've lost one of their own agents.

Jim is back on the line. He sounds excited. 'Greece, you've snared two brothers from one of the most influential crime families in Colombia, if not all of South America! We have a price tag on these guys worth two million. We need you to bring the one that's still alive to the US immediately. We've ordered a private Department of Justice jet from Dallas. It's about to take off for Mexico City, with a medical team on board. It'll take three hours to get there. In the meantime, you need to get to the airport, with the cash and the wounded Colombian.'

'What?' I'm screaming into the phone. 'You can't be fucking serious! You want me to walk out of this hotel with ten million cash and a half-dead Colombian? For a start, there'll be at least twenty Colombian bodyguards watching for me to leave and hotel security who will steal the fucking cash. Even if I get out the Mexican police will find the three dead bodies and start looking for me. They'll close all roads to the airport and I'll be stuck in the middle. Forget it! No fucking way!'

'Have you got a better idea?'

'Yes, I have. Get your fucking Marines down to the hotel, set this place on fire and I'll walk out with the money. Get your helicopter onto the roof and fly me to the airport. The Marines can get the Colombian and put me in a private jet to somewhere safe where I can bank the cash.' I haven't drawn breath. 'For Christ's sake, Jim, I've got a family back in Australia. I've got to get out of here safely.'

I shoot a glance at the time on the bedside clock. I've been here exactly one hour and the Colombian's people will be all over this floor any minute. 'We've been talking on the telephone for over fifty minutes. You've told me countless times that telephones in Mexico are tapped by the police. Considering I'm not supposed to be operating in Mexico at all, that I'm persona non grata, I don't exist, I'm fucking surprised the cops and cartel hitmen haven't knocked the door down and dragged me out by my teeth to the nearest telephone pole and hung me upside down with my balls in my mouth!'

I pause, momentarily. 'Fuck, Jim, we had a deal. I did the job, got paid and went home.'

'Greece, we can't directly involve anyone from the US embassy. You've been told that already. We haven't informed the Mexican government of our activity in Mexico either. What we have to do now, you and me, is work together and get you and the Colombian to the airport, with the cash, as soon as possible. We have no choice. I'll have one of the hotel drivers take you both to the airport and charge it to the room.'

The Colombian is lying inert, his eyes half closed and I'm running out of steam. 'What do you want me to do?'

'Dress him and take him down the service lift. Under no circumstances use the guest elevator. We will arrange for the police to arrive. Before you leave the foyer, we'll phone the fire department, the hospital and the TV stations so that, as you're leaving, they'll be arriving, which will cause total chaos. The bodyguards will head to the room, but you'll be long gone before they get there. We also have one of our trusted Mexican policemen heading to the hotel now, to remove the security tapes so there's no record of you entering or leaving. That's the only thing he'll do. He doesn't know anything about what went on in the room. You clear with all this, Greece?'

'Jim, what about Claudia and her children? They're at risk as well.'

'We've got that sorted. Don't panic. Morgan has sent agents around to the house and schools, and they'll be in an aircraft heading to New York within the hour. They'll be in a safe house tonight. Once you arrive in Dallas, you will board a flight to New York, which is where you'll stay until further notice.'

'What about my Australian family?'

'We'll sort that, too. They'll be safe.'

'What about the room? They'll know I was here.'

'You came to collect the money and left, it's that simple. Now get the hell out of there.'

My cellphone is ringing.

'Hi, Keith, it's Adriana.' Adriana is a Mexican friend of Daniel's, who is looking for an equity partner for her own business. Daniel recommended me to her because he was anxious that I also did business with people unconnected to the drug cartels in order to appear less suspicious. The

DEA are also happy with this arrangement. Adriana is ringing for some financial advice, but I quickly interrupt her.

'Adriana, where are you?'

'I'm at Alsace, finishing up lunch.' Alsace is a French restaurant a few blocks away.

'Can you get to the El Grande right now?'

'Yes, why?'

'Because I have a client here who is really ill. I need to get to the airport as soon as possible so he can get treatment in the US. I'll throw in a thousand dollars to cover the cost. But we need to leave urgently.'

She doesn't ask any more questions. 'Sure, Keith. I'll come.'

'Can you drive to the carpark, first level, and meet us by the service lift?'

'Yes, okay, I'll be there in ten minutes.' She hangs up, with no idea what she has let herself into.

The DEA team has heard my conversation. 'Great work. Your transport is sorted. I can confirm that your flight has left Dallas and will be there in approximately three hours. We have requested that, when it lands, the plane will park close to where embassy staff can gain access, away from the public. We've notified the Mexican authorities that it's a diplomatic flight carrying senior officials from Washington, DC for our embassy in Mexico City, so we've got clearance. There'll be no Mexican customs. Check you've got everything – your briefcase and the Colombians' cash. How's he holding up?'

'He's still lying in the same spot, but he's stopped talking.'

'You need to move now. Hang up and make sure you keep Al's cellphone. Good luck.'

The service lift is twenty-five metres from the room. I sling the shoulder straps of the briefcases over my neck so they sit halfway down my back and try to pick up the Colombian. He is so heavy it takes me several minutes to get him up. Slumped over my right shoulder like a sack of flour, I drag him to the doorway and heave everything into the lift. The corridor is still empty and I push the down button to the first floor carpark as the Colombian's cellphone in my pocket starts ringing. We've got two minutes, max, to get out of here.

Police sirens are blaring as we hit the carpark. Adriana is waiting outside the elevator door. 'Keep the engine running!' I scream, dragging the Colombian into the back seat and closing the door.

Adriana is suddenly hysterical. 'What the hell's going on, Keith?'

'Don't ask questions, Adriana. Please! Just get me to the airport and don't stop for anyone: not police, fire engines, no one! Get us there safely and there's five grand in it for you. Hit it!'

She accelerates like there is no tomorrow. I look out the back window to see if anyone has followed us out of the service lift. All clear. The Colombian's cellphone is ringing non-stop. Adriana slows down at the carpark exit, flashing a strained smile at the security guard who grins back at her, lifting the bar to let us out. Thank God for her good looks.

We exit via the back entrance to the hotel. As we pass the intersection I can see a half-dozen police cars, fire trucks and TV vans with police trying to make some sense of the mayhem. The DEA have done their job this time. It looks like a major disaster scene.

Adriana starts yelling at me as soon as we pass the hotel. 'What the fuck is going on? The guy in the back seat is saying he's been shot and needs help. I have a young baby, Keith, and I can't afford to be involved in this, whatever it is, five grand or not. Tell me what's going on or I'll stop the fucking car and you can find your own way to the airport!'

'He's a banking friend of Daniel's,' I lie. 'He's been shot. We're rushing him to the airport, because Daniel's American connections have sent a private corporate jet to pick us up.'

Her hands grip the steering wheel more tightly and her face drains of colour. 'I've got a baby at home, Keith. I've got to stay safe.' Muscles twitch in her cheekbones but she keeps her foot on the accelerator.

'Try to trust me, Adriana,' I say, leaning over the back seat and looking anxiously at the Colombian. 'Hang in there, mate. Hang in there.' The last thing we need is for this bastard to die.

Al's phone rings. 'It's Jim. Where are you?'

'On the road, a couple of kilometres from the hotel.'

'The police have found the bodies and, as expected, it's absolute chaos at the hotel. They've sealed off the airport already, and Cali people have been to the room. They know you and their man are missing. They'll be at the airport as well. We have reason to believe they may have spotted your friend's car, so you have to switch vehicles now.'

I look over at Adriana, and groan. This is a nightmare.

'She will have to come to the States as well, Greece. There's a possibility they have her car registration number and, if they do, they'll be at her house within minutes and will kill anyone who is there.'

'Okay.' I'm trying to keep the panic from my voice, for Adriana's sake. 'Adriana, who's looking after your baby?' I ask her.

'My mother, at her house.'

'How far is that from here?'

'It's halfway to the airport, about two miles off the main road.'

'Okay, get off this road and head there. We're going to pick up your baby daughter and your mother.'

'Why?' Her fear is now palpable.

'Because that was the Americans on the phone and they have ordered it. They're a bank in Washington that Daniel has worked with. Just do it, Adriana. Please.' She doesn't answer me. 'Does your mother speak English?'

'A little. But not very well.'

'Does she have a car?'

'Yes! Why, for God's sake? What's this all about?'

'Does she have a landline telephone?'

'Yes!'

'What's the number? Washington is asking.'

I repeat the number to Jim.

'Okay,' he says, 'stay on the line. We're ringing her now and telling her to get the baby and jump in her car. Hang on. Right, got her. She understands what she has to do, she's heading out to the car now. We've left the line open with her, she has a cellphone. Take Adriana's cellphone. The Cali boys will have that number in minutes and will track her through it. Throw it out the window, along with the Colombian's phone. Now.'

22

Adriana, deathly pale, hands the phone over without question. I open the window and throw both phones out, turning my head to see them bouncing along the road.

'Greece, switch your cell off as well. The Calis will track Daniel Gómez down to get your number. Adriana's mother is now in the car with the baby. She is widowed. Adriana has three sisters living in Mexico. One is married and lives in Los Cabos, the other two are in Mexico City. We have contacted our team at the US embassy in Mexico City, and they're arranging to have the families collected today and placed on a flight to the States tonight, as a safeguard.'

'Right.'

'Don't tell Adriana yet about her sisters. Her mother is heading to the shopping mall about one mile from her house. She'll park outside McDonald's and wait there. And, Greece? Your family in San Diego has boarded the flight to New York and are safe.'

Morgan is now on the line. 'We've just been informed the Colombians are on the lookout for Adriana's car, as are the police. They've been issued an alert to stop the vehicle when they see you.'

'How much further to the mall, Adriana?'

'We're here.' Her mother is gesturing wildly and gibbering in Spanish as Adriana picks up her baby from the child seat. I can't understand what she is saying, but the gist of it is clear: she is petrified and wants to know what is going on.

'Tell her it's all right, Adriana. Calm her down. It's all right.'

I lift the Colombian from the back seat of Adriana's car and haul his weight into her mother's vehicle. She is hysterical. The last thing we need is further attention. 'Tell her to shut up!' I demand, sounding more panicked than I would like. 'She's making things worse.'

Adriana puts her arm around her mother's neck, drawing her close to her face and making soothing sounds. '*Cálmate madre. Todo está bien. Estaremos a salvo.*' Quiet, Mama. Everything is all right. We will be all right.

'Take the numberplates off Adriana's car,' Jim instructs. 'We'll have some of our people there soon to tow it away. We don't want the police or the Calis to find it, because it will be covered in your prints and the Colombian's.'

After a few minutes I manage to wrench off the number-plates using a crowbar from Adriana's boot. We drive for fifteen minutes when Al's phone rings again.

'You've got to switch cars again!' Jim's voice has an urgency I haven't heard before. 'The Calis have made the connection to Adriana's mother and are moving faster than we expected. Ask Adriana how long before you get to the airport.'

'Twenty minutes, maybe longer, depending on traffic,' she answers.

I know that the Calis will have their hitmen on motor-bikes, one driving and the shooter on the back, and they will be covering all roads leading to the airport. With the police on full alert as well, we've got Buckley's chance of getting through. 'How the fuck do you suppose we're going to do this?'

'We're working on that. In the meantime, just get off the main roads heading to the airport and find another shopping mall.' He gives me the exact location, checks it twice and continues. 'Park underground. I'll call you back to check you're in the right place.'

At the mall, we pull a ticket out of the parking machine and race through when the bar rises, steering the car into the first available space.

I jiggle up and down on the balls of my feet, waiting for Jim to call back. 'Near Escuela de Tiro, close to the airport.'

'Hold on.' He passes instructions to Morgan, who makes another call. 'You there, Greece? You're all going to have to sit tight. We've arranged a car for you, and it should be with you within the hour.'

'Fuck, Jim, I can't hold everyone for that long!'

'You've got no choice,' he says. 'Just stay there, and make sure everyone remains in the car.'

I turn to Adriana and her mother and try to speak as confidently as possible. 'Someone is going to be here shortly to collect us,' I say, my ashen face betraying the truth. 'We've just got to sit tight and be patient.'

23

The Colombian is still making noises, mumbling in his native tongue and drifting in and out of consciousness. I don't know the extent of his wounds, but the DEA has a medical team on board the aircraft on its way to get us. God only knows what will happen when they get him into their custody.

I'm worried sick about Claudia, as well. Her move with the children from San Diego by federal agents would be really distressing for them and she would be desperate by now to hear from me, to find out what is going on. The cartels, I know, have already gathered all the minutiae of my relationship with Claudia and the children and our lives in San Diego: where we shopped, went on weekends and had coffee; which beach we went to; where the children went to school and which way Claudia and I drove to work. I coached rugby at Point Loma University, and I know I was being observed when I was with the players.

Jim is on the phone again. 'The Colombians arrived while our team was loading Adriana's car onto the tow truck. They now know you're in her mother's car, and they've been to her house and were searching it when the police arrived. We don't know if they have the details of Adriana's sisters, but we expect they do. We're rounding up the sisters and their families now. It's a race against the clock. Because the car was found in the shopping mall carpark, they will search every mall from there to the airport. So there's a change of plan. You need to move. Find a hotel carpark. Get going!'

'Is there a hotel carpark close to here, Adriana?'

She is beyond questioning anything. 'The Internazionale is about fifteen minutes away. That's only twenty minutes from the airport.'

'We're heading to the Internazionale, Jim. You need to find out where that is.'

We park in the hotel's underground carpark. Al's phone battery is dying and I can't charge it in the car. I need to find a phone, urgently. I go up to the lobby and wave my credit card at the young woman in reception, interrupting her as she checks in some guests. 'Sorry, I don't mean to be rude, but this is an emergency. I need to use a phone, please.'

She arches an eyebrow and excuses herself, glancing at the guests as she does so. Her expression says it all: bloody rude foreigners. 'Are you staying in-house, sir?'

'Not as yet. I'm about to check in,' I lie. 'Look, sorry, but this really is an emergency. Where is your phone?'

She shoves it towards me with a glacial stare. 'Dial 00 to get out,' she says, with pursed lips.

Jim answers immediately. 'Where the fuck are you, Greece? I've been trying to call you for ten minutes!'

'The battery's died. I can't use it. I'm on the reception phone at the Internazionale.'

'That's all we need! We're still working on a plan to get you to the airport. You'll have to phone me back in fifteen minutes.'

I explode. 'Fuck off! We need to keep moving!' I slam the phone back on its hook and interrupt the receptionist again.

This time she holds her hand up to stop me. 'If you don't mind,' she says in an officious tone, 'I'm dealing with other guests at present.'

'I can see that. But I've also explained to you that this is urgent. I need to hire a car to get to the airport to meet a flight. I will check in when we return.'

'We have our own airport buses,' she says, 'and cars with drivers.'

'No, I want to drive myself.'

'Then you need to ask the drivers outside the hotel.'

I jam cash from the briefcases into my wallet and run outside to the first car. 'How much is it to the airport?' The Mexican sizes me up. *Americano, expensive hotel.* 'Sixty American dollars,' he says, grinding his cigarette underfoot and starting to open the taxi door.

'I will give you a thousand American dollars if you allow me to drive myself and you follow in a taxi.' I have to bribe him with money; there is no way, otherwise, that the driver will allow me to drive his car, and I don't know how to get there under my own steam. Adriana and her mother are in no state to take control.

His jaw falls open. '*Sí, sí, señor!*' he says, scrambling to compose himself. 'I can do this.' I peel a thousand from my wallet and wait for him to step out of his vehicle. He hands me the keys in exchange for the cash. '*Sí, sí,*' he repeats. 'I will follow.'

I drive into the carpark and pull up beside Adriana's mother's car. No one says a word as we exchange vehicles and move the Colombian into the back seat, throwing a blanket over to hide him. Adriana and her daughter sit in the front with me.

We have been driving for five minutes when I spot two motorbikes with passengers on the back. They are peering into car windows as they wheel past, weaving in between vehicles. I know they are Cali hitmen.

'How long before we get to the airport?'

'Ten minutes.'

I change direction at the first turn-off and head towards the major highway to get to the airport. The driver following me in the taxi must think I am either lost or have lost the plot. I know Mexico City Airport very well, having flown in a dozen times to meet Daniel Gómez and other clients. It has only one main entrance, and I expect that if we drive in that way we will be greeted by a welcoming party of police, army, airport security, the Calis and Mexican cartel hitmen. And I have no idea where the Americans park their plane. Adriana directs me to the back entrance of the airport where the cargo planes park.

We pull up at an area for corporate jets and I walk into the office and ask to see the manager. 'Good afternoon. I want to fly my family to Los Cabos. What's it going to cost?'

He affects an air of consideration before answering, computing figures into his desk calculator. 'About three thousand American each way,' he answers.

'That sounds fair,' I smile, knowing he's at least doubled the price. 'I need to phone my boss in Chicago and ask him to approve the payment. Do you have a telephone I can use? I'll pay for the call.' I hand over a hundred-dollar bill, which he takes before pointing towards a private office. He knows the call will only cost twelve dollars.

I phone Morgan's cellphone and give her the office number. 'Jim will ring back and ask to speak to John Wilson,' she says. 'Stand by for his call.'

Jim phones back in half a minute and I quickly run through what has happened since I left the hotel. 'Great work, Greece,' he says. 'But the police have found the mother's car, and they know which driver's car you're using. The Calis know as well. They listen to the Mexican police radio network. The plane's still forty minutes away and we're very concerned about landing now, as the Mexican army and police will surround the aircraft. They have guessed we have the Colombian and that you're somehow involved. The Calis have high-ranking Mexican army men and police on their payroll, so we're expecting trouble. They have informed us that the security is for our own protection, which is bullshit, but that's what's been relayed to us from Washington. We'll keep you posted.'

'Fuck me, Jim, we can't all continue playing hide-and-seek!' I'm talking to myself. He has hung up.

Now I have to hide the car, the driver, Adriana and her family for at least the next hour until the plane is prepared for take-off. I need the manager again. 'Can I park the car in the hangar?' I ask, peeling more cash out of my wallet.

'Sure,' he grins, picking up the money and stuffing it in his pocket. I follow him outside and he opens a gate onto the airfield, allowing me access to the hangar. 'Follow me,' he indicates with the crook of his finger. 'You and your family will need a room where you can rest.'

I leave the Colombian in the car and shepherd the rest of the crew into the tiny room off the hangar and close the door. Adriana is pale with fear but doesn't ask any questions. I don't think she wants to know the answers. What a fucking mess I have dragged them into. They won't be able to return to Mexico for years, if at all. I head back to reception.

I'm too scared to think about what is happening to Daniel Gómez. He has assured his people that I can be trusted: *se puede confiar en él*, and his life is now in danger. The Cali hitmen will be with him, holding him until they work out where I fit in the scheme of things. I have to bank the cash, make sure it is transferred to the Calis' account in Switzerland, ring them and give them the receipt. The next task will be to convince them that I actually left the hotel before the dead bodies turned up in the room.

My plan is to tell them that Al was a Colombian recently recommended to me and that I had no idea he was an undercover DEA agent. I have to turn this to my advantage. If I bank the cash and they buy my story, then Daniel will be free to go home. Once I'm back in the States, our safety is more assured. But if they find me in Mexico, we're all dead.

The phone rings and the receptionist beckons me to the desk. 'How's everyone holding up?' It's Jim, and he does not sound relaxed.

'As well as can be expected, under the circumstances. They're all as nervous as hell. The driver has no idea what is going on, nor do Adriana and her mother.'

There is a slight pause. 'Okay, understood. Greece, we have a problem.' My heart sinks and I feel my blood pressure rise. 'The Mexican police and army believe that our aircraft, which is only twenty minutes away, is going to be used to take the Colombian to the US. Once we land, they're gonna surround the aircraft and check everyone leaving and boarding. DC is working to persuade the Mexican government that it's certainly not the case and that they're not to come near the plane, but we've been negotiating with them for nearly forty minutes now and they won't interfere with the army or the police.'

I'm grinding my teeth and clenching the phone so hard my knuckles are white. 'Christ, Jim! If we're going to be discovered within the next hour, we have to get out of here!' The panic is clear in my voice and I involuntarily turn to see if anyone can hear me. 'We can't stay here. They'll kill the lot of us!' I can see Adriana holding her baby close to her chest, rocking the child with the soothing rhythm of a protective mother. 'There's a baby here with us, Jim! The longer we stay, the more suspicious we look to the driver and the people here at the airport. Fix the fucking problem!'

'Stand by,' he says.

I slam the phone back on the receiver. There is no time left to idly stand by. The police, army and cartel people are close and it is just a matter of time until they find us. I check on the Colombian. He is still moaning, slipping in and out of consciousness. Through the small hangar window I can see a parked twin-turboprop light aircraft.

'That aircraft,' I say to the manager, pointing out the window. 'How far can it fly on a full tank and how many people can it have on board? It is urgent that my friend gets some medical help.'

'Six people and the pilot. You can get two-and-a-half hours' flying time.'

'Is it available?'

'*Sí.*'

'Fill it up. We're heading to Tampico, on the coast of the Gulf of Mexico. How long will that take?'

'About two hours. But I thought you said you wanted Los Cabos?'

'Change of plan. We need to get to Tampico.'

'That's five thousand dollars,' he says, without a hint of embarrassment. This greedy bastard obviously thinks all his Christmases have come at once.

'Right,' I agree. 'I'll pay cash, but we leave now.' I go to the car, open a briefcase and count out five thousand.

'We're moving, now,' I tell Adriana. She nods mutely, stands and tells her mother to follow. In her mid-seventies, her mother has said virtually nothing since their heated discussion in the car, but now she starts gabbling in Spanish. She is utterly petrified and I doubt she has been on a plane before. 'Tell her she is going to be all right, Adriana. Please,' I say. 'We need to move quickly.'

I pull the Colombian out of the car, dragging his full weight towards the aircraft. It is a Herculean effort to get him on board. The driver's initial reluctance to join us on the plane softens when I bribe him with another thousand of the cartel's money.

The pilot turns to speak to me. 'I have filed a flight plan for Tampico,' he says, ignoring the obvious fact that there is a seriously wounded passenger on board his aircraft. 'We have been given permission to leave.'

Adriana's mother is wildly moving her hands in the sign of the cross, gibbering under her breath to a god she hopes will save her. Adriana has the glazed features of one who has resigned herself to the worst possible scenario and the Colombian is slumped, half-comatose in the rear seat.

We taxi out of the hangar as I watch the private jet from Dallas that we were due to board lower its landing gear and hit the runway. It taxis towards the international cargo terminal, followed by six army trucks and nine police cars. I can't believe our timing. We need to get this plane in the air while the focus is on the American jet.

Our pilot manoeuvres to the runway, makes contact with the control tower and is cleared for take-off. I look behind. The jet, now at a standstill, is surrounded by army and police. We bump along in the small aircraft for a few seconds before gathering speed as we race down the runway. After five hundred metres, the aircraft is airborne. Mexico City is now beneath us: her sprawling, over-crowded neighbourhoods, the Ajusco mountain, the Xico volcano crater.

I slump back in the seat and heave a shaky sigh of relief. It is not going to take long for police to find the car, work out we are in the air and have the air force hunt us down. I need to change course and not follow our flight plan.

24

Moctezuma is inland and closer to Mexico City. I take another ten thousand dollars out of one of the cartel's briefcase and tap the pilot on the shoulder. 'We need to change course and head to Moctezuma,' I say, putting a thousand dollars into his lap. 'Have no communication with the control tower. Don't use the radio. We need absolute silence from now on.'

His eyebrows furrow with a quizzical look, but as he looks at the cash, it is obvious he has made his decision. 'No problems. It is good weather. We go to Moctezuma.'

The flight is smooth, but the mottled clouds are darkening. We won't arrive at Moctezuma until 7.30 pm, another hour and a half. The Colombian's breathing is slightly laboured but I'm grateful his condition appears to be stable. Adriana and her mother hold hands, the baby snuggled on Adriana's lap, and the driver seems unperturbed about this unexpected adventure.

Jim and the DEA team will be worried about us, but they are monitoring the Mexican police and army, so they will know we haven't been caught yet. There is nothing more I can do before we land, but it is pointless trying to rest. I drift off into a meditative state, staring out at the gathering darkness and thinking about the dead men in the hotel room, their bodies bloodied and crumpled.

I have seen dead bodies before. Once, jogging around my neighbourhood of Brighton in the dark hour before dawn, I noticed a vehicle parked in a carpark, its interior light on. The driver, no older than his mid-twenties, was collapsed over the wheel, dead from the toxic fumes that flowed from the hose connected to the exhaust pipe of his car. Another morning, a year later, I saw two bodies washed up on the Brighton sea bank. Both people had clearly jumped from the West Gate Bridge, the current dragging their bodies along the shore. Straggly hair clung like wet strands of wool to the nineteen-year-old girl's face, and the older man's body was broken. Their images stay with me.

The pilot has been given clearance to land at Moctezuma. We taxi towards the small cargo sheds where a few other light aircraft are parked. There are no signs of the Mexican police or army, but that is no guarantee that cartel members aren't around.

The hotel driver looks anxious as the plane comes to a halt. 'I need to get back to Mexico City,' he tells the pilot in excitable Spanish. The pilot looks at him, and shrugs.

'We are leaving again shortly,' I assure him, pressing another thousand into his hands. 'Okay? You stay close to me.' I turn to the pilot. 'We need to refuel and leave again.'

'Sorry, not possible.' He shakes his head. 'Not possible.'

'Maybe this will help,' I say, my voice betraying sarcasm. 'Three thousand for fuel and two thousand in cash for you.'

He holds his hand out and grins. 'Where we heading this time?'

'Madero, on the coast of the Gulf of Mexico.'

'Madero? I will need to fly to a flight plan.'

'No, you won't,' I correct him. 'You can work out the details without informing anyone where you're going.'

'It is dangerous to fly like that. Besides, I need to check in with the office.'

I cut him off, irritably. 'You can tell them in the morning.'

He lingers like a hotel porter and I take the hint, handing him another thousand out of my pocket.

'No problems,' he drawls. 'I will find the fuel depot and fly you anywhere.'

Adriana is peering at me and has found her voice. 'How much trouble are you in, Keith?' Her chin is trembling and I'm afraid she will start crying.

'A lot,' I reply, stuffing my hands in my jacket so she doesn't see me shaking. 'But once we get to the US, we'll be all right. Don't ask any more questions, or I'll have to lie to you. I'm going to get us some coffee. Don't let the driver leave.'

Languid fans stir the night air in the cargo shed, where a couple of young women are working. 'Do you speak English?' I ask and one looks at me with huge chocolate brown eyes and shakes her head, pointing towards an office. I smile at her and she looks away, shyly giggling. 'Thank you, señorita,' I say. The situation seems absurd, as if I should doff an imaginary hat.

The man in the office speaks almost perfect English inflected with a thick Mexican accent. 'I need to find some food and drinks, please, and also make a telephone call. May I use your phone to call the US? I'll pay for the call.'

He looks dubious, and I move through the now familiar routine of handing him some cash. 'Dial 0, then 1 for
the USA, and then your number,' he says, handing me the
telephone.

Morgan answers the phone. 'Where the hell are you?'
she shrieks, switching us over to speaker. I fill them in
on what has happened since we last spoke. 'Very impressive, Greece, very impressive,' Morgan chortles. 'Jim wants
a word with you.'

He comes straight to the point. 'How's the Colombian?
You obviously haven't had any opportunity to get him
medical help?' Even at this distance, clearly he has little
sympathy for him.

'He's still out to it. He seems to be in a lot of pain, but
he comes to now and again. He doesn't have any idea
where he is. Hopefully he'll stay that way until I arrive in
the US.'

Jim doesn't comment.

'What's happening at Mexico City Airport?' I ask.

There is a slight pause which gives me an ominous
feeling. 'The situation isn't good, I'm afraid. Our aircraft
is surrounded by army and police and no one has
been able to leave the plane as yet. We haven't opened
the doors. We have two vehicles from our embassy in
Mexico City heading out to the airport. They're stuck
in traffic, of course, but should be there within the
next hour. The vehicles are being escorted by traffic
police and helicopters.' He doesn't pause for breath
now. 'The Mexican police are convinced we have the
Colombian on board, and perhaps you, as well. Thankfully they have no idea who you are, or what you
look like. All they know is someone was in the room,
made several phone calls and that there is a strong

possibility that you left in Adriana's car. They know all about her and her family, and they have full details on the driver. They're convinced you and the Colombian were in the vehicle heading out to the airport and that Adriana and her mother are paid decoys. We believe that the cartels are also of that opinion, because no one has seen the car at the airport. It hasn't been discovered yet.'

'Right.'

'They can only sit on the tarmac for another hour, tops. We are still trying,' he stressed, 'through DC to negotiate with the Mexican government to move their vehicles away from our aircraft, but they are insisting that the police and army are there for our protection. It's a Mexican stand-off, so to speak. That being said, Greece, what's your plan?'

'We're heading to Madero. According to the pilot, it will take one and a half hours, and we'll refuel there. Then we will push on to Brownsville, which will take about the same time again. All up, around three hours.'

'You'll be just inside the USA in Brownsville,' Jim replies. Brownsville is on the Texas/Mexico border. 'We'll have federal agents, police, a medical team and a DEA jet to bring you to Dallas from there. We'll hold the fort for the next two hours, by which time you'll be close to the border. It won't take the Mexicans long to figure out what we're up to. I think they'll find your car, know which aircraft you're on and be looking for you within that hour. With luck, you will be across the border before they can get to you. We'll speak again when you land in Brownsville.' He is about to hang up. 'By the way: we've heard that the Arellano drug cartel family are looking for you. Miguel was their man.'

'Fuckin' great,' I mutter. I'm almost too scared to ask about Daniel. 'I can't sit on the phone much longer, Jim,' I say. 'What is happening with Daniel Gómez?'

'The Colombians have him and his family, and they're waiting to hear from you. Don't worry,' he adds as an after-thought, 'we'll take care of you.'

25

Within minutes of climbing back on board we are rolling down the bumpy tarmac. In another three hours, all going to plan, we will be in the United States. But this is no ticket to safety for me. Unless I can convince the Colombians and the Arellano family that I am not involved in the hotel shoot-out, I will spend the rest of my life looking over my shoulder. It's not an appealing prospect.

We have been flying for almost an hour. 'How long before we land?' I ask the pilot, straining my eyes to see any lights below us. All I can see is inky darkness.

He looks at his watch. 'We should see Madero in fifteen minutes. We have made good time because of a strong tail wind.'

One hour. The embassy vehicles will be at the airport in Mexico City by now. I pray Jim can hold everyone off long enough for us to get to the border. Everyone is still asleep, except for me and the pilot.

'How much fuel is left?'

'About another hour's flying, maybe one and a half hours if we're lucky.'

I pass him another five thousand dollars. 'Keep flying, follow the coast to Brownsville, just across the border in the US. At five thousand feet, with that amount of fuel we should make it.'

'No way.' He shakes his head, determinedly. 'No way. I have no authority, no passport, and the US customs won't allow me to enter.'

'Don't worry about that. I made some phone calls when we landed at Moctezuma and I have arranged everything.'

'How?'

'You don't need to worry about how.'

He looks at the cash. 'I will need more money for expenses and for fuel to get back to Mexico City.'

'When we land, you'll get another five thousand dollars.'

He smiles. 'You have a deal.' He heads north towards Brownsville.

We are four hundred metres offshore. The pilot waits until the lights of Madero are far behind and then slowly points the aircraft downwards. When he reaches five thousand feet, he levels off and flies along the coast. Intermittent patches of lights define small coastal towns and, in the distance, I make out the brighter lights of cities and towns. The pilot points ahead. 'That is the US. We are making good time and should be across the border in another forty-five minutes.'

'Great. Don't use the radio until we have crossed.' I turn and look at the passengers, still sleeping. Is the driver married with a family? I wonder. I have thrown their lives into utter turmoil.

The pilot interrupts my reverie. 'That's Brownsville, about ten minutes away.' He points to the radio and passes the air phone to me. 'Control tower. You sort it out, okay?'

The man's voice is distinctly American. 'Brownsville control tower. Identify yourself.'

'This is DEA Special Agent Greece from Mexico City. We are carrying six passengers.'

The response is immediate. 'Cleared for landing.'

Two corporate jets are sitting on the tarmac with their lights on, flanked by a dozen police cars. It's a large welcoming party, but the pilot is not impressed. 'Who are all these people?'

'It's okay,' I assure him. 'They are on our side.'

'I hope so,' he mutters. 'You are not carrying drugs? We are all fucked if you are.'

It occurs to me that he should have thought of this earlier, but it's not the time to tell him. 'No drugs. We're all safe.'

We touch down and race along the tarmac with several police cars following. At standstill, more police vehicles surround the aircraft, their lights flashing.

'I'm going to get out first,' I tell Adriana, who is now wide awake and petrified. 'Please don't panic. It's all right.'

Four men are waiting for me at the bottom of the aircraft steps, DEA written on their jackets. The tension of the last twelve hours has taken its toll. For the first time since we left Mexico City, I break down. 'There is a wounded Colombian on board who needs urgent medical help,' I'm yelling. 'A mother with her daughter and granddaughter. A taxi driver and the pilot. They don't have papers. And they are terrified.'

One of the agents is checking my features against a photograph he is holding in his hand. 'Greece, over here,' he says, moving me away from the crowd. He shakes my hand. 'Well done. Excellent work.' He hands me a cell-phone. 'Jim is on the line.'

He doesn't wait until I speak. 'Shit, Greece! You made it! Just in time, too. The Colombians and Mexican police have found the car and are tracking your flight. They now know you've landed in the US.' I feel exhausted, but listen to him as he rattles on without pausing for breath. 'Our people were off-loaded in Mexico City and they locked up the aircraft after the Mexican police searched it and the vehicles. They are now aware that the whole thing was a decoy and they're seriously pissed off. Stiff. You're now in the US, and that's great. The DEA manager and his team will travel with you and your passengers to Dallas and sort it all out there. Greece, you did a great job. We'll make a fully-fledged agent of you yet.'

'I don't want to be a DEA agent,' I mutter, wearily. 'I just want to see Claudia and know that my family in Australia are safe.' I hand back the cellphone. The other DEA agents, with a medical team, have taken the Colombian off our aircraft and put him on a corporate jet. The plane man-oeuvres to the runway and within seconds is racing down the tarmac and rising into the night.

A female agent is talking to us as we are shepherded towards the second jet. 'We need to get on board and get out of here,' she says, smiling at Adriana. 'Please rest assured you are safe. We will let no harm come to you.'

Once again we strap into our seats and climb into the air. I am struggling to stay awake but there is still business to be dealt with. I take another twenty thousand out of a bag and once we reach our cruising height, I give Adriana ten thousand and hand the promised five thousand to our Mexican pilot. The driver of the car also gets five thousand. They take it wordlessly and quickly put it away.

I look at my watch. It is just after 11 pm. We have refuelled in Dallas and are en route to Washington, DC, another two-hour flight. I catch a restless sleep before we come in to land, the usual cheer squad waiting for us at the DC airport: a squadron of police, FBI and DEA officers.

The Arellano Félix organisation, I know, have had some major setbacks over the last decade. Ramón, whose capture carried a two-million-dollar price tag, was killed in a shoot-out in Mazatlan on 10 February 2002. Weeks later, Benjamín was arrested at his safe house in Puebla, just outside Mexico City, on charges of operating a drug-smuggling organisation, kidnap and murder. The mantle of leading the cartel then fell to brother Javier, who kept a tight rein with the help of brutal henchmen. His subsequent arrest paved the way for a power struggle on a scale authorities had not witnessed before, and also led to the capture of his loyal lieutenants.

The Arellano family, seven brothers and four sisters, were all involved in the business. But if the DEA thought that the rest of the clan did not have the brains and muscle combination of Benjamín and Ramón, they were dangerously wrong. After Ramón's death and Benjamín and Javier's arrests, they became more powerful and far more violent, with one brother, Eduardo Arellano Félix, wresting control of the family's drug organisation. As the DEA was to grimly discover, Eduardo was the mastermind behind Benjamín's financial genius, and well placed to assume leadership. Worse, he also possessed Ramón's cold-blooded appetite for murder.

Following Benjamín's arrest, the Mexican government harnessed thousands of troops and police to restore order to the border city and expose corrupt police officers. The result was a weakening of the Tijuana cartel's power base outside its main centre of operation, but the crackdown fell far short of crushing the cartel entirely. They are still very powerful, very wealthy, very dangerous and very violent. I pray to God they're not waiting for us.

26

We are escorted to separate apartments, secured by DEA agents. No one can enter or leave without them knowing and a pass is required to access our floor. They have thought of everything, it appears, including clothes and a vanity lined with toiletries. 'Have a good night's sleep, Greece,' the agent says as he closes the door. 'Lock up after we leave and don't open it until you hear from us. Here's one of our cellphones. We will ring you first on this, three times, and then knock. Check through the spyhole first. We'll be back at 10 am. Please be ready to leave.' It's already 2 am. I crash onto the bed and am asleep in seconds.

Special Agent Gary is at my door at precisely 10 am. 'Morning,' he smiles. 'Hope you slept well?'

'How is everyone else?'

'Fine. They are in good hands.' He is polite, but obviously does not wish to tell me anything more. I refrain from asking him where we are going.

Ten kilometres from the apartment block, we stop at a set of imposing gates, two men with ID tags hung round their necks standing guard. They check the two agents' identification, nodding for them to go through and pressing an internal button to open the gates. The car stops in front of an historic two-storey house. We walk wordlessly down a wide hallway into a massive lounge with a dining-room table in the corner and French doors overlooking a garden of magnolias and roses.

A man approaches me and extends his hand in introduction. From the smile on his face, I'm obviously on friendly turf. 'Good morning, Greece. I am Anthony Campbell, Deputy Director of the DEA. Please, take a seat.' I'm underwhelmed by his presence, despite his apparent warmness. He looks tired and his grey pallor is testament to long working hours with little sunshine and greasy food on the run. He makes an expansive gesture with his hands, ushering me into a plush brocaded chair. He remains standing. 'Coffee?'

'Please. White and two.'

'First, Greece,' he starts, 'congratulations are in order. You have achieved a remarkable outcome for the agency, a first-class job. Everyone is impressed, from the director to the team in San Diego.'

'Thank you.'

He takes a seat, awkwardly. 'Okay, down to business. The Colombian? He's recovering in hospital and will be a wealth of intelligence for us. He'll sing, and you've brought this guy to us on a silver platter, so we thank you for that. The pilot and the driver: neither is married, their families don't live in Mexico City, and,' he gives a sarcastic laugh, 'surprise, surprise, both have asked to stay in America. We have, of course, obliged.' He is standing again, pacing now. 'They will be given new identities and job opportunities here in the US. Both will be out of

DC within forty-eight hours, and you won't have to worry about them.'

'Adriana, her baby and her mother?' I have opportunity to speak, finally.

'Yes, about them.' He coughs. 'The three of them, plus Adriana's sisters and families, are a different story. All will have to be relocated to the US. They're making it difficult for us, but they will play ball in the end. They know they'll be better off here, and we will find them employment and a housing loan at a zero interest rate, to make it easy for them to settle down.'

I fail to control my anger. 'You're telling me these people have been wrenched out of their home and country, that they can never go back, and that you're doing them a good turn?'

He ignores my outburst. 'As for the bodies in the hotel,' he continues, 'they have all been recovered and Al's family have, with our help, made arrangements to fly him back to the US. The surveillance videos in the hotel were picked up by our man there and there is no direct link to you. He also removed the surveillance video of the hotel where you were staying, so there is no record there, either.' This time, it's me who says nothing. 'You have the cash?' he suddenly asks.

'Yes, it's all there. Except for expenses.' I itemise what the expenses are, one by one, while the two agents make notes. 'I have to bank the balance into the Colombians' account. Then Daniel Gómez and his family will at least have a chance at safety.'

'I don't give a flying fuck about Gómez,' Campbell snarls. 'But I can understand your own safety concerns. Take our commission out and give us the account number in Switzerland. We'll wire the funds today.' He turns to

Gary. 'Take out our commission, less the expenses already paid and bank the cash at Washington Mutual Bank on Tyson's Corner. We have an arrangement there. Greece, do you have their bank details?'

'Yes, I do.' I take out the written instructions from a briefcase.

'Okay,' Campbell says, 'you had better go as well. Do the banking first, then come back here and we'll have some lunch. The director wants to see you personally to say thanks.'

The bank manager is expecting Gary but casts a suspicious eye over me. We empty the bag and start counting the cash, withdrawing the five per cent commission – half a million dollars – less expenses already paid. I pocket four hundred and forty thousand. 'I need the receipt from the receiving bank as well as Washington Mutual,' I explain to the bank manager. 'I also need the wire to come out of this bank in New York, not Washington, DC.'

He doesn't look up but writes out the wire instruction form, stamps it and confirms that Washington Mutual has received the funds and has wired them to a numbered account with the Union Bank of Switzerland in Zurich. He then scans the document and sends it to their main branch in New York before phoning one of the senior managers there and explaining the situation. Within ten minutes, he receives a call back from New York, walks to the printer and hands me the receipt of the wire to Switzerland. Gary seems overwhelmed by the transactions, but I am beginning to enjoy myself.

'The joys of technology,' I quip.

The manager looks back at me, blank-faced. 'The actual

proof of funds in the account in Switzerland will be available in the morning, and the clearing bank will be the Bank of New York,' he says, completely deadpan.

In my mind, I follow the money trail. When the funds are wired, Washington Mutual – the clearing bank that handles international exchanges – will do the actual transfer. Money being wired from Barclays Bank in London to Wells Fargo Bank in Denver will be cleared through the Bank of New York. I'm satisfied that the money has been processed correctly, but wonder how much of the commission I will get and what percentage of the two-million-dollar reward for the Colombian? I think I already know the answer.

We are ushered into the dining room on our return, the table prepared for lunch. Anthony Campbell grills me about the banking transaction. 'What will happen to those funds?' he asks, looking at me intently.

'They will move through a series of banks and may end up back with the Union Bank of Switzerland, but we will lose trace of the money once the funds are moved to the next bank.'

Campbell shakes my hand as he prepares to leave. 'I'm afraid I will not be joining you for lunch, but I will be here for coffee. Thanks again. Your team from San Diego will be here after lunch as well: Morgan, Jim and the rest of the crew.' I bet they will, I think grimly. This is a golden opportunity for them to be noticed by the Director of the DEA.

'Tomorrow,' he continues, 'we will deal with the Colombians and work out a means for Daniel Gómez and his family to be released. Enjoy your lunch.'

The mention of Daniel has made me lose my appetite

and I send the food back. This is not a time for fancy lunches and backslapping. Gómez would be terrified for his family and doing his best to resolve the issue. And if the Colombians think he is in any way involved with the deal that went so wrong, he is a dead man walking.

The director arrives with Anthony Campbell on cue with the coffee. 'Well done, Greece,' he says, shaking my hand for a brief moment. 'We are all very impressed with your escape from Mexico City. You think very quickly on your feet.'

I barely have time to acknowledge the compliment before a photographer appears from nowhere. With immaculate timing, Morgan and Jim enter the room and give me a passing hello before joining Campbell and the director for a group photo. I watch, bemused, as they grin and preen at the camera as though they themselves had been in the hotel shoot-out. They invite me to join them in the second photo before the director leaves. He doesn't have a coffee. He is in the room no longer than ten minutes.

Campbell addresses me and from his tone I know immediately that something is wrong. 'Greece, we want you to take back control of the Colombian money that you have deposited. Move it into Essex Finance's account in London. We want the cash. There is no way we can allow it to flow to the cartel. This is a direct instruction from the President to the director.'

For a moment, I lose my voice. When I do speak, it is choked with disbelief. 'Please tell me you're joking.'

'I'm afraid not. This is a directive from the top.'

'Do you realise the implications of this? It will cause major problems for me, Daniel Gómez and our families. You don't mess with the fucking cartels! A deal is a deal!'

'There are no options here, Greece. We have contacted

the Union Bank of Switzerland and advised them accordingly. They will play ball. We want you to move the cash to our account today. The Swiss bank is awaiting your instructions.'

'Do you realise the problems this will cause?' I am repeating myself, but I don't care. 'It's going to create a nightmare situation.'

'We know,' he says, puffing out his chest. 'But we can handle that. What did Miguel and the Colombians want you to do with the cash?'

'Just bank it. Just bank the cash into their account; nothing else.'

'Did you discuss the concept of moving the cash into Essex's account in London?'

'No, I didn't have time, and it's a bit hard to talk to dead men.' I can't keep the sarcasm from my voice.

'Understood. But would you have discussed it if they were still alive in the meeting?'

Now I can see where he is heading with this. 'Yes, I would have.'

'Good. So that is what you will do: move the cash to Essex and then we have control. We will consider what we do after that. This is our cash now, and there is no way they will ever get their hands on it.'

There is a drumming noise in my ears, loud and unmistakable. I'm trapped, and I know it. 'Yes, sir.' I hate myself as soon as I say it and my accusatory inner voice starts the incessant chant. *Coward, coward, coward. Do something.*

'Gary, take Greece to the bank. And, Greece, make sure you get a receipt. Move the funds to our London account.'

'Sir, I will need to move the funds via France first, to a French bank called Caisse d' Épargne, and then on to

London. It's part of my usual strategy. I need to be consistent with our plan. Daniel Gómez knows of this system. It isn't what the Colombians wanted, but it is what we do. So when I tell Daniel, he will understand, it will make sense to him. Hopefully he can advise the Colombians as well.'

Campbell eyeballs me. 'You have complete control over the movement of funds, is that correct?'

'Yes, sir.'

'Well, do it, and come back here straight after so we can set up the telephone call with Daniel Gómez. He and his family are still in their house with the Colombians in Mexico City.'

'This will create major problems for me.'

'Don't worry, son, leave that to us. We will look after you.'

Son. The word grates. How does this patronising bastard think they are going to look after me? Like they have in the past? Or will it be the lonely road of the witness protection program – a new identity, a suburban house in Iowa and working at the local university, lecturing in economics, blending into the environment around me?

27

Gary and I meet the same staff at the bank as we had the previous day, asking the manager to immediately transfer the funds to Essex Finance Limited's account in Caisse d'Épargne, Paris. No doubt the Director of the DEA has persuaded the president of the Swiss bank as to how important it is to co-operate with the Department of Justice, especially if they wish to continue operating in the US.

I decide to hold the funds in France for a day or so until we can work out the next step. The funds, I know, will be in our account and under our control after lunch. We head back to the DEA complex and receive our next instructions. I understand clearly now that I am nothing but a pawn in the DEA's game, that the chances of surviving this operation are very slim.

The government will now move with lightning speed to seize all assets, houses, bank accounts, property, shares in public listed companies and pharmaceutical factories as well as everything we have been involved in through the network of bank accounts, offshore trusts and company structures. They are shutting Essex down. Within the next few days, the US Department of Justice, through the DEA, will have under their control cash and assets worth in excess of nine hundred million. They already have one of the top Colombian drug cartel leaders in custody and will swoop to make several other arrests around the world within days.

When the orchestrated stage production is over, the DEA will bathe in the media spotlight, accepting the plaudits and bouquets while I start to mark down the days until the Colombians find me. And they won't stop there: neither Susan and my children, nor Claudia and her children will ever be safe again. The cartel's vengeance is ruthless and exacting.

We return to the lounge, where Morgan, Jim and five other agents are waiting. 'You have the bank details?' Morgan asks.

'Yes.' I take the receipts from my inside pocket and hand them over.

'Great, Greece, now we need you to phone Daniel.' I knew this would be their next move and know also there is nothing I can do to avoid it. 'You know what to say?'

'Yes. But I need to put on record that I really do not want to do this. Playing Judas is not my thing.'

'No choice, Greece. Sorry.' I look at Morgan. I have seen her soft side in the past, heard her concerns for my safety, but this is completely different. This is business and she has her orders. 'We've arranged for different headsets so we can listen in to the conversation. We may pass you some notes, but keep it simple, Greece, short and to the point. Don't get into a discussion about the events in Mexico City. The Colombians will be listening as well, remember that. Okay? Ready?'

'Yes.'

'Okay, go for it.' I pick up the phone. I know Daniel's numbers well and dial his office, guessing it will be diverted to his home. As I dial, the team picks up their headsets, recording the call. A girl answers the phone. 'Hello, may I speak with Daniel, please?' My voice has a slight tremor in it and I will myself to sound calm.

'Who is speaking, please?'

'Keith. Tell him Keith is on the phone.'

'Wait, please.'

It takes two minutes for him to come to the telephone. 'Where the fuck are you?' he bellows. There is no mistaking his fury.

'I'm in New York,' I lie.

'New fucking York! Keith, you're in trouble, big fucking trouble! You have to return to Mexico City tonight, do you understand? Tonight!'

'Daniel, listen to me. I've banked the money from Miguel's client and I've got the receipt number and confirmation from the Union Bank of Switzerland. But I don't have a fax number to give the client a copy of the confirmation, and I can't get hold of Miguel to ask him, either.'

'What the fuck are you talking about? Miguel's dead! And the clients: one is dead and the other is missing, I suspect in the hands of the DEA in America. This has got your name written all over it!'

'Dead?' I try to feign surprise, but it sounds feeble and disingenuous. 'What do you mean, dead?'

Daniel is shouting over my questions. 'Secondly, your so-called friend Al is dead also and he has been identified as a DEA agent who was based in Colombia. How the fuck do you explain that?'

Morgan has passed me a note. *Stay calm. Speak clearly.* I am so nervous that my hands are shaking.

'I have no idea what the fuck you are talking about, Daniel. I went to the hotel with Al who, as you know, was introduced to me by my investor who helped fund Essex. We met Miguel at the hotel, I met the two clients briefly and they handed me the cash. I counted it and we agreed on the amount of ten million. They were arguing with Al, but the whole conversation was in fucking Spanish and I couldn't understand a word. It was obviously a very heated argument, so I left.'

'Cut the shit, Keith! You were on the fucking plane! The people at the airport said it was you, with Adriana, her mother and the fucking driver.'

'When I left, I saw police cars arriving at the hotel, Daniel. Since I was carrying so much bloody money, I didn't want to be caught with it. I would have been killed, even by the Mexican police, and the cash would have been stolen. You've told me that a hundred times.'

I'm talking faster than I should be, but I'm desperate to get this conversation over. The lies come easily. 'I had made an appointment to see Adriana, which I'd forgotten about. She turned up and agreed to take me to the airport, as I had already made my own arrangements to leave Mexico with the cash. Adriana had to see her mother first, then on the way she heard the news on the radio that something had happened at the hotel. It wasn't until we got to the airport that we found out they were looking for me. So I took precautions, Daniel, and the rest is history. I've done my part and the cash is banked.'

'Hang on a moment.' He comes back on the line three minutes later. 'The cash was banked last night from New

York, but you transferred it this morning. What the fuck is going on, Keith?'

'It was agreed by the clients that I would transfer the cash to Essex's bank account in Paris and later move the funds to London. You know I have done that for dozens of clients.'

'But how the fuck did you move the funds from the client's account in Zurich?'

'I had written authority from them.'

'Hang on.' Morgan pushes me another note. *Great work. He is going off-line to get instructions from the Colombians.* Daniel is back. 'Keith? Okay, move the funds to London and then we'll advise you where to send them. And keep in touch! I expect to hear from you within forty-eight hours. The client wants to see you in person and he will locate you. Be prepared to tell him the truth.'

'Hold on, Daniel. I thought you said that one client's dead and the other is missing. If that's the case, I'm going underground, and will get back to you later.'

'Don't be a smart prick, Keith. They will find you and they will want to know the truth about their missing family member. Don't fuck with them and don't take their fucking money! They will locate you within days. Have you got that?' Two seconds silence. '*Adios*,' he says, and the phone goes dead.

I'm going to be dead, too, within days unless I can work something out.

Jim, quiet until now, chips in. 'I think Daniel will be okay. But the Colombians will now try to find you, Greece, so we must move you quickly. We've decided on a safe house for a few weeks until we can reassess everything, so you'll move today. We have agents who will be based close to the house. It is all set up, fully furnished, and Claudia will arrive with her children tomorrow.'

I'm beyond speaking, simply nod my head in agreement.

'Let's get moving. Greece, we will need you back here in a few days, as we take control of the cash in the different international bank accounts.'

Morgan gives me a hug as I leave. I get the feeling she senses I'm not going to make it. I've got exactly the same feeling. It won't take the cartel long to find out where the information has come from. Even if they suspect I am not involved, they'll kill me just to ensure my silence.

28

By mid-afternoon, Jim and I arrive at our destination, a small town that feels like nowhere. Annapolis has one main street, several cafés and restaurants and one movie theatre. The focus of the town is its Naval Academy, a massive campus attended by thousands of students. The town is so bland, so typically American, I could be anywhere.

On the way, Jim has given me instructions. 'There's a local school that we have arranged for Claudia's children to attend, effective Monday. You're John Keith Wilson from now on – Dr John Keith Wilson – and you have a PhD in American Naval History. All the paperwork has been done to support that, including your driver's licence and academic qualifications. We've prepared a complete history on you and Claudia, so study the profiles. Claudia and the children are still from Germany and you both met in Berlin, where you were a visiting professor two years ago. You will be teaching at the academy.'

'Teaching! I don't know the first bloody thing about American naval history!'

'It's okay. You won't need to. You won't be in a hands-on teaching role. You are a civilian, not a professor with a military background, and the academy has arranged an office on campus in the main education building for you.'

He stops the car. 'This is it,' he announces, pointing to a faux-colonial two-storey house with an attractive front garden and double garage. It never fails to amaze me how he keeps his sangfroid, despite the circumstances. Then again, it's not Jim himself who has to move in a hurry and go undercover from drug cartels. 'You and Claudia will need to stay here until we think it appropriate for you to move on.'

'And Claudia?' I ask. 'Who is she?'

'She's your loving wife!' Jim grins. 'How do you fancy that idea! Her name is Claudia Wilson, and the kids will maintain their own names: Martina, Anja and Klaus.'

I'm only half-listening, looking at the empty driveway. 'What about a vehicle? How do we get around?'

'Organised. A Ford van, eight seats and all the bells and whistles you could possibly want. We've attached a tracking device on the car for your own safety, plus an alert button which is under the front seat. Press it and the alarm will go off at DEA headquarters. It's parked in the garage and the keys are in the house.'

'And what do we do for money?' This is all moving so fast. A new identity and a new life.

'We've opened a bank account in joint names, with your ATM cards in separate names. The limit on each credit card is twenty-five thousand and there is twenty-five thousand in your joint savings account. You will be paid a monthly salary by the academy, twelve and a half thousand a month less tax and benefits. Your first pay is the end of this month.'

I'm becoming weary with all the information. 'Sounds like you've thought of everything,' I say, with more than a hint of sarcasm.

'The removal van was here yesterday. It had Boston registration numberplates, so the locals will think you have moved from Boston. Two of the female agents who will be watching you went shopping this morning and the kitchen is well stocked with supplies.'

We have moved inside the house. 'You will head to the academy in the morning at 8.30 am. You have the appropriate identification pass, which also has the code key to your office. When you arrive, you will be met by Commander Stan Lysterfield, who is aware of your status. Your office is set up with a fitted video surveillance unit. The phone is automatically linked to DEA headquarters and the office is fitted with two alert buttons.'

'Claudia and the children?'

'Agents will bring them here around 2 pm tomorrow. They will be told that the agents are from a relocation company in Boston. Now I'm going to show you around the house.'

They haven't missed a thing. Beds made, our clothes from San Diego hung in the wardrobes, house fully furnished, flowers on the coffee table and photos of Claudia, me and the children on the mantelpiece. 'How the hell did you get these photos?' This has become seriously spooky, like I am living in a parallel universe.

'We raided your house in San Diego and also downloaded some from Claudia's computer.'

'Good to see we've got plenty of privacy, then. Do you think you could have asked first?'

'No time for that. Okay, security arrangements. There is a recording device and video surveillance in each room of the house, including your bedroom. Alert buttons are in every room and security lights outside. When you enter the house at night, switch on the outside alarm. This will ring if someone enters the property, including the garage. We have a team on standby around the clock and they are only minutes away.

'We will phone the house every morning at 7 am and you must answer the phone. If Claudia or you answer and there are people in the house and you are at risk, simply advise the caller they have the wrong number and we will be here within ten minutes. When Claudia takes the children to school and collects them in the afternoon, we'll have a car with two agents monitoring the drop-offs and pick-ups.' Even Jim is starting to flag. 'If you want a day out, we'll arrange a surveillance team to be with you. Any questions?'

'Yeah. How long is this nightmare going to go on for?'

'Until we're satisfied you're all safe.'

29

The morning is overcast, but no rain. I walk down Prince George Street towards the Naval Academy, my security pass around my neck and other identification papers in my pockets. The duty sentry stops and checks my pass in a computer list against my photograph. The DEA have certainly done their work. The guard hands back my security pass. 'Thank you, Dr Wilson. Have a nice day.'

Commander Lysterfield's office is on the ground floor. He greets me warmly. 'Hi, John, welcome to the US Naval Academy. Please call me Stan.'

'Thanks, Stan, it's nice to be here.'

He shows me my office and takes his leave. I sit down at my desk, switch on the computer and search the *Washington Post* for any information on Mexico City stories. Nothing new. I look around my office and ponder the absurdities of my situation. Masquerading as a university professor is all very well, but it doesn't change the reality that I'm hiding out from a drug cartel. A posting to Iraq would have been a safer assignment.

The academy has the US Defence and Fire Departments

on site. Since the catastrophe of September 11, the campus has been on heightened security readiness and awareness, which gives me some small comfort if the cartel's hitmen arrive in town. I choose the library as my safe house, a large building that will allow me time to make an urgent phone call to DEA agents. The sounding of the alarm will bring the navy police to the building within minutes. I decide to learn every aspect of the library's layout. From now on, I will visit there every day until I know every brick, every staff member and every hiding place. I also need to work out an escape route. There is no easy way out. The best bet is for me to be extra-vigilant about where I am on campus each day.

Claudia is settling in with the children when I arrive home. Martina is the first to hear me come through the door and runs up to give me a hug, followed by Anja and Klaus. Claudia is behind them and I am shocked when I see the change in her. Tired, stressed and frightened, she looks stricken. I feel so ashamed that I have brought her to this. Her face is expressionless, but I know what she is thinking: *What the fuck is happening here?*

I move to her and take her in my arms. She leans into me and weeps. 'I'm so sorry,' I repeat, stroking her hair. 'I'm so sorry. Let's settle the children and we'll chat tonight. It will be all right.' She smiles and kisses me and I nuzzle closer in the intimate way of lovers, burying my face in her hair. 'I love you, Claudia. It will all be all right.'

We raid the pantry and make a snack: sandwiches and cordial for the children, biscuits, cheese and white wine for us. All the while I know our activities are being watched via video-link back at the DEA's bolthole. We sit close together as the kids huddle in front of the television.

'Okay, Keith, what's the plan?' Claudia has broached the subject and I can no longer avoid answering her.

'I've got a position at the Naval Academy and we have this house for the next twelve months,' I tell her, speaking slowly and praying I don't slip up. 'Once the children are settled into school, I thought you might like to look at the possibility of working in the Naval Hospital on campus?' She has a puzzled look on her face, but I know she won't press me further with the children around.

When night falls, we settle the children into bed and light a fire in the lounge room. Soft music plays in the background and the only light is from candles. Claudia is seriously beautiful: 1.7 metres tall, hair that falls halfway down her back, full lips, and almond skin. I hope that the DEA surveillance team will have the decency to switch off the video and allow us this privacy. I lie beside her on the carpet and she rests her head on my shoulder. The music is gently soothing and we say nothing as we sip our wine and stare at the flames in the fireplace. Claudia snuggles into me. 'Tonight I want to be loved, Keith. No stories, no talk. Just love me.' She doesn't have to seduce me.

As Claudia dozes with her head on my shoulder, I think of how my life has changed. The past few years have sorely tested my sanity: three years in solitary confinement, two months in Arthur Gorrie, the bashings from Malcolm Pearce and firebombing of the family cars, extortion threats, and working here in America and in Mexico on one of the most dangerous assignments I could have been handed. Claudia is the best thing that has happened to me in a long time, but with the nightmare that I am living, I don't know how long I can keep her.

The following morning, the DEA call me as planned. If they have seen the spicy surveillance video, they give no indication. As promised, they are in the process of freezing accounts, transferring all the cash held on deposit in Essex back to DC, seizing assets, properties, art works and public companies. They have also issued notices to sell stock and will need to step up protective measures around us.

Jim is, as usual, bluntly to the point. 'Our team will be raiding your office in San Diego tomorrow morning,' he says. 'The media will be there and will be told that we are seizing records and that the directors and CEO of Essex are to be interviewed. They will be given no more information. We have placed a court order suppressing names, so no need to worry about that.

'Also, Daniel Gómez and his family flew out of Mexico City last night for a European holiday, so he's safe. His group will watch his back.' I am vaguely confident that Daniel will survive if he can stay away from Mexico for a while. He managed to stay in hiding for four years when he was on the run.

Jim is more animated now. 'Sorry, Greece, but the shit is going to hit the fan tomorrow. The cartel will come looking, but we're very confident that neither the Mexicans nor the Colombians can find you.'

My gut is roiling. 'Fuck, Jim! How can you be sure they won't? They have their people everywhere, they will find us!'

'We don't think so. There will be no trace of you anywhere, believe me.'

I am pacing the study. 'So far you guys have made a heap of promises, but the only person who has got me out of the shit is me.'

'How are Claudia and the children?' He has deftly changed the subject, a tactic he uses every time a situation becomes tricky.

'They're fine, as well as they can be. But I still haven't worked out what to tell Claudia. I can't tell her about the cartels, she's already worried sick about what the fuck has happened so far. And just how long do you think I can continue not telling her the truth?'

'That's up to you.'

Claudia is standing in the doorway, looking at me. She knows something is wrong, but hopefully she will stick with her policy of waiting until I tell her in my own good time. 'Is everything all right, Keith?'

'Couldn't be better,' I smile, wrapping her in my arms.

In truth, I can see us needing to move again and again to avoid the moles and double agents who work on the inside of the DEA. I've heard about Felipe, who worked for the Beltrán-Leyva drug cartel while simultaneously 'working' for the DEA in Mexico City. Felipe received more than four hundred thousand dollars a year from the cartels for information. With so much black money involved, it is ludicrous to believe that Felipe was a one-off, or that there are no more rotten apples feeding information to the cartels from DEA offices throughout the United States.

At best, we would have two or three weeks before we have to move. At worst, a matter of days. I have to think of something, fast.

Within twenty-four hours, I am back at Deputy Director Anthony Campbell's complex, transferring the funds in the accounts under my control. With Morgan and Jim watching, I make all the transfers and close accounts.

Then I trawl through the share portfolios of all my clients, checking the list of nominee companies and the stocks I have purchased through them. I check whether I have the share certificates in trust, which in many cases I do. People who need to hide their wealth from authorities use nominee companies. The companies have directors and a secretary, who are paid a fee, but the real owners are hidden in complicated mazes which take time to unravel. It is sometimes impossible to find out who they are. I hold most of the certificates, with other important documentation, in a number of safety deposit boxes with Wells Fargo Bank in San Diego, the contents of which are now on the boardroom table in front of us. Finally, I check the sell orders to make sure I have all the certificates.

When I'm done, I relay the news to Morgan and Jim. 'Everything is in order.' I'm depleted and frightened. By taking the cash, the DEA has brought significant pressure on me. I may as well wave a red flag to the Colombians and Mexicans, inviting them to seek their revenge.

30

The announcement that millions in cash and assets have been seized from the cartels will make international news, a carefully choreographed stage show set against the backdrop of the White House, with President Bush and the DEA director as the leading men and Jim, Morgan and other senior team leaders as the chorus line. The irony does not escape me that while I'm the least visible, hidden away, I'm the most exposed.

Claudia is becoming agitated and it is increasingly difficult to hide the truth from her. 'I need to start working again, Keith,' she announces over breakfast. 'I can't spend my days doing nothing.' I try to placate her by promising to check with the Naval Hospital administration. This time, my soothing words don't work. 'Keith, what the hell is going on?' she demands. 'We've come here and are provided with everything we can imagine, but why? I want to know.'

'It's the bank in San Diego,' I lie. 'It's owned and funded by the US government and my job was to gather information and handle clients' business for them. A few weeks ago it was discovered that some of the clients have criminal connections, and the Justice Department froze those accounts and closed the bank.'

'Right. But what has that got to do with you?'

'As a precaution, purely as a precaution, they moved us here and found me a job.'

She is silent for a while. 'You went to Mexico a lot. You spent several weeks in Mexico City and Los Cabos. Most of your clients were from Mexico, and some of them would have to be connected to the drug gangs, wouldn't they?'

I gulp. 'Some, yes.'

'Level with me, Keith. How much trouble are we in?'

'There is no trouble. I helped the US authorities freeze the accounts and I keep them informed about the bank's activities. I did what I was required to do by the government, so I haven't done anything wrong. They simply moved us here as a precaution, and we're protected by the Justice Department. They've paid for the house and car, given me some cash and found me a job. It's their reward to me for doing the right thing.'

She listens to everything I say without interrupting. When I finish, she squeezes my hand. 'I've got three young children, Keith, and I know you wouldn't do anything to harm them.' She gets up and starts clearing the breakfast dishes, signalling the conversation is over.

I watch the children play in the lounge room, frolicking on the couches and pulling silly faces. They don't deserve this, nor does Claudia. I can't bring myself to admit to her that we are under twenty-four-hour surveillance and that a DEA tag team is in town to monitor our every move. We need more than protection. Right now, it feels like the only thing that is going to keep us safe is a bulletproof bunker.

I head out to the university, stopping to pick up the papers. The seizures have made headlines in the *Washington Post* and the *New York Times*: 'DEA seizes millions in drug cartel bank accounts throughout the world'. I grab a coffee and find a table, shaking as I read the article which outlines the closure of an investment bank in San Diego and the freezing of cartel accounts which hold approximately eight hundred million in different countries around the world. The DEA has also sought a suspension order on the details of the company until such time as the bank's CEO and directors have been interviewed. The director will be making a full statement within the next few days. I put the newspaper down.

These stories would have been run overnight by radio and television stations in Mexico and Colombia. Jim was right: the shit is about to hit the fan. I race to the office at the university and dial DEA headquarters.

'What's up, Greece?' Special Agent Gary has answered the phone and can hear the tremor in my voice.

'What's up? Are you kidding? Have you seen the fucking papers?'

'Yes.'

'Well, why didn't someone warn me about this yesterday, so I could be prepared?'

'We thought about it, but decided not to.'

'I'd prefer to know in future, thanks very much, so I can tell Claudia. She will find out before I have a chance to talk to her!'

'She already knows. She switched on the TV when she got home after dropping the children off at school, and is walking down to your office now. She left a couple of minutes ago.'

'Well, fuck me! Thanks a lot!' I slam the phone down and wait for Claudia. She has been to my office before and will arrive soon enough.

'Is this true?' She is breathing heavily from the exertion of rushing over here and is waving the *New York Times* in front of me.

'Yes, it is. Sit down, Claudia. Please.' She slumps into a chair and covers her face with her hands. 'Look, as I explained to you this morning, I've been helping the government and that's why we're here. They have frozen accounts which belong to a number of Mexicans.'

'I've asked you repeatedly if we are in trouble.'

'The government is helping us.'

'But drug cartels, Keith! They are so dangerous.' She is pacing the room now, and stops in front of me. 'Keith, you have to tell me the truth.'

'I am,' I lie. 'I am aware of how dangerous the cartels are but we are well protected. They'll never find us.'

'Don't be too sure about that. Can you ask them to provide you with further protection until this passes?'

'I have asked for round-the-clock surveillance and they've agreed, effective immediately. There are emergency buttons in the house which send off an alarm, and they have a team stationed here in Annapolis who can be with us within minutes if that is activated. And the calls in the morning are to ensure we're okay.'

She tries to manage a smile. 'I thought it was odd that the phone rings every morning at seven o'clock.' She pulls me close and kisses me. 'We're in your hands, darling.' Not for the first time I marvel at how calm this woman is. But I know we are not safe. They will find us, it is just a matter of time.

In the quiet of my office when Claudia leaves, I lay my forehead on the desk and try to calm my breathing. This nightmare has shifted a gear. I can no longer rely on the agency or anyone else to protect us. I have to analyse my options and work out my next move. Like a game of chess.

I need to work out a contingency plan for our disappearance.

31

I have kept meticulously detailed reports of my activities with the DEA since I started working for them, including seven tape-recordings of my conversations with the Mexican drug cartels. Now, they are no longer safe in my possession. I need to get them to my lawyer, but I can neither call him to make an appointment or send him an email, as both my phone and computer are monitored by the DEA. The best bet is to send them by courier and buy a phone card to call him from a public phone in a shopping mall. The DEA is watching our backs and working on the assumption that Colombians or Mexicans would make a hit on us at our house, when we are driving to or leaving the shopping mall, at the university or in a park. They would not hit at a crowded shopping mall with banks of security cameras.

The reason I keep records of everything is because of advice from a former agent, who warned me to record all my conversations with the agencies and take their photographs as well. During meetings with cartel members, the DEA always has someone taking photographs. 'Make no mistake,' the agent told me, 'if the DEA is ever asked if you work, or had worked for them, they will vehemently deny it. You will become persona non grata. You will simply cease to exist.'

I take the ex-agent's advice, recording each meeting with government agencies, whether it be DEA or FBI, taking notes and burying the tapes. I have also kept the letter from Justice Armstrong, who wrote to my lawyer advising that he had met with a representative of the US embassy in Canberra and had given permission for me to work for the US Department of Justice. He copied this letter to the DEA. I hide them where I know they can't be found. The cartels will always ransack a house, as will the agencies, to ensure nothing is recorded.

The ex-agent also gave me other advice. 'Be prepared for the police to come knocking on your door with a search warrant at any time. Never keep documents on display and hide any notes or memos on your computer amongst photos and porn. Heaps of porn.' I didn't understand what he meant.

'Anyone switching on your computer automatically goes to document folders, and their eyes pop out at the sight of countless rows of pornographic images. Make them as explicit as possible, to divert attention. Also, leave a lot of useless notes around on any subject: women, sport, anything at all which means nothing to you. They may or may not know when you are returning, but it slows them down when they search your house.' I take his advice, writing piles of rubbish and scattering it like confetti on my desk. It offends my natural sense of order, but it may save my life. I also print out a number of photos of women and put them in photo frames. If they photograph all the information in my hotel room, they will be confused as to which girl is mine.

The agencies pay in cash, providing credit cards to cover additional expenses. On a particular day each month, I fly to San Diego and meet two agents at a Starbucks coffee shop near DEA headquarters, following them to a vehicle where they hand over my pay. All three of us check the cash and, when finished, I sign the receipt in my code name, Greece. I never use my real name.

I try to engage DEA agents with the question of what I should do if the cartels come looking for me. I don't know why I bother; their reassurances never work. I prefer my own mantra, taken from the Special Air Services motto: 'Proper Planning and Preparation Prevent Piss-Poor Performance'.

Jim is on the phone. 'Greece, we've got a problem. The Mexican Juárez group has put a reward on your head for two million dollars. And we understand the Colombians have offered a similar amount, dead or alive. We received this confirmation a few minutes ago.' There is a slight pause, the only time in all my dealings with Jim I have heard him stumble. 'Also, the Mexican Attorney-General's office is making noises about issuing an arrest warrant for you.'

'What?' My head is spinning. 'Arrest warrant for what?'

'The murders of Al and Miguel. We are speaking to the government of Mexico now and have been assured that the warrant will not be issued.'

'This is a fucking debacle!' His assurances that the DEA have this under control are doing nothing to boost my confidence in their claims that they are watching out for me. 'I can't believe this! I can't stay in hiding for the rest of my life! I want to be relocated to Europe somewhere, with a top job and a heap of cash. You fucking promised me this!'

'I know what we promised, Greece. But believe me, we can give you twenty-four seven protection with the best surveillance teams in the world, and we have the resources here in the States, not in Europe. We will protect you, Claudia and the children, and your family in Australia. You have my word on that, and it's endorsed by the director.'

'With the greatest respect, Jim,' I reply, 'that doesn't mean much to me anymore. What do you propose I tell Claudia?'

'Nothing. Not a word. I've been in touch with the naval police on campus and advised them that your building has been found on a target list. Effective from today, their police will be in that building around the clock for additional security. We've advised them to check everyone entering the building, and surveillance will be in place by late today.'

'That makes me feel so much better, Jim.' I put the phone down, hoping he has tuned in to the sarcasm.

I post the recordings to my lawyer, Steven May, who has his practice based in Chicago, and purchase a couple of phone cards. He isn't in his office but his PA assures me he will be available in the morning. I have known Steven for more than thirty years. Steven and I played rugby against each other in London and when he toured with his club in 1972, he was billeted with me. His rugby days are long gone. Overweight, he is short with a stocky build. In 1997, he opened his own firm with three partners, specialising in corporate law.

When I arrived in the US, he was the first person I contacted. Steven was always concerned about the DEA. 'Keep asking the questions, Keith,' he warns over a dinner in San Diego. 'They have a history of not carrying out what they promise, and you need to know if they will go in to bat for you when you need them.'

I hand him a copy of the letter from Justice Armstrong. 'This is great: firm evidence that you were in contact with them. But they will duck and weave better than any rugby player we know. The agencies have the ability to concoct stories and they work on the assumption that no one will believe you, that it is all a flight of fancy on your part.'

He raids the cheese platter for his favourite camembert and continues talking. 'If the agencies have been carrying out covert operations in Mexico, without the approval of the Mexican government, you will have some explosive evidence. They don't want to make these operations known, because of certain people who have helped their security.

'Try to record a few conversations with the agencies: that would be excellent evidence. Make notes of meetings and tape-recordings of the drug cartels in Mexico City as well.' It is the same advice the DEA has given me. 'Believe me, if you can do this, we'll have their balls in a vice!' Steven is not given to histrionics, but there is urgency in his voice. 'Record everything, protect your ass, and get the information to me. I've a number of friends in Washington, DC, in both houses of Congress, so if push comes to shove I can make them dance. Believe me, Keith, the agencies fear embarrassment more than they fear their nation's enemies.'

I understand only too well the veracity of what Steven is saying to me. 'Charlies' – undercover agents – are graded by the agencies. If you are not that important, then you will be hung out to dry with no help given. No one will step up to defend you. It is not unheard-of for Charlies to be killed. 'Never heard of him,' is their usual line, if asked. 'He's lying.'

A friend of mine who worked for the CIA was promised a payment of one million dollars for information which would lead to the arrest of some terrorist cell leaders in the US. The information was given to the CIA, but they refused to pay the Charlie. Instead, they said these orders came from above and washed their hands of all knowledge. Fortunately, he had a video camera in his house which recorded the agreement to pay him the money. He took the video to his lawyer, and within days the CIA paid up.

I know my involvement with the DEA is never logged, much less acknowledged. The name I use is concealed as much as possible. Nowhere in any dossier is there the slightest clue of a Washington connection. In addition, certain people in government would go to significant lengths to keep my name and my covert operations in a 'black hole'. Their reasoning – that they are doing this to protect me from the drug cartels and the Mexican government – is clearly skewed in their favour. The truth is, when it comes to compensation and other promised benefits, they can confidently say, 'We can't help, because you don't exist.' But the gunshots in the hotel room in Mexico City and the instructions from the DEA operation centre to bring the wounded Colombian and the cash to the US would certainly verify the truth. As much as they would like to claim so, this isn't fiction.

I walk over to the Student Union complex and find a public phone to call Steven. He is, as usual, upbeat. 'I received your package this morning,' he says. 'Are the recordings explosive?'

'Yep.'

'Thank God for that. I'll have copies made today and they'll be locked away where no one will find them. I'll also send instructions to another friend of mine, a lawyer in Canada, in case something happens to me. This means that he'll be able to locate the tapes and find you, if necessary.'

'Steve, I'm in deep shit,' I offer. 'The fucking drug cartels and Colombians are looking for me. The DEA has seized all the bank accounts, frozen their assets and taken their property and shares. I'm on the run, so to speak, protected by the DEA and in a safe house on the East Coast.'

There is an elongated pause on the other end of the phone. 'Tell me you're kidding.'

'I wish I was. This is real. You'd have seen the news on the investment bank in San Diego being closed down? That was Essex.'

'Keith, you've got to get away from the DEA. They will screw you really badly. You can't trust them.' He pauses. 'How are Susan and the kids? And Claudia? How is she handling all this shit?'

'Susan is safe. Claudia doesn't really know what's going on. She has some idea, but doesn't understand that I have a price tag on my head.'

'Can you get to DC?'

'Yes. Why?'

'I can meet you somewhere there, record your details and lock them away. We may need to press the government into making sure that you, Claudia and the kids, and

193

your family back in Australia are taken care of. The DEA will dump you as soon as they can. History has proved that. When can you make it to DC?'

32

Steven starts recording as soon as we settle into the hotel room. He bombards me with questions and, forty minutes later, has most of the information he needs. His businesslike demeanour doesn't change as he works, but his mask drops when he is finished.

'Keith, I can't tell you enough how concerned I am about your situation,' he tells me. 'You have got to make your own plans. If things go wrong, you need to move fast. With a family in tow, that's going to be very difficult. You must think about what you can do.' He is tapping his fingers on the desk. 'You are going to need money. I will only charge you for expenses, nothing more. My time is free.'

The stress of the past few weeks finally takes its toll. I slump into the chair and start crying uncontrollably, my shoulders heaving. I'm beyond feeling any shame for breaking down. Fear and exhaustion envelop me, and I can't stop.

'I'm so scared, Steve,' I sob. 'I don't know where to turn anymore. I've put everyone's life in danger around me and I can't see any way out.'

'The only thing you can do, my friend,' he says, shoving a cold Budweiser that he has grabbed from the mini-bar into my hands, 'is rely on your own instincts. Make solid contingency plans. And be prepared to move . . . fast.'

I call an urgent meeting with the agency. Jim and Morgan have returned to San Diego, and Gary is the agent in charge.

'Hi, Greece,' he greets me in a cheerful voice. 'What can I do for you?'

'I don't want to talk on the phone. Can we meet somewhere today? There are some issues I need to discuss.'

'Are you free this afternoon?'

'Yes. I'm in DC, but will be back in Annapolis in a few hours.'

'Okay, we'll pick you up from Gate 1.'

We head to Truxton Park, where we can walk and chat without being overheard. 'What's on your mind, Greece?' he asks me.

I clear my throat. 'You need to inform me of the current situation with the Mexican and Colombian cartels. Are they close to finding me?'

'The word from our informers is that they are looking and the reward is for finding you, dead or alive. That hasn't changed.'

I stop in my tracks and make eye contact with Gary. 'I've asked you a direct question. How close are they to finding me?'

'According to our intelligence, they're looking for you in New York and California. So we're very confident they won't find you here. Furthermore, the Mexican government is now aware you were working with the US government as an undercover DEA agent, and they will not be charging you with any offences, nor seeking an interview with you. The matter regarding you is now considered closed.'

'How did this come about?'

'We made contact with the Colombian government and advised them we have one of their drug cartel leaders, who's also linked to Mexico's Sinaloa cartel, in custody. They were not impressed that we plucked him out of Mexico City and moved him to the US. Not happy at all. However, the White House has successfully pushed a four-hundred-million-dollar aid package for Mexican and Colombian anti-drug forces, and provided significant amounts of weaponry to both governments. This has calmed them down.'

'Well, Gary,' I interject, 'since we're on the topic of money, how about the two million reward for the Colombian that you guys promised?' I figure I already know the answer, but if I'm going to be running for the rest of my life, I may as well give it a shot.

'Greece, you are not entitled to the reward because you work for the DEA. You are an employee and we are still paying all your expenses and your salary at the academy. So, no commission and no reward. Sorry to tell you, but no agents have ever collected a reward. It is part of our job, you know that.'

'What I know is that you bastards promised me the world before I came to Mexico City.' I don't tell him that I have them recorded on tape, stating commissions would be paid. 'If things go wrong, we will need to get Claudia to Europe with her family where she is safe, and tucked away. At least assure me you can do that.'

'I'll see what we can do.'

I phone Steven straightaway. 'Just as you predicted,' I tell him. 'The pricks are wiping their hands of me. The recordings I've given you, can you copy the first one several times and see if you can edit it? It's from the hotel room where Al and I arrived to meet Miguel, ending with their deaths. Can you copy to the part where I am walking around the room, and then cut it?'

'I guess so. But why?'

'I may need it. If I have to, I can play it to the end of the shooting. I may be in a better position then to try and convince a few people that I left immediately after getting the cash.'

'Okay. I can see your reasoning in this. Good idea. How did you get the tape?'

'Al had the recorder in his pocket. When I turned his body over, it fell out. The light was still green and it was still recording, so I kept it. I recorded everything.'

'Surely the people you met in the hotel room would have known if you or Al were carrying a wire?'

'Yeah, but it's the latest type. It looks just like an electronic car key and can hold four hours of recordings. The DEA were convinced that if the Mexican police found the device, they would think it belonged to a car and forget about it.'

'Fuck, Keith! You took a bloody risk!'

'I know, but it's the only evidence I have that proves I had nothing to do with the deaths. Guard them with your life, Steven.'

'Will do.' He whistles. 'These are red-hot, my friend. The Mexican government would love to get their hands on them. The US has repeatedly said they respect Mexican sovereignty, yet here they are running around Mexico, doing covert operations and you have the fucking tapes to prove it!'

'I've got to go, Steve,' I say, looking at my watch. I've promised to meet Claudia and the kids for an early dinner. She doesn't know I've been to DC today and I don't want her to become suspicious. 'Thanks so much for all your help, mate. I owe you one.'

We are heading into a wide boulevard of cafés and restaurants when Martina pipes up from the back seat. 'Keith, two men on a motorcycle are following our car. They've been there since we left the shopping centre.'

I try to keep the panic from my voice and shoot a petrified glance into the rear-vision mirror. I can't see a motorbike. 'Where are they?'

'On the left. Just behind.'

Martina is right: a motorcycle with rider and passenger wearing black leathers and full helmets is behind us. 'What are you worried about?' I say to Martina. 'They're probably going the same way we are.' My lame attempt at calm is not working and Claudia looks stricken.

'No, they were in the carpark!' Martina insists. 'They followed us when we left!'

The bike is tucked in behind us and suddenly pulls alongside. I'm trying to watch them and the oncoming traffic. I look on from the corner of my eye in horror as the passenger raises a black metallic object and holds it close to the window. Claudia has taken charge, quietly demanding the children put their heads down in the back seat as he takes aim.

Click, click. They snap their photos, weave between traffic and disappear.

'Why did that man take pictures of us?' This time it is Anja speaking.

'They do that here,' Claudia counters. 'They just take photographs of people who are out and about, and sometimes they put them in the paper. I don't want our photos in the paper, so I got you to put your heads down.' The explanation seems to satisfy them. With the innocence of childhood, they start talking amongst themselves about something entirely different.

The photographs would have been organised by one of the cartels. Shaking, I abandon the idea of going out for dinner and head straight home via a circuitous route. How the fuck did they know we were at the shopping centre, let alone in Annapolis? Claudia sits in silence, her face slate-grey. She is petrified, and so am I.

I phone Gary as soon as we get home. 'We've been spotted. Two blokes on a motorbike. One took our photos.' I am shaking with rage. 'The fucking kids were in the car! You bastards promised to look after us!'

'Settle down, Greece. Stay put. We have all the video cameras on in your house. Lock all the doors. We'll notify the local police to keep patrolling the streets. I'll get back to you.'

This time, I can't pacify Claudia. 'We've got to get out of here, Keith, and you know it. I just can't believe they found us so fast. Get hold of the people in charge and demand we move now!' She is close to hysteria, and rightly so. I wrap my arms around her but she moves away, shrugging me off.

There must be a leak within the DEA. That is the only logical explanation as to how they located us so quickly. I pick up the phone again and Gary answers immediately. 'We heard Claudia's response on the phone tap,' he says. 'Look, if need be we will move you, but right now we are trying to understand how they got on to you so quickly.'

'There has to be a leak from within the agency! You are the only people who know where we are.'

'That has occurred to us, but only a handful of agents know your whereabouts.'

'Whatever. We need additional security and we need to make arrangements to move immediately.'

'Sit tight tonight. You're safe and we will make plans to get you out of there tomorrow. I have four agents looking out for you there and another four will arrive in a couple of hours. We have the video cameras operating and every room will be on camera throughout the night. If anything happens, we will be at the house in minutes.'

'If the people who took the photos are cartel men, we won't even have minutes to live when they burst through the door. You know that!'

'We'll have a van with two agents parked around the corner from your house. If anything goes wrong, they'll be in the house in thirty seconds. I could move agents into the house now, but we don't want to scare the children. Send the kids to school in the morning as usual. There will be two agents there all day tomorrow as back-up, so the children will be fully protected.'

There seems to be no more I can do for now. It is bitterly cold, threatening light snow, and the wind is strong. A cold, moonless night in a town where I know the cartels' hitmen are circling like sharks. Claudia drifts into a restless sleep and I lie awake, listening for every sound.

33

Sleep finally captures me in the quiet stillness of pre-dawn. My uneasy dreams do not last long. At 6.30 am, I am jolted awake by Claudia's screaming and the cold metal of a gun pressed hard against my temple. I am instantly aware of three strangers in the bedroom and hear their unmistakable accents: Colombian. An icy terror overcomes me.

One is guarding the door, another holding the gun to my head and the third is dragging Claudia across the floor by her hair. By the passage light I can see she has a bloody nose that looks to be broken and a swollen, damaged eye. Another two are roughly herding the children downstairs. Martina and Anja are screaming out for Mummy, but I can't see or hear Klaus.

I start thrashing and kicking my feet, but it is useless. Tape is being wound around my arms, immobilising me, and the man with the gun is shouting in fractured English.

'Asshole! Try move and we'll cut little throats.'

I know it is no idle threat. They want information. They will torture the girls until they have what they want from me, and then dispose of us, one by one. They will cut the

children's heads off, then rape and kill Claudia. My turn
will be last.

Where the fuck are the agents? The girls' screams have
stopped and there is silence downstairs. Claudia is struggling violently and yelling out in her native German, but
the bastard is putting his boot in, kicking her face and
body. He has ripped her nightgown off and she has wet
herself with fright, cowering from his assault.

My assailant's grip suddenly loosens. He falls to the
ground and I realise instantly what the sound was I had
heard a millisecond before. A gun with a silencer. The
bullet has blown away part of his head.

There is another shot, and then no more sounds, except
Claudia screaming hysterically. Her attacker has fallen
on top of her, with a hole the size of a tennis ball in his
forehead, and he is staring up at me with glazed eyes. A
female agent is standing over them, her gun raised in one
hand as she drags his body off Claudia.

The agent is calm, her voice measured. 'Are you okay?'
she asks Claudia. I don't hear the answer.

The third assailant in our room is wrestled to the ground
and handcuffed. Someone is removing the constraints from
my hands and, in shock, I am incoherently mumbling an
apology for the mess I have made. I have vomited on the
doona and my boxer shorts are wet, the urine dribbling
down the inside of my legs.

A blanket is wrapped around me and I am ushered
downstairs into a waiting van. Claudia is stumbling ahead
of me, also covered by a blanket, helped by two female
agents. They escort her to another van where Martina,
Anja and Klaus are sitting, huddled together in terror. In

the mayhem, I realise police cars have surrounded the house and at least a dozen DEA agents, in their distinctive blue jackets with yellow writing, are also there. The vans suddenly start up and race away from the house, police cars in tow.

An agent hands me a coffee. I am shivering with cold and my mouth is parched. The cloying nausea I feel explodes in projectile vomit when I notice my attacker's blood and brains all over me. I watch as the suburban landscape flashes past. I have no idea where we are, or where we are headed. Right now, I couldn't care less. Shock has numbed my senses and I can't stop shaking, despite the warmth in the van.

A DEA agent is sitting in the front seat next to the driver, and I am in the middle rear seat wedged between another two agents, both spattered with my vomit. I can make out the road now, by the signs we pass. It is the main highway back to DC. There has to be a leak within the DEA for the Colombians to have found us and entered the house without the alarms going off. Some bastard is on the cartel payroll.

I can hear snatches of conversation from the agent sitting in the front passenger seat, talking to headquarters on his cellphone. 'The group were Colombian. No identification. The boy heard noises and hid under the bed.'

Even in my fuddled state, I realise Claudia will have to return home with the children. Her former husband, Paul, has made offers and the kids miss their dad. I am no substitute, not with this nightmare I am living. We are lurching from one crisis to the next and our only saviour is witness protection away from the DEA. Under witness protection, the US Marshals would guard us and relocate the family, finding employment and housing. But that is not an option because it would mean I could never see my Australian family again and Claudia's children could not see their father or grandparents.

I am jolted from my reverie by the terrible realisation that the Colombians in the house were not the ones who took our photographs from the motorbike. 'They could be following us!' I yell, stuttering out what I have remembered. 'They were different people.'

The agent in the front seat spins around. 'Are you sure? They were wearing helmets and leathers.'

'A thousand per cent. They were completely different builds. I just know.' The agent jumps on his cellphone and phones the vehicle carrying Claudia and the children. He talks so urgently I can't make out a word he says, then hangs up and makes two further calls.

We race along the highway until we reach a major intersection and signs pointing to Baltimore-Washington International Airport. We don't go near the commercial aircraft, instead veering off towards a zone that looks to be operated by private enterprise. The vans and cars come to an abrupt halt beside two helicopters.

'Hop out, please, Greece,' a female agent says, extending a hand to me and helping me out the door. Claudia and the children stumble from their van, dazed and confused. I awkwardly try to cover the vomit on my pyjamas and blanket before they see me. I needn't have worried: they are ushered into a chopper geared for immediate take-off, its blades slicing through the air. I am helped by agents on both sides to run to the second helicopter and be strapped into my seat. Within seconds, the doors slam shut and we too are gone. Our escorts watch as we gain altitude and the airfield shrinks beneath us.

The chopper lands in the grounds of the National Naval Medical Centre in Chevy Chase, Maryland, only a few kilometres from the White House. I am shown to a private room and offered a shower, which I gladly accept. Shaving gear and a dark-blue tracksuit have been provided, neatly folded into a square on the chair. The naval doctor gives me a perfunctory check-over, announcing I have no major wounds and only a few cuts and bruises.

'Your partner's children are fine but she has not fared as well,' he tells me as he washes his hands. 'Her nose is broken and she has several fractured ribs. You may get a shock when you see her; she is extensively bruised. But she will be okay. No psychological damage that we can see, as yet anyway. She is remarkable, put up a great fight. You can go and visit her.'

She looks so pitiful, lying in the hospital bed, her face bandaged. I creep over and she extends a hand, wrapping her fingers in mine. 'I'm so sorry, Claudia,' I whisper. 'I'm so sorry this has happened to you.' I stroke her hair and say nothing more, overwhelmed with shame that I have brought her to this. 'I'll come back later,' I say, kissing the top of her head, careful not to hurt her.

The children are playing in the next room, watched by a female DEA agent. 'Nice kids,' she grins when I walk in. I want to know how they managed to escape unharmed and we walk to a quiet corner of the room. 'The Colombians took them downstairs, and two agents entered the house,' she says, her voice composed. 'They were shot.'

'In front of the children?' I am horrified that they have witnessed that.

She shoots me a level gaze. 'Greece, they had guns. We had no choice. Who would you have preferred to be killed?' She changes the subject. 'The girls are like their mother, very strong. Klaus has been awarded the DEA badge for his bravery. He didn't panic, simply got out of bed and hid under it.' I turn my back on the children and hunch into myself so they don't see my tears. 'Everyone will be all right,' the agent consoles me. 'It will take some time, that's all.' I don't share her confidence. This night-mare experience will stay with all of us for the rest of our lives.

I surf the television stations to find any news of the attacks. It is dramatic footage: television crews outside the house giving pieces to camera, earnestly reporting that the recent occupants of the house had been mistak-enly identified by Colombian drug cartels as witnesses in a major drug trial and attempts were made on their lives. The report switches to the Annapolis police chief, who confirms that the police task force and DEA agents have killed five Colombian hitmen and the family has been injured in the shoot-out.

The message is out there: we are in a serious condition, but still alive. The police should have told reporters we were all killed. The DEA will now need to move us from the hospital within hours. Not only because of the mole within its ranks, but because the Colombians will start to search hospitals from Baltimore to Washington, DC. I demand to see Special Agent Gary, to find out how the hell we got in this situation.

I can barely muster more than a snarl when he arrives but I admit to a grudging respect for the bloke. He is, as usual, blunt. 'Look, Greece, we knew there was consider-able danger, but we thought you were all safe in Annapolis. It's now obvious to us that the Colombians are being fed information. They had details of your new identity, work location, home address, cellphone numbers and knew where the children went to school. They knew the whole damn lot about you.'

'I warned you there was a leak!' I am shouting now, unable to control my rage. 'This could have been prevented if you had listened to me!'

'We're investigating how the information got out,' he says, talking over me. 'We have decided to break the team down to eight people, and only that team will know your whereabouts. No one else will have that information. In the meantime, we need to move you within the hour.'

'Claudia isn't well enough to move!'

'There's no choice. You can't stay at the hospital. It's not going to take the Colombians long to work out where you are. Perhaps a couple of hours, max. There is no time to wait.' He hasn't finished. 'We need to hide you until we have found you a new job and a new school for the children. Everything back at the house stays there. This is a new beginning, and in time, once we're satisfied you're safe, we can bring you your computers and personal belongings.'

Within the hour, we are dressed in new clothes they have brought us and Claudia is on crutches. We exit the hospital via a back door and move into a waiting ambulance. 'Hop in,' Gary says. 'It's a cover for us leaving the hospital. You'll be taken into DC to Union Station.'

Three hours after leaving DC, the train pulls into New York's Penn Station. Claudia has dozed for most of the journey, the painkillers at least taking the edge off some of her discomfort. She doesn't complain. We are greeted by our new DEA team: Leanne, Kris, Jerry and Phil.

'We'll be here with you at all times,' Phil announces, 'and only Gary and Brian will be the back-up team. There are two other agents back at headquarters who know of your whereabouts, that's it. We're going to split up. Kris and Leanne will take one taxi with Claudia and the girls, Greece and Klaus come with me and Jerry. We're all going to the same place.'

Phil instructs our taxi driver where to go. 'Le Parker Meridien Hotel, 57th Street, please.' There, he guides us to the carpark on the second floor and fishes out a set of keys from his pocket, pressing the electronic security button. Within minutes we are back on the streets of Manhattan in a new Ford van.

'This is the Waterside Plaza, your new home!' Phil has pulled up outside a block of classy residential apartments. 'It's a fantastic place,' he spruiks, sounding like a real estate agent. 'A three-bedroom apartment with all the mod cons you will need, plus breathtaking views of the water and the city of Manhattan!'

He sounds so excited I'm tempted to ask if he wants to move in himself. He saves me the trouble. 'We have taken the two apartments either side of you. Kris and Leanne are staying in one, and will provide protection for Claudia and the children, and I'll be with Jerry. When there is a change of guard, it will be Gary and Brian. You already know them.'

'Stuff the views,' I retort. 'What about security?'

'Jerry is the whiz-kid on technology and will have this place under surveillance in no time. We'll be able to watch and listen to you guys twenty-four seven.'

I'm not happy about this. Claudia and I need some space. We can't live like this for months on end. 'I need a walk, some fresh air,' I say. 'Can Claudia and I go out for a bit while the kids watch television with Kris?'

'Of course,' Phil nods. 'Leanne will cook dinner for us so you can both have a meal out and Jerry will get the wiring done while you're gone. But I'll have to follow you guys, sorry. Just pretend I'm not here.'

We say goodbye to the kids and leave the apartment, followed by Phil. Claudia is frail and badly bruised, but she is able to walk unassisted. It is a chilly New York evening, a cold wind blowing off the river. Snow is on the way. Claudia takes my arm and we lower our faces into the wind as we walk towards the nearest bar.

Claudia bombards me with questions as soon as we get our drinks. 'What is happening, Keith? How the fuck did the DEA agents get to the house so fast? Was the house wired with video cameras?'

I take a deep breath. 'Yep, the DEA had the house wired, and under constant video surveillance. They'd have seen the Colombians enter the house. That's how they got to us so quickly.'

She is staring at me, speechless. 'We would have been murdered,' she says, finally. 'The guy who attacked me said he was going to rape me in the ass, Keith.' Tears are streaming down her face. 'He said he was going to slice my breasts off, and then my head. Keith, I can't handle this. They'll continue searching for us until they've got us in a corner, won't they? You know that, don't you?'

'Yes.'

'What are you going to do?'

I hold her hands in mine. 'I do have a plan and I will act on it. But not yet. I need more time.'

'Time? You need time? While these dogs are hunting us

down?' She has raised her voice and looks around the bar, suddenly embarrassed. 'What's the plan, Keith? You have to tell me!'

'When it's time, I'll tell you straightaway.'

She looks stricken. 'You don't want us to head back to Germany?'

'It did cross my mind, yes,' I admit. 'For the children's safety, as well as your own.'

'I am not going back to Paul!' Her face is flushed. 'I can't handle him!'

'Well, you know it's going to be tough, very tough. We're not out of the woods yet, and we'll be on the run for a while. I don't want what happened this morning to happen to any of us again. Ever.'

'Have you got a price on your head, Keith?'

'Yes, two million dollars.'

'They'll never give up, not for that kind of money.' She hides her face and gives way to tears again. She is near breaking point, and so am I.

The idea comes to me as I watch a cloudy pink dawn creep over the East River. Claudia and the children are fast asleep, but I have been awake all night, a wired, jangled mass of nervous energy. All this time we have been the DEA's responsibility, and I now have little, if any, faith left in their ability to look after us. It is time to make a break.

I need to start withdrawing cash if we are going to be on the run, as credit cards are traceable. If I play my cards carefully, within another week I should be in a position to settle with the cartels. My own way.

34

I ring Steven May in Chicago at 9 am, filling him in on the past few days. He doesn't mince words. 'You have to leave the US straightaway! You're going to be killed if you stay there.'

'I've thought of that, Steven. I'm also sending Claudia back to Europe with the kids. It's too dangerous for them here.'

'That's a shame, Keith. I'm sorry to hear that. What are you going to do?'

'I'm planning on returning to Mexico and doing a deal with a cartel family I know.' There is a long silence, and I think we have lost the connection. 'Are you still there, Steve?'

His voice is incredulous. 'I'm here. You can't be real, Keith. Fuck me, you'll be murdered! You know that. They'll skin you alive. For Christ's sake, don't be so fucking stupid!'

'Steven, I've given it a lot of thought. The cartel family I know controls the drug market in Mexico City. I've always done the right thing by them, and they haven't had any of their accounts frozen.'

'Doesn't make any difference,' he warns. 'You're playing with fire.'

'Perhaps. But you know that the DEA and the Justice Department will always deny I worked for them. They'll only protect me when it suits them, like now, but at some stage they'll cut me loose. We can't be on the run forever. It's got to stop, and this is the only way out that I can think of. I've got to do something.'

I keep talking, hoping to gain his approval. 'Look, my insurance with the DEA is the tape-recordings that you're holding for me. You told me yourself this is my best protection. And the DEA aren't exactly popular with the Mexican government.'

That, we both know, is an understatement. When the DEA first established a bank in Mexico, they attracted the small players in the drug business, not cartel families. After a number of transactions, they invited the account-ants and lawyers of the clients (who used the bank to launder their funds) to America for a lavish dinner. Several of them took the bait, and were arrested on arrival.

The DEA boasted to the media about the sting, but the operation backfired, creating a huge political storm. All hell broke loose. The Mexican government, unaware of the covert operation in their country, were less than impressed, particularly after the Director of the DEA stated that no one in Mexico could be trusted. Then President Clinton waded in, promis-ing no further covert operations would be carried out without Mexican government approval or involvement. Promises, promises.

I think Steven is getting the message that I'm serious. 'I need to put on record, Keith, that I am not at all comfort-able with your decision and that as your lawyer, I am advising you against this. Having said that, if you continue I will, as your friend, support you if you need my help. I have copied the recordings as you asked me to, and the copies are in safekeeping.'

'Thanks, mate.' My words sound hollow and insignificant. The truth is, without Steven I'd be stuffed. Apart from Claudia, he's about the only person I trust at the moment. 'Thanks so much, Steve,' I repeat. 'My plan is to start withdrawing cash today from the credit cards. I hope to withdraw fifty thousand over the next few days and wire the cash to you, via Western Union. I'd appreciate it if you would set up a deposit for me in your trust account. This way, when we decide to run, we'll have access to the cash we need.'

'Okay. When do you expect to send the first amount through?'

'I'll withdraw eighteen thousand tomorrow and send you eight thousand. I'll phone you from a public phone with the transaction details.'

I suddenly have an overwhelming urge to call my family in Australia. But I would be opening up a death-trap if I did: my Melbourne number is tapped by police and all calls are monitored. The DEA would have access to the information and with their leak, the Colombians and Mexicans would know very quickly where my family live. One phone call could be fatal. The call could also be traced back to me in New York. I resist the urge.

The next day, I locate a Bank of America and, using my American Express credit card, take out a cash advance. I have a limit of five thousand dollars. I then walk to Wachovia Bank and take out another eight thousand in cash. If I'm going to be on the run, it is cash, not traceable credit cards, that will prove my best ally.

I look around. No Phil. I've got to give it to these guys, they keep their distance, allowing me freedom, focusing instead on protecting my back, focusing on who may be following or watching me. I head into a restaurant and pay for lunch, smiling as I hand the waiter a thirty-dollar tip. 'Can you bring me my coffee in ten minutes?' I ask him. 'And is there a back way out of here?'

'Yes.' He looks bemused. He has been given a tip before I eat the food and I want my coffee deferred. 'Through the kitchen,' he says, pointing behind him.

'Can I use that exit?'

'You're not supposed to. But yes, I guess you can.'

Phil is standing idly outside the front of the restaurant when I return, with another five thousand cash withdrawn from my MasterCard safely in my wallet.

I now have thousands of dollars in my pockets that I need to off-load to Steven. I wander up Fifth Avenue with Phil trailing behind and spot a newsagency that has a Western Union outlet. Perfect. I fill out the paperwork and take my place in the line behind a bushy-haired woman who seems to take forever to complete her business. I hand over eight thousand to the pasty-faced attendant, in thousand-dollar bundles. Bored and patently uninterested, he thumbs and flicks the notes like a bank teller, pushing the receipt back to me and signalling for the next customer. I quietly heave a sigh of relief. I select several magazines and the *Washington Post*, pay and leave. The whole exercise has taken no more than ten minutes. Phil is still outside, waiting patiently.

I put a phone call through to Steven from Grand Central Station. 'Steven, it's Keith,' I start, but before he can say hello, I interrupt him. 'Here's the first number: Western Union, JTP 187.'

'Got it.'

I hang up, and walk as casually as possible to another café, where I order coffee and read the paper. So far, so good. Phil hasn't seen me. Another two days of this, and I will have the fifty thousand dollars I need.

I take Claudia home a bottle of her favourite Two Paddocks pinot noir. She pours two glasses and offers me one, smiling as she kisses me. I have forgotten how beautiful she is, even with her broken nose. Wisps of her honey-blonde hair caress my face. For the first time in a long time, it feels like we are alone. I resist the urge to bang on the apartment wall next door and tell Leanne to switch off the security video. Over a drink, I tell Claudia of my plans to collect cash and wire it to Steven without the agency knowing.

She seems confused. 'Why do you need to do that?'

'Because they will know that if I'm hauling cash, then I'm planning a runner. Tomorrow we should walk down Fifth Avenue and pretend to sightsee. We'll find a restaurant and I'll go out the back way and get the cash. It shouldn't take me more than forty minutes.'

In the restaurant the next day, we order food and wine before I slip out the back door and run down the street. Inside the Bank of America, I withdraw another five thousand in cash, folding the bills as inconspicuously as possible and head out looking for two more banks, where I repeat the procedure. It takes longer than I had anticipated, more than an hour.

When I return to the restaurant, Claudia has cancelled my lunch, eaten her own and drunk the wines. She is now sipping on a coffee. 'All done?' she smiles. I nod. 'Where are you hiding the cash, since we're being watched?' Claudia asks, summoning the waiter to bring the menu for me.

'I've cut a hole in the inside lining of my woollen jacket. This jacket is now my second skin.'

I need to contact the agency for another briefing. No one has told me anything since the Colombians broke into our house and I have no way of knowing if they are still following me. There has been no further news on television or in the papers. No word from head office, either, and no messages about my Australian family. Just an eerie silence.

'I've got to organise another wire,' I tell Claudia, picking up the bill to pay.

'Why?'

'Because the DEA can't be trusted and I need to have them on tape at all times.'

I share an anecdote with her to illustrate my point. 'A friend of mine worked for one of the Australian agencies. He had meetings with them weekly and he taped every one. Just in case. He was working on a sting involving bank cheques and gave the agency weekly updates. Out of the blue, he was raided by the Major Fraud Investigation Group. They searched his house, took his computers, and started a full enquiry.'

The waiter is hovering for me to pay and I do so before continuing. 'He phoned the Australian agency to advise them what had happened, and their reply was, "It will work itself out." In the meantime, the group was convinced he was part of the scam. But the agency didn't step in and say, "Hold it, lads, he's working with us, and we know everything about the whole operation." They hung him out to dry.'

Claudia is listening intently, looking mortified.

'He wanted the information on his computers protected, so he took the matter to court. He wrote an affidavit explaining why he didn't want the group examining his computers and that he was working for the Australian agency. On the day of the hearing, the agency's lawyers asked him to omit the part that referred to his work with them. He couldn't understand why, and no reason was given. The lawyers treated him like dirt.'

'So what happened in the end?'

'Nothing! I suppose the agency put in a good word for him. But he still isn't relaxed about it. If nothing happens over the next few years, he will assume he was protected. If not, then he has a major problem. Or they have a problem, if he goes to the media with the taped evidence he has.'

We stand to leave. 'He learned that he had to record every conversation with the agency: their promises, the approval to proceed, comments on his activities; the lot. And to send copies of the recordings to a safety deposit box in another state, under a lawyer's authority. Insurance.'

'I don't understand,' Claudia says. 'If you work for them, they should protect you at all times.'

'Well, they don't. They can get very nasty, too, and some-times threaten you, so you don't feel inclined to push the issue. Bottom line: keep insurance, and if they don't back you up when you need them, produce the tapes.'

35

I wake next morning to the sound of cartoons on the television, the kids glued to the screen. It is raining outside, the sky slate-grey. I shiver in my boxer shorts and grab a jumper. Claudia is looking concerned. 'We haven't heard from the agents this morning. Normally, they're knocking on the door and checking to see what we're doing.'

'Maybe they've decided to have a late start as well,' I reply. I yell out for the children to join me in a swim. It's the best way I know to relax and forget my troubles. They eagerly change into their bathing costumes and we head down to the lower level. The indoor pool is deserted and silent, no agents within cooee.

'Where are they?' Claudia asks, looking around.

'I don't know, but I don't like this at all. Something is wrong.' I change my mind about the swim. 'Get the kids, Claudia. We're going back to the apartment. Hurry.'

The memories of her attack are so recent, the bandages still covering her face and body, that I can see what she is thinking. I open the apartment door and do a quick check. No one there.

'Dress the kids quickly and pack their backpacks. Nothing else. I'm going to knock on the other doors to see where Phil and Leanne are. When I get back, be ready to leave.'

Claudia is close to tears, and the kids can sense something is wrong. 'What the hell is happening, Keith?'

'Lock the door after me. I'll be right back.' I grab Klaus's baseball bat and knock on the girls' apartment door first. No answer. I try Phil's. Still no answer. I try the handle of the door and, to my amazement, it opens. There is no sign of life. The bedrooms are empty, though someone has slept there. The video camera is still working, and I can see Claudia and the children packing in our apartment. I clear the tape and smash it with the baseball bat, and anything which connects us to the apartment block. Then I go to the other agents' apartment and do the same.

Back in our room, I stuff our cash and passports in the inside lining of my jacket and grab my laptop and backpack. 'Let's go!' I command in a voice that frightens Klaus. His lip trembles and I pick him up. 'It's all right, mate,' I tell him. 'We're just off on another adventure.' Claudia and the girls don't smile.

'What's happening, Keith?' Claudia needles, following us to the lift.

'I don't know, but the agents wouldn't just leave like this. I smell Colombians. If they're not here already, they're not far away.'

She is starting to lose it. 'We can't handle this on our own!'

I'm starting to panic, too. 'I know. Look, let's just get out of here, okay?'

I flag down a taxi. The driver is from Somalia and doesn't speak a word of English. 'Penn Station. Quickly!' I command. He understands that word, screaming past cars and dodging jaywalkers.

It's 11.30 am when we get to the station, and I run to purchase tickets for the DC train leaving at midday. I usher Claudia and the children into a small café. 'Stay here until the train is about to leave, and then get on board. It's our best cover.'

I find a public telephone and call Steven's direct line, drumming my fingers as I wait for him to answer. Instead, I get his PA's voice message: 'You have called the office of Steven May, attorney at law. The office is currently unattended. Please leave a detailed message after the tone.' I slam the receiver down. No way am I leaving a message.

I scan for Colombians or Mexicans, but it seems no one is looking for us, not even DEA agents. I check my watch. Eight minutes to go before the train leaves. Then I see them: two Colombians, both checking the train. One climbs on board, the other is walking down the platform peering into carriage windows.

I can see Claudia and the children walking quickly towards the train. I can't yell out, and before I can do anything they are aboard. The Colombian checking the windows hasn't seen them, but they are in the third carriage from the front and the Colombians are making their way down towards them. I wait until the one on the platform isn't looking and jump on board. I hurry through the carriages and find the family settling into their seats.

I grab Claudia. 'Go into the toilet and stay there till I tell you to come out. Take the kids, and if someone asks if anyone's in the toilet, answer in German. You speak German, Claudia! No English! The Colombians are on the train.'

White with fear, she rounds up the three kids and they make their way to the toilets. I get off and head back behind the café. Eventually I run back and jump on a middle carriage with seconds to spare before the train leaves the station.

I can't hide Claudia and the three children in the toilet all the way to DC. The next stop is Newark International Airport, forty minutes away. A Colombian is walking towards me, scrutinising the passengers. His sidekick will be coming from the other direction.

One has stopped at the toilet. He knocks on the door to see if it is vacant. 'Hey, mister, I'm next! There is a queue,' a teenage girl with piercings and attitude tells him. 'You can't push in.' He glares at her and moves on.

I head to the next carriage, knowing the Colombians are only seconds from entering. I sit beside an older woman with a cross around her neck, who looks to be in her fifties.

'Please, I need a hug, please.' She looks startled. 'I've just heard my father has died.' She smiles, and puts her arms around me.

'I'm sorry for your bad news,' she consoles me. 'I am sorry to hear of your loss.'

I turn as the Colombians pass us, walking back through the carriages. 'Thank you,' I tell her. 'Thank you.'

Three people are now waiting to get into the toilet and they are becoming agitated. 'Sorry, folks, the children have lost their father this morning,' I tell them. 'They are very distressed. Please understand.'

The teenage girl is ready to rip Claudia apart, but her expression softens when she hears of their loss. 'Sorry,' she mutters. 'I've been banging on the door for them to come out.'

Claudia and the children walk out, their expressions convincing all and sundry how sad they are. Martina and Klaus have been crying, which is even more convincing. We return to the third carriage and take our seats, facing the way the train is travelling.

I trawl the carriage in search of someone with a cell-phone, tapping a young man who is listening to his iPod. 'I need to make a call to San Diego,' I tell him. 'Would you accept a hundred dollars to cover the cost if I borrow your cellphone?'

He smiles with dollar signs in his eyes. 'Hey, no problem,' he says, handing it over.

I go to the bathroom and dial Morgan Taylor, my heart singing when I hear her voice. 'Hi, Greece. I didn't recognise the telephone number. What's up?'

I fill her in on what is happening and where we are. 'The agents wouldn't do this,' she says, incredulously. 'They wouldn't just desert you.'

'Well they have, and there are two Colombians on the train. Morgan, I want you to do the following. Ring the FBI. Make sure they have a group of agents at Newark International Airport Station. We arrive in fifteen minutes. Get them a photo of me. When they board carriage three, I'll lead them to the Colombians. They can hold them until the train gets into DC.'

'Why don't you stop the train? Find an inspector and have them stop.'

'Because if I do that, the Colombians will know we're here and we'll never make DC. Do you understand? Their arrest has to be unrelated to us. Let them make up a story about a terrorist threat to bomb the train. Don't use the DEA. That's where the leak is coming from. Tell the FBI to drive the Colombians around for two hours before they arrive at their offices, otherwise they'll be on the phone to their lawyers. Contact me on the same number I've just called you on.'

I return to the carriage and ask my train companion if I can have his phone until we reach Newark International Airport, offering him another hundred dollars. 'Sure thing!' he says, stuffing the money in his pocket. 'No problems at all!'

Jim phones back in five minutes. 'Greece, we have arranged for the FBI to board the train in Newark and they will come to carriage three. They'll be undercover, plain-clothes agents. The head of the team is Stewart and he has your photo. He's been told that there are two terrorist suspects on board and that you're a DEA agent on holiday with your family. They will take the Colombians to FBI offices in New York. We are checking on the whereabouts of your missing agents from New York. They are still missing. They haven't checked in with us and their cellphones are not working. The FBI and our New York DEA team are at the apartments now.'

36

The train pulls into Newark Station. The Colombians don't get off, and only a couple in their early thirties enter our carriage. The train pulls out of the station and heads to the next stop, Philadelphia, an hour away.

The man who has boarded with his female partner comes over to me as soon as the train leaves the station. 'Are you Greece?' he asks. I don't know who he is. 'I'm Stewart, and this is Erin. We're from the FBI.'

She smiles an acknowledgment. 'There are six other agents on board,' she says. 'We will collect them as we move through the carriages. Let's go.'

I spot one of the Colombians in carriage seven, drinking a coffee. Because he hasn't noticed me on the train, he appears confident I am not here. I point him out to Stewart. 'He's armed, obviously. And his companion is sitting a few seats behind him.'

There are now four agents with us and Stewart instructs two of them to go through to the next carriage. 'Find Peter and Nick and block that entrance. If our targets try to leave, arrest them. Erin and I will block the rear exit.'

He addresses me. 'We won't touch them until we get to Philadelphia. Thanks for the tip-off.'

I return to where Claudia and the children are sitting. They are becoming fractious, tired of the constant travel. Claudia barely speaks to me, staring blankly out of the window at the passing scenery.

'It's okay, darling,' I reassure her. 'We won't be having any more trouble from the Colombians.'

She speaks, finally, without looking at me. 'I can't do this any longer, Keith.'

A large crowd is waiting to board at Philadelphia Station, including twenty police and FBI agents. I pick up Klaus and grab the girls' hands, running to the taxi stand. At the airport, I scan the departure screens for available flights. Within the hour, we are winging it to Chicago. I have no idea what my next move is. But I know I can't trust the DEA anymore. This is the second leak. I doubt we will be so lucky the third time. I book us into an apartment under an assumed name. Hopefully that will buy us some time if we are tracked to Chicago.

The former Prime Minister of Norway, Grete Stellenberg, is an acquaintance. We were introduced years ago through a business colleague and, though she is no longer in office, her name carries a lot of weight. I have made a decision to contact her and see if she can help find a solution regarding Claudia and the children. If Claudia is reluctant to return to Germany, perhaps Grete can help find a house for her to rent and a position with a university in Norway.

I call Steven to update him on where we are and what has happened in New York. 'Christ!' he says when I have finished. 'What happened to the DEA agents?'

'I've got no idea.'

'Are they dead?'

'I don't know. I really don't know.'

'What are you going to do, Keith? You can't keep running like this.'

'Grete Stellenberg owes me a couple of favours. I'm going to phone her today and ask for help.'

After I explain the connection, Steven agrees. 'Sounds reasonable. But what are you going to do?'

'I want to arrange a meeting with the head of the Santiago family in Mexico City and give him some tapes. Maybe I can convince him that I wasn't involved. It's a long shot, but it's my best chance, because he's linked to the Colombians.'

'You can't be fucking serious! Aren't they the cartel that police think are responsible for the decapitated bodies found around the airport in Mexico City?'

'Yep. They also control the importation of cocaine and methamphetamine from Colombia through Mexico City Airport. Rommel Santiago, while being Mexican himself, has the right connections with the Colombians and also has the government and police eating out of his hand. His rival, El Chapo Guzmán, will probably try and have me killed, but I've got to do something.'

'I can't believe what you're telling me, Keith. Are you out of your mind? You can't go back to Mexico! What makes you think they won't kill you, or hand you over to the Colombians for the two million reward?'

'I control Rommel Santiago's bank accounts, Steven, he was the first client Daniel Gómez introduced me to and I have a list of all his stock holdings, worth millions. I know all his property assets in Florida, Spain, Britain, Canada and New York. It would take him at least two years to unravel the money trail I've set up. His accounts are in Europe, and he can't move the funds without my signature. I did it that way for my own insurance.'

'Do the DEA have all this information?'

'No, they've got no idea. I kept this to myself. As you've always said, you can't trust the agencies. This was an insurance package for me in case the shit hit the fan. And it has.'

Steven exhales a long, deep breath. 'Jesus, Keith. You know the Mexicans can't be trusted either?'

'I know that, but I've got no choice. I'm going to need the cash now. We have to move fast.'

'Where are you heading to this time?'

'I don't have a clue. But we need to be on the move and one step ahead of everyone.'

'Come by in my lunchbreak tomorrow and I'll give you the cash and the tapes. In the meantime, watch your back.'

I haven't spoken to Grete Stellenberg in more than a year, but I know she will remember me. She greets me warmly, with the smooth charm of the Norwegians. 'Well, I never, Keith. How are you?' Her accent is as endearing as ever.

I cut to the chase. 'I'm fine, Grete, but I need a favour. A big favour.'

'I owe you one. What is it?'

'I need to send my partner, Claudia, and her three children to Oslo the day after tomorrow.' Thankfully they don't need visas. As German citizens, they are part of the European Union and free to travel immediately. 'She needs to find a house to rent and a job, preferably with a university in Norway. I can send the funds to cover all the costs, but we need it to happen as soon as possible.'

'Why the rush, Keith?'

I decide to tell her the truth. 'The bank in San Diego was a DEA sting operation. I was their banker. We dealt with the Mexican and Colombian drug cartels. The rest you can work out for yourself.'

Grete groans. 'Good God, don't tell me you've got the cartels after you?' She doesn't wait for my answer. 'Hasn't the DEA and the American government stepped in and helped you? They should!'

'They have, but there's a leak somewhere within the agency. There have been two attempts on our lives within days of us being placed in a safe house.'

'You're surely kidding me!' I fill her in.

'I can't believe this!' I can hear her tapping a pencil on her desk. 'Okay, go ahead and make the arrangements. When they arrive I will have my driver pick them up at the airport. I'll make a booking at a nice hotel and will ring some senior police to give them protection. And what about you, Keith? Are you not joining them?'

'Afraid not, Grete. I wish I was. I very much appreciate your help.'

'No problem.' We discuss how I will wire the money that Claudia needs into her account, allowing for the cost of the hotel, the first month's rent and a second-hand car and she gives me further contact details, including her private fax number.

'Grete, I'll book the flight to leave the day after tomorrow and fax the information to you.'

'Fine. I will make sure they are well looked after. You have no need to worry.'

37

Steven is as good as his word the next day, the cash waiting for me at his office. 'What's your plan?' he asks, looking at me intently with the resolute stare of a lawyer.

'I'm going to phone Claudia's ex-husband, Paul.'

'They don't get on, do they?'

'Yes, I think they do. The children used to ring him once a week in San Diego and right now, they need their dad. They've been dragged all around the countryside and are confused. Claudia will need someone to talk to as well, someone who listens. Paul loves her.'

He raises one eyebrow. 'And you don't?'

'I do. But living like this is not fair to her. I'm worried sick about their safety.'

'What happened to end the marriage?'

'The usual. She found out he was playing up with a research student from Germany. By the time Paul arrived home from a conference in Amsterdam, she had changed the locks on the house and filed for divorce. She applied for a position at the University of Southern California, and was offered the job within three months. You know the rest. Speaking of Paul ...'

Steven gestures for me to use the phone on his desk. 'Perks of the job,' he grins. 'Long-distance calls on the company.'

I dial Paul's number and he answers straightaway. He sounds perturbed. 'Keith, I haven't heard from Claudia or the children for a week and the phone to your house is dead! What's going on?'

'We had a break-in,' I lie. 'Scared the shit out of the children and Claudia.'

'Are they okay?'

'Physically, yes. Psychologically, no. They are still frightened. Paul, I think it's time they returned to Europe.'

'Has something happened between you two?' There is a cautious edge in his voice that he didn't have initially. 'Why would they not stay with you?'

'I wish they could, Paul,' I answer, honestly. 'But the truth is, right at the moment that is not a good idea. They need to return to somewhere they feel safe.'

'Door's open and always has been,' he says, sounding relieved. 'I don't need to tell you that, Keith. I'd give anything to have Claudia and the children back. What does Claudia think of this?'

I was hoping he wouldn't ask me that question. 'It's best she discusses that with you. Look, they're not going back to Germany, and I'm sorry if I misled you on that. They are booked to fly to Oslo tomorrow and, if you will allow me, I would like to pay for your flight, so you can go and take care of them for a few days. I'll fix up your accommodation as well.'

His tone is cynical now. 'This is all very generous of you, Keith, considering you are Claudia's lover. Would you like to tell me exactly what is going on?'

I don't appreciate his question. 'No, I wouldn't. Are you available to travel, or not?'

'I will make myself available,' he says, and backtracks. 'Sorry, Keith, I didn't mean to offend. When would you like me to go?'

'The day after tomorrow.'

I put the phone down. Claudia won't like this at all, but she and the children need to be somewhere safe. That is the only priority right now. Steven briefs his PA to make all the necessary arrangements for me. So far, my expenses are up to thirty thousand, eight hundred dollars. They are way too high, nearing my limit. I dash to the bank, withdrawing a further thirty thousand, compliments of the DEA. They will be really pissed off, but they have started this mess.

When I return to Steven's office, he hands me a receipt of transactions and details of flights. He shakes my hand as I leave his office, and offers me a caution. 'Mate, whatever you do, make sure you look over your shoulder. Don't trust anyone. And keep yourself safe.'

I wait until the children are asleep to deliver the news to Claudia. 'It's not safe here, you know that. The chances of the Colombians closing in on us are high, the risks far too great for you to be here with the children. We would be on the run all our lives. I need to sort this out, on my own.'

She takes the news better than I expected. 'I understand. But where are we going? Not back to Germany, I hope.'

'No, Norway.'

'Norway? When?'

'Tomorrow. I've organised the flights, and my friend Grete's people are meeting you at the airport. You'll be in the best hands, Claudia, until I get there.'

'How long do you think you'll be?' She is taking this

extraordinarily well. 'Maybe two weeks. It could be longer, but not more than a month.'

'All right.' She has closed her eyes and is leaning on my shoulder. 'I'm tired, Keith. All this running around is exhausting, particularly for the children.' She has another thought. 'The agency has to pay you what they promised. They will, won't they?'

'I doubt it. The bonuses on the funds are frozen and the commission on the Colombian money as well. There's no way they will pay any of the two million reward, and relocate us to Europe. It just won't happen. They've never honoured their commitments. But I've got my insurance.'

Claudia changes the subject. 'What time's our flight?'

'Tomorrow night at 7.45. Direct to Oslo. We will have to be there much sooner to clear customs.'

'Well, at least we have tomorrow together.' She has curled into me now, her arms wrapped tightly around my chest. 'I'll miss you, darling, I really will. So will the kids. You will join us as soon as possible, won't you?'

I've got to tell her about Paul. 'I think it would be nice if your ex-husband went to Oslo to see the children as soon as possible. What do you think?'

'He can't afford it, that's what I think.'

'I'll organise it.'

Claudia stares at me, her eyebrows knitted. 'You've already organised it, haven't you?' Her tone is accusatory, bordering on angry.

It's best I tell the truth. 'Yes.'

'You have to be straight with me, Keith, from now on. When does Paul arrive?'

'The same day as you.'

'And where is he staying?'

'The same hotel. Different room.'

She says nothing for a long moment. 'Okay. Thanks for organising it.'

I can't detect any sarcasm in her voice. 'Are you sure you're okay with this?'

'Positive, Keith. It's for the best. Just make sure you come back to us as quickly as possible.' She smiles at me. 'Let's go to bed.'

Morgan is preparing for work when I call her the next morning. 'How's Chicago?' she asks.

'How do you know where I am?'

'Because you booked the flight using the identity we gave you. The Colombians have picked up on it as well. We have confirmation from our sources that they are in Chicago. They arrived yesterday, looking for you. So pack your bags and get the hell out of town. Today.'

'Fuck, Morgan! This information is coming from someone in the DEA! And you know it!' My blood pressure is rising.

'Yes, we know that, but it will take us time to find out where the leak is. So get out of town and head west. Get back in touch with me as soon as you can. Just trust me at this stage, no one else. Okay?'

'Any news on the missing agents in New York?'

'Yes,' she replies. 'But I'm not going to discuss this on the cellphone. It's being monitored by the DEA and whoever is leaking information will get it to the Colombians.'

'You want me to head west?'

'I want you to think. You and I have discussed a few options. Think about what they are and act fast. You've survived so far and you will continue to do so if you remember what we have talked about.'

'Yep, I remember. I will pick up a hire car and leave this morning. Thanks again, Morgan.' She is gone.

I lied. I won't get a car. And she has told me to head west, which means north. She wants me to go to Canada. I run back upstairs and yell out to Claudia. 'We've got to leave, now. Pack for the airport. Let's go.' She doesn't ask any questions: she can tell by my voice it's urgent. 'Get the kids ready and pack my stuff, too. I'm calling Steven.'

I don't wait for the pleasantries, launching straight in. 'I need a lift to the airport, mate. It's urgent. We're heading north but we can't cross the border legally. We'll have to sneak across without being seen, otherwise we'll be tracked to Canada.'

I think Steven has become inured to the dramas. 'Where are you?'

'At the apartment.'

'I'll be there in half an hour.'

I know that both the Colombians and Mexicans will have people at the airport, but I have to take the risk. I don't have a choice. Post-September 11, security at US airports is extremely tight. Morgan will also let everyone know she has received a call from me, and that we are in a car heading west. This will be leaked to the Colombians.

Steven arrives on time, as usual. 'We need the International Terminal to get Claudia and the kids on their flight to Oslo.'

He cruises around the block at the airport while I run inside, served by a woman with a face as sour as a lemon. 'The ticket counter isn't open yet,' she spits.

'My family needs to get out of the main part of the airport. Can they go through customs?'

'Nope. Not without a boarding pass. Please step aside, sir, so I can serve other customers.'

We're stuffed. I wander through to the Domestic Terminal and scan the available flights, settling on one that leaves for Minneapolis within the hour. 'Gate D-67, boarding in forty minutes,' the guy tells me as he hands back our tickets. At least he smiles.

Steven is on his second round of the airport. There is no doubt that by now the Colombians will have covered the complex and will have information on Claudia's flight to Oslo. I give the tickets to Steven. 'Please cancel this flight at 6 pm, not before. The Colombians know who is on that flight, and will be waiting. Second, your brother lives in North Dakota, right?'

'Yes, he does. Why?' He is trying desperately to keep up with my train of thought.

'Because I need him to drive us to the Canadian border tonight.'

'What?'

'We are leaving for Minneapolis now and will get a connecting flight to Fargo. It would be terrific if you could get your brother to drive. It takes three hours, I think?'

'Yes, it does. What are you going to do then?'

'Make our way to Toronto.'

'Keith, if the Colombians can track you to Chicago, they will track you to North Dakota and into Canada.'

'I know, but I am a few hours ahead of them, and that's all we need right now. They won't be checking domestic flights, only international.'

I herd Claudia and the children out of the car. 'If you

could speak to your brother, Steve? I'll call you from Minneapolis.' We walk quickly to the gate and board with the last passengers. Within twenty minutes we have climbed into the sky.

The kids are grizzly and Claudia's patience has run out. 'How much more of this, Keith?' she asks. 'Canada tonight, Norway tomorrow. We've had enough.' I turn my head away lest she see the despair and shame on my face. I can think of nothing to say anymore to offer her any comfort.

I call Steven again from a public phone at Minneapolis Airport. His brother has agreed to pick us up and take us to Canada. 'I've offered him expenses, Keith,' he says. 'There is some risk involved here.' I have only met his brother twice, and suspect that Steven will be glad to see us safely out of the States.

'Of course,' I agree, not asking how much. In truth, I no longer care. 'Steve, could you also organise flights for all of us to Billings, Montana, and phone Grete and let her know that Claudia is delayed.'

On board the flight to Fargo, I ponder the absurdity of our situation. I feel like we are flying around in ever-decreasing circles. We are ahead of the cartels' hitmen for now, but for how long I don't know.

38

North Dakota is freezing, the city of Fargo blanketed in snow. Steven's brother, Frank, a burly and cheerful man, is there to meet us as agreed. I don't know him well and he is surprised when I tell him there is a change of plan. 'Do you know anyone who will rent a car in their own name and drive to Seattle, via Billings in Montana? I will pay for the car and throw in one thousand dollars cash, a return air ticket and accommodation.'

The answer comes to him immediately. 'My son would do that!' he grins. 'He's at university and could do with the money. I'm sure he'd be keen.'

'Terrific. And, Frank, I need yet another favour. A backpack, drinks and light food, a map, compass and five jackets. And,' I try to make it sound as casual as possible, 'a guide who can walk us across the border into Canada. Tonight.'

Frank's grin has turned to a frown. He is suddenly not so chirpy. 'What's the story, Keith?'

'Nothing sinister, I just can't go through Immigration or Customs. It's a safety thing. We all have to sneak across the border. There has to be no record of us leaving the US or entering Canada.'

'You're not carrying anything illegal? I don't want to know about any of it if you are.'

'No, nothing like that. Please, trust me on this. Steven wouldn't have asked you to do anything that wasn't right.'

Frank looks thoughtful. 'I go shooting with a friend of mine, Arnold Davies, who lives in Drayton, near the Canadian border. I'll give him a call. He knows the area like the back of his hand and he could walk you guys across at night with a blindfold on.'

Frank is on the phone to Davies for almost half an hour, their conversation broken by laughter and moments of seriousness. 'He's agreed to do it,' he says, when he finally hangs up. 'He's got all the gear and is happy to walk across. Apparently he's crossed the border many times chasing deer, and no one's ever approached him. North of Fargo and along the border, there's a big movement of people from Canada to the States. It's easy money for the local hunters. Which brings me to my next point: he will charge a thousand dollars for the trip. He has told me where to meet you guys on the other side of the border, so we're set. Let's hit the road.' It's just after 5 pm. 'The trip to Winnipeg and the walk will take hours. We'll be pushing to make it by midnight.'

We have been travelling for almost fifty minutes when Steven phones back on the pre-paid cellphone I picked up before the trip. 'Keith, you can't get out of Winnipeg tonight,' he says. 'The best is a 6 am flight to Toronto, arriving at 8.45 am. I've booked Claudia and the children on the first flight to Oslo and have booked you guys into the Hilton

Suites at the airport. Do you have a pen? Write down the following flight details and reference number for the hotel. I'll fax a copy of the flight bookings to the hotel.'

Arnold Davies is waiting for us in Drayton. He has packed everything we need, including warm coats that swim on us. We drive slowly, no cars in sight. 'Okay, Frank,' Davies says after twenty minutes. 'Stop here. Everyone out.' We are just short of the border crossing. It is dark and light snow falls on our faces.

Claudia speaks to the children in German, soothing them when they complain about being tired. They are not frightened, and we don't let on that we feel any fear.

Arnold straps on his pack and slings his rifle across his back. We quickly head into the bushes on the side of the road. He takes a compass bearing and orders that we follow him in single file. Further on, he stops and checks his compass. 'Are you all okay?' he asks.

I check the crew. 'Yes, we're right,' I nod.

We walk on into the bush, the children now exhausted and struggling to keep up. Thirty minutes later, Arnold stops and enquires again how everyone is going. I check my watch. It is just after 8.30 pm. We have been travelling two and a half hours since leaving Fargo. Thank God the land is flat.

The next hour goes very quickly as we trail Arnold. Klaus walks directly behind him, followed by Martina, Claudia and Anja. I am last in the single line. Arnold suddenly stops, and we all come to a standstill behind him. He asks us to sit and we follow his instructions, gratefully. 'Well, folks, Canada is just across the border! How is everyone?'

Klaus cannot keep going, but the girls soldier on. We agree that I will carry Klaus on my shoulders and set off again. There is no sign of activity, border trucks or guards. It is pitch black, no stars overhead, nothing but small torch lights and Arnold to guide the way. The next thirty minutes is extremely hard work. We have slowed down significantly. So far, we have walked six miles.

'Good work, guys,' Arnold says. 'Now we're gonna head to the road, which is probably another hour's walk, to where Frank will be.' This time, the reaction is different: at least the end is in sight.

We arrive and Arnold instructs us to wait about a hundred metres back from the road while he looks for Frank. He can't use his cellphone, as there is no coverage, and we huddle together until he returns, talking quietly to the children.

He is gone for about thirty minutes when we hear a car pull up, and Frank calls out to us. The half-hour had felt like three hours, as we crunched the snow between our fingers. I summon Claudia and the kids to get their things together quickly and we dash over to the car.

'Pile in, guys,' Frank says, and we do so, grateful to be out of the bitter cold. The car tyres squelch in the snow and he hits the accelerator. The children are asleep as soon as they get in the car and Claudia is so exhausted she can barely speak. The drive to Winnipeg is slowed down by heavy snowfall, and we limp in to the Hilton in the early hours of the morning. We have been travelling eleven hours since we left Chicago Airport.

Waiting for me from Steve is a fax detailing our tickets to Toronto and Oslo. We have to be up again in a few short hours.

We arrive at Winnipeg Airport and board our flight, heading to Toronto. The flight takes two hours and forty-five minutes, enough time to get some badly needed rest. Claudia and the children don't need to go through customs until 3 pm. I have wrestled with the problem of explaining to the Canadian Immigration how we arrived in Canada. In their country, you need to clear customs when leaving. But the Canadians are like the British: they only check the passport photo to the passenger, instead of checking the computer.

Thirty minutes later, I have organised my flight to Mexico. I have to stay overnight in Toronto, but I'm reckoning the cartels will be focused on the US and waiting for information to be leaked to them there. It should take them several days to work out I was in Canada, by which time I'll be long gone.

Claudia's flight is boarding. We hug each other and I promise Claudia I will be in Norway within weeks, if not earlier. The children wrap themselves around me and look back when they get to the gate, waving. Claudia doesn't. Crying as she leaves, she raises one hand in the air as a farewell and keeps walking forward. She is gone. For the first time on this escape journey I feel lonely, tired, and frightened. I find a bar and order a beer, overcome with a terrible desolation. In my heart, I know I won't see any of them ever again.

I arrive at Terminal Two and clear customs. Within twenty minutes of boarding the flight we are in the air, climbing to thirty-five thousand feet and heading south to the Mexican tourist city of Cancún. I sit back in my seat, thinking of what may happen if anyone in Immigration or customs realises who I am. My code name is Greece, so all communications with me from the US agencies is via that. I am travelling on my own passport, so there isn't any connection there, I hope. The tapes from both hotels have been removed, so there aren't any pictures of me. My real name has never been used, not even with the drug cartels. They only know me as Keith Wilson. And I have another passport, not Australian, which is added protection. There is always a chance of not getting through, but I am confident.

The flight is just over three hours. As we approach Cancún Airport I can see the cobalt sea of the Gulf of Mexico and feel the rising tide of terror and nausea enveloping me.

I advance in the line at Immigration. The female officer smiles, takes my passport and asks how long I am staying. 'Three weeks,' I say, smiling back. 'I am looking forward to some beautiful Mexican sunshine.' She punches my name on the computer and stamps my passport. 'Have a nice holiday,' she says. I walk quickly out of the area, collect my bags and head to the taxi stand.

Officials in tourist areas are very relaxed, but I can't expect the same in Mexico City. There, Internal Security agents drag people off flights for random checks, ransack luggage and ascertain whether the passenger has any involvement with the drug trade. There is no way I could have taken the risk of flying there directly or have come back in via the United States. If I am interviewed and photographed, the photo could be shown to cartel members, who will verify my identity. The rest doesn't bear thinking about. I will be thrown in a warehouse somewhere by Mexican police and handed to hitmen, who will skin me alive for information before executing me and sending my head in a brown paper box to the US embassy, complete with a message: 'This is what happens to DEA agents.' It has happened numerous times.

I decide to spend a couple of days here in Cancún and work on my plan for confronting the cartels. I check in under an assumed name and they ask for my passport. 'I've misplaced it,' I lie, handing over two thousand dollars for two nights' accommodation. No further questions are asked.

I need to ring Claudia. I locate the public phones in hotel reception, cash in some US dollars for pesos and am connected to her room. Grete has delivered on her promises: the family were greeted at the airport and taken to the hotel, and Claudia was given a brown envelope containing one thousand euros. 'I feel safe, Keith,' she tells me before we hang up. 'But we miss you.'

'I miss you all, too,' I tell her. 'Hang in there, darling.'

My options are limited. One is to get a new identity from the DEA and live in Europe. But the Colombians and Mexicans are hooked into the agency's systems and it wouldn't take them long to track me down. I could buy my own new identity, but that is extremely risky. I could be caught by other authorities and charged with holding false papers, and either put in gaol or deported. The best option is to simply disappear, fade into oblivion. This requires three things: false papers, a shitload of cash and no family that I would wish to contact. I can't do that.

39

I've made my connection to Mexico City safely, but the Colombians can't be far behind. I need to move again, quickly, but I also need to talk to Morgan. 'Where are you, Greece?'

'Mexico City.'

Her silence says it all: it is as though I have lobbed a grenade into the conversation. 'What? I thought you were in Canada!'

'I wish I was. I have to broker a deal with the cartels. You guys can't look after me, and I can't be on the run forever.'

'You won't be able to do a deal! They'll murder you, and the agency can't allow that to happen. Sorry to be so blunt, but you know too much. Stay where you are and I will have the boys at the embassy pick you up and bring you back to the States.' She pauses. 'I will personally take responsibility for you, Claudia and the family. That's a promise.'

'Thanks, but no thanks. You know we can't be protected. The best deal is for us to move to Europe and for me to be placed in a position within the UN, with around-the-clock protection. Your government does it all the time: a new identity, wiping a person's history and getting recommendations from the Justice Department and US Senators. That's our best chance, but it still won't stop them. Claudia has three young children, Morgan. They can't be compromised any longer.'

'Stop right there,' she says. There is a catch in her voice that I haven't heard before, bordering on panic. 'The agency owes you and we need to make sure that you are protected. I know we have leaks and we are trying to sort that out. I can place you in the armed forces and slip you into Germany. No one would know except me. We'll buy you a house and get you a good salary. We have to look after you, for fuck's sake. I know you have tapes. Bury them, because if they ever get out, we're all goners. Every man jack of us, from the director down. The President and director gave their word that we would respect Mexico's sovereignty and not push its government on extradition issues for cartel members.'

'I've given you guys plenty of chances. And you've fucked up. By the way, what happened to the agents in New York? You said you had news of them?'

'They've disappeared, that's all we know. We're still looking for them.'

'Was one of them the mole?'

'I can't discuss that with you, Greece. Sorry. I can tell you they have disappeared. Where they are, or with whom, we have no idea.'

'And you want me to trust you! We've almost been killed twice! You won't pay me the bonus or the reward, as promised. I have to deal with the cartels and the Colombians. I have no other choice!'

'Greece, give me a couple of hours. I'll talk to the director and see what we can do.'

'Okay. But the only deal I will entertain now is a job in Europe, security for the family for life and a fully furnished house. Plus five million dollars.'

'That's ridiculous.'

'It's either that, or I cut a deal with the cartels and the Mexican government. I'm sure they'll be very interested in what I have to say. Don't take it personally, Morgan, but you've got two hours. I'll call you back.' I hang up. I know the director won't play ball. They will place us in a house and find me a job, well paid, but that's about it. They will beef up security, short-term, and then scale it back until I don't need it anymore.

My one remaining client, Santiago, is my only chance. He can broker a deal with the Colombians and Mexican government and protect me in Mexico City. I want word to leak out to the other cartel leaders that I was set up by Al, that he was the DEA agent, and that I have fled to Mexico City for protection because the DEA were now looking for me.

Morgan launches into a tirade as soon as I call her back. 'Greece, the director is furious. You need to be picked up within the next hour. We know Claudia and the children are now safe and we can hide you in the US. We have a plane waiting for you at the airport and you'll be taken under protection. You will be given a fully paid house in Washington and a job with the US government as a consultant. Security will continue until you feel safe. We can't offer that indefinitely. We'll give you a hundred thousand in cash and two cars totalling another hundred thousand. That's more than generous, better than anyone has been given in the past. But all the tapes, including any copies, must be handed over. And we'll give you a letter signed by the director thanking you for the work you have done for us, and forward a copy to your own government stating the same.'

I can't believe what I am hearing and wish the conversation was being recorded. This time, when I most need it, I don't have a recording device with me. A letter from the Department of Justice would satisfy the Australian Minister for Immigration to approve my application to stay in Australia. It would give me back some credibility to seek employment back home and go a long way towards helping with my chances for a pardon. I am desperate to get some proof that I work for the agency, but there is no way they will come through with this promise.

Morgan is still talking. 'The DEA will also pick up the tab for Claudia and the children's costs until we feel they're safe to return to the US. We'll work with the Norwegian government to make sure Claudia and the children are continuously monitored for their safety. The director will provide a written contract and a US government cheque for two hundred thousand dollars, sent to your lawyer today, confirming what I've just outlined. You'll have it within the hour. That's it. This is a fabulous deal for you and Claudia.'

'Is it?' I can't keep the sarcasm from my voice. 'Give me an hour.'

I consider my options. If I accept the government deal, financially I will be set for life, living in one of the best suburbs of Washington with money, protection and a plum job. But the cartels will never stop looking for me. I will still be on the run. Then there is Claudia. If they can't get to me, they will take their revenge out on her and the family. Morgan's deal is generous. But it can't save my life.

I phone her back.

'What's your decision?'

'Morgan, for me to take your deal I would have to have diplomatic cover for the rest of my life, so I can't be troubled by the local authorities. The protection has to extend to Claudia's family as well. The offer of two hundred thousand is bullshit. You guys promised the commissions, which are well in excess of half a million, and I should get the two million reward as well for delivering the Colombian alive. And I still prefer Europe.'

'We can't provide protection for you outside the US. But I'll see what I can do.'

'Okay, and the payment would have to be two million into my attorney's trust account, by wire transfer, and a watertight contract to my lawyer on my conditions. We need to move fast, Morgan. Time's running out.'

'I'm aware of that.'

'The big issue is security. How safe are we going to be?'

'We've promised to give you the best.'

'Listen to me, Morgan. The top federal prosecutor in Mexico City was gunned down yesterday at a busy intersection. It was a murder of precise choreography. These killings are done by professionals who are hooded and gloved. They trap their targets in coordinated ambushes and strike with overwhelming firepower. Your best isn't good enough. I need time to think. I'll call you when I've made a decision.'

'When will that be, Greece?' I can tell what she is thinking: *You stuff up on this one, we're all dead.*

'I don't know, Morgan,' I tell her, honestly. 'I don't know.'

PART FOUR

Jeopardy

40

I have to see Santiago and find out what he can do. He was the first customer for Essex Finance, through my friendship with Daniel. I have done a number of successful transactions with him and still have all his details: bank accounts, assets and offshore contacts. I phone him.

'Where are you, Keith?'

'I'm not far away.'

'Good. Let's meet. The coffee shop at the Hotel Nikko in one hour.'

Santiago will have his people at the shop within minutes and he will arrive after I do. I feel sick with terror. This man, who towers over me and whose every movement is covered by bodyguards, has a menacing presence and the power to nod his head and have a person executed on the spot.

I try to console myself with the knowledge that he can't afford to kill me because I control his bank accounts, but my efforts to stay calm don't work. He can force me to transfer the funds across, and then murder me. His list of stocks and assets is my best insurance. They will be difficult to off-load, and I have sole discretion on them. I could give him written authority to switch them, but his name would send off alarm bells. His other option would be to switch to an accountant in Mexico, but that would take time and the US authorities would question and delay him. Any switch would take months. Alternatively, he could change to an American lawyer, accountant or investment trust, but once again time is the crucial factor and he is on the FBI radar. He is only too aware of this.

If I am murdered within the next few months, he will lose millions. He needs me, and if the list falls into the hands of the US government they will freeze the accounts for years. He can't afford that to happen. I weigh up the Colombian situation. If they believe I had nothing to do with the death of a family member, and they have their cash, I have a chance. I don't have the same hope with the Mexicans.

My body is pumping adrenaline as I enter the coffee shop. The place is surrounded by bodyguards: two at the entrance, four inside and two behind the counter. There is only one waiter and the shop is closed to the public. Santiago would have arranged that. He will be waiting in a van outside for me to arrive, with at least a dozen or more bodyguards with him for his own protection in case he thinks I am a stalking horse for the DEA. The waiter, a gaunt young man no more than eighteen years old, brings coffee and water. He is a nervous wreck, his hands shaking uncontrollably as he pours me a coffee. I try to relax with some deep breathing but that doesn't work. I check my watch: 2.35. My gut is roiling.

Santiago arrives at 2.54, trailed by eight bodyguards. He is not smiling. He pulls up a chair in front of me and does not offer a handshake.

'Play the tape.'

His eyes are cold, his mouth set in a thin hard line. I switch on the player I have brought with me, willing my hands to stop shaking as I start to play the version that Steven has edited. Santiago listens intently, his head slightly bent towards the machine. The voices are clear: Miguel, the Colombians, Al, me. And the gunshots, five in all. Then me again, heaving this time as I roll Al's body over and my gasp of shock when I see his face. My breathing is harsh, rasping, and I heave again until I dry-retch. The tape comes to an abrupt end and Santiago sits stock-still, saying nothing. Two minutes later, he points a bejewelled finger towards the player.

'Play it again.'

I depress the start button and the voices again resound in the restaurant: Miguel, the Colombians, Al, me. This time, at the end of the tape, Santiago taps his plump fingers on the table.

'Play it again.'

Over the next hour, I play it five times.

'Explain to me how you were hiding under an assumed name in Annapolis and New York?' He is looking at me again, now, his bodyguards standing behind him, arms crossed. The interrogation has begun. Obviously his sources have done their work.

'I was on the run and used my own resources, same as when I left Mexico City,' I lie. I force myself to return his gaze without flinching. He seems to be buying it.

'Explain how the DEA were looking after you in both Annapolis and New York.'

'They weren't. I didn't know they were watching the house until we spotted them in New York. That's why I went to Canada and then down to Mexico.' I pause for effect. 'Santiago, if I was being protected by the DEA, I wouldn't be here.'

'What about the shootings in Annapolis, and the DEA and police all over the house?'

'I didn't have a clue what the fuck was going on until I woke up with a gun to my head! The DEA came crashing into the house because they were watching us. I had no idea. With all the chaos, I thought the best thing I could do was just disappear. Then I kept moving with the family. I needed to be a few steps ahead of the DEA and the Colombians.'

'Where's your family now?'

'Safe. Out of harm's way.'

'They are in Europe?' He has moved slightly closer to me, his bodyguards shadowing his every movement.

'Yes. They are in Europe.'

'Germany?' He has a good memory: the DEA instructed me to tell Daniel that my relationship with Susan was over, in order to protect my family. I had also told him that I had found a new, German girlfriend. Daniel had, in turn, told Santiago. 'Germany? No. But close.'

'How close?'

'Close enough.'

He sits back in his chair. 'The Colombians' money. Where is that?'

'It's under my control. In Paris.'

'So you are saying that the Colombians can have their funds?'

'Yes. I banked the money and it is still in their account. If they had killed me, they would have lost the lot. It would have been a very costly exercise for them just to prove a point.'

'I see.'

This is my opportunity to bargain for my life. 'Your accounts have not been closed and your stocks, property and offshore trusts haven't been frozen or seized. They will stay that way as long as I stay alive.'

'Why have you come to me?'

Santiago is known for his conceit and arrogance. *Flatter his ego*, I think. *Tell him what he wants to hear.* 'Because you are the main man, the one the Colombians trust.'

Santiago controls the flow of drugs through Mexico City Airport and across the border, protecting shipments into the US. He also controls the drug empire in Mexico City, paying off officials and anyone else on the take, from senior police, customs officials and military personnel to members of Mexico's Congress. When Santiago speaks, the Colombians listen. If they buy the story I tell him, then I have a chance.

'So what do you want from me?'

'You set up a meeting with the Colombians. I have to have your protection. I will play them the tape and explain what I have told you, and transfer their funds to an account anywhere in the world. Hopefully they will listen, and save themselves ten million.'

'Less my fee!' he interjects.

'Your fee?'

'Yes, Keith. I will charge a fee.' He smiles for the first time, an aloof smile that looks more like a grimace. 'The fee is for arranging this for you, and you will deduct it from their money. Let me be very clear about this. I protect you, and in return all my accounts are safe: cash, property, stock holdings and my offshore trusts. Correct?'

'Correct. But if something happens to me, regardless of how it happens, the US government will have all your information within twenty-four hours.'

He doesn't like being challenged and leans in close to my face. 'I could sell all my stock and property, close my accounts and transfer the cash to other accounts. And then I could have you killed.'

'Of course you could. But if I die, the US government will still have all the information and seek you out. You will still lose millions. The US will put pressure on other governments, including Mexico, which will prove problematic, because this will be the only place you can park all your assets and cash. Even if you are protected by the Mexican government, it will be at a significant cost to you. Millions, once you factor in the exchange rate. I estimate it would cost you between twenty million to fifty million over a period of years.' I pause and wait for the information to sink in. 'I have always done the right thing by you, Santiago. I have risked my life protecting you, your assets and your cash and at no time have I exposed you.' I've played all my cards now, and think it best to retreat.

'First things first,' he says, drumming his fingers on the table again. 'The joint accounts? Close them and transfer the funds over to my other accounts. Secondly, you will move into my house this evening where you will be under my protection. No harm will come to you. That is a promise from me. You will stay there until I can do a deal with the Colombians. I will ensure you are protected from the other families, also.'

He stands up abruptly and mutters in Spanish to his guards, who suddenly appear less threatening. I figure he has told them I am now under his protection.

Three black vans are parked outside the hotel. We climb into the middle van, flanked by bodyguards. The front and rear vans also carry bodyguards, and four motorbikes sit near the vehicles, each carrying a driver and a shooter. The motorbikes weave their way through the traffic, checking for signs of an ambush. Santiago's security arrangements are not overkill: rival cartel families would assassinate him at any opportunity.

We race through the streets of Mexico City until we reach an upmarket suburb twenty minutes from the city centre. The circular driveway to Santiago's house is lined with palm trees and guards stand sentinel at the fortified front gate. Drugs and corruption have afforded Santiago a luxurious lifestyle: gardeners tend to manicured lawns and hundreds of rose bushes, a tennis court and swimming pool are housed in a separate pavilion. The mock-Georgian mansion, with marble foyer and sweeping staircase, boasts twelve bedrooms, each with an en suite bathroom. Santiago employs almost fifty people: bodyguards, housekeepers, gardeners and his personal secretaries. His wife, a willowy Spanish beauty half his age, greets us at the door.

He settles us in his airy study and calls for drinks. I decline his offer of beer or wine, settling instead for water. My throat is parched and I can't control the trembling in my hands.

'Close the joint accounts, now,' Santiago demands, pointing to my laptop. Within minutes, I have linked into the banking system and transferred the funds into his nominated accounts in Spain. I then close the existing accounts and send copies to his email.

Satisfied that the transactions are successful, Santiago dismisses me. 'Laura will show you to your room.' A maid who has stood discreetly by the door now steps forward with a shy smile. Santiago continues. 'Refresh yourself, and we shall meet back here in thirty minutes for further discussions. I will reach out to the Colombians and see what we can arrange.'

The bedroom is luxuriously furnished with a small lounge off the bedroom and handmade soaps in the bathroom. I sink onto the bed and do some breathing exercises to try and calm myself, surfing television stations to find an English channel with news headlines.

That morning, a Mexican beauty queen who dates one of the leaders of the powerful Juárez drug cartel was arrested outside the city of Guadalajara when soldiers stopped the vehicle in which she was travelling at a military checkpoint. Inside, authorities found a large stash of weapons, ammunition and three hundred and eighty thousand dollars in cash.

Juárez is one of the largest cartels in Mexico, controlled by their leader who is known as the Lord of the Skies because he flies planes packed with cocaine directly into the States. The beauty queen's partner and his brother were responsible for supplying a massive twenty per cent of Mexico's coke and marijuana sold on American streets, their enterprise earning close to one billion a month.

Their family are chasing me as well, because their assets and cash, which I handled for them, were seized by the DEA. This was a major setback for them and the word is out that I am a DEA agent. If they find me, they will ensure I die a very slow death. And they aren't my only problem. The Juárez cartel is allied with the Beltrán-Leyva organisation and I am also on their target list. I handled significant amounts of their cash and bank accounts for them, which have been frozen and seized after my meeting with the DEA deputy director.

I once met the Seagull, a Beltrán–Leyva cartel leader, at his compound, a heavily-fortified mansion set on the edge of an artificial lake. It is here that drug deals are sealed, bribes negotiated and girls supplied, along with cocaine and champagne. When the deals are done, everyone leaves. The only people living on the property are household staff.

The complex houses an impressive collection of rare big cats, including an albino tiger, black panthers, African lions and a chimpanzee. These animals provide gruesome entertainment, guests taking bets as to how long a person who has fallen out of favour with the Seagull will live before he is eaten alive by a wild cat.

I was picked up in Mexico City and blindfolded so I would not be able to identify the location of the property. At the house, I was searched and ordered to remove all jewellery and shoes and to hand over my cellphone before being shown into a luxurious study. Like the Lord of the Skies, the Seagull uses seaplanes to smuggle cocaine, hence his nickname. But there is another reason for it: his features resemble the scavenging bird. His face is narrow, his nose pointed and his eyes as small and hard as marbles.

The Seagull is known as one of the most sadistic cartel leaders. His favoured torture method is to strip his victim naked, tie his legs and arms behind a chair and insert a plastic ball into his mouth. The person's head is then placed in a box with trapdoors. When they open, rats rush out and chew off the victim's face.

The Seagull walked towards me with his hand out-stretched. 'You come highly recommended,' he remarked, his face taut. 'I have little time. I want you to tell me how you will bring my cash back into Colombia. It is in the Cayman Islands.'

I ran through the procedure, using Essex Finance as the trap. 'It can be finalised within seventy-two hours,' I said when finished.

'Good.' He shook my hand again. 'Would you like to stay here and have some fun, or go back to the hotel?' I opted for the latter. The less time I had to spend with this monster, the better.

El Chapo Guzmán, head of the Sinaloa cartel and the most-wanted drug lord in Mexico, is also baying for my blood and the Gulf cartel, with their group's paramilitary enforcement arm, Los Zetas, have their people hunting for me. They want to know who is responsible for their losses and they will kill me before I can wreak any further havoc on their financial bases.

Santiago, who controls Mexico City and Mexico State, is waging a war against these cartels, but I am only too aware that he could also do a deal with them and hand me over for a fee, or in exchange for more territory. Santiago has a strong relationship with the Arellano Félix cartel and he will definitely talk to them. I did an assignment for them where they used my services to bank cash and their accounts haven't been used for a while, so they are unaffected by the DEA seizure. But I am not confident about the level of protection Santiago can provide. As powerful as his network is, he is outnumbered by the other cartels on his turf.

I am ushered into the study again. Santiago is on the phone, but indicates for me to take a seat.

He hangs up. 'The Colombians will see you tomorrow at 9 pm, at a location they feel is safe. I am to guarantee this safety. They want to talk to you, see the cash is transferred and listen to the tape. Then they will make a decision about whether you live or not. It is fifty-fifty, in my opinion.'

He says it so casually, as though he is discussing the weather. 'You cannot stay in Mexico City. Several of the other cartels know you are here and they will kill you within days. You have to leave and move to Baja California where the Arellano Félix organisation will protect you. They are still grateful for the small work you did for them. I can't look after you myself. I don't have the resources. I have spoken to Eduardo and he will use your experience to bank some cash and provide the protection. You cannot go to Tijuana, or anywhere in northern Baja, as the DEA have too many agents and they will spot you. We have confirmation you are now wanted by the DEA.'

'None of this gives me much comfort,' I scowl.

His glacial smile returns. 'You have cause to feel discomfort, Keith. Much cause.' The conversation is over. 'We make the decision tomorrow night, after our meeting with the Colombians, as to where you go. In the meantime, enjoy my hospitality.'

I would laugh, if I weren't so petrified.

41

I barely sleep. The prospect of trying to do a deal with the Colombians, whose trigger-happy bodyguards could execute me on the spot, doesn't exactly encourage rest. My other major issue is the DEA. I have control over the Colombian money in the bank in Paris, but the DEA will want to move those funds back to the US. The Mexican operation has been a great success for them. They have seized millions in cash, shares and property and have bagged a known Colombian drug leader. I decide to tell Morgan after I make the transfer to the account at the Caja de Madrid bank in Spain. She's not going to be happy.

Santiago and I, entourage in tow, head to a downtown hotel. Cartel leaders often use the facilities of five-star hotels: they provide a perfect cover, cloaking them as Mexican businessmen carrying out kosher deals. Each hotel has its own security and few would risk trying to murder a rival cartel leader in such a public place. As we pull up, the bellboys rush to open the van doors, but the bodyguards are quicker and block the way. Santiago and I step out like movie stars.

Santiago leaves me in the hotel coffee shop. 'I am busy today, but I will return at 8.45 tonight, in time for the meeting,' he says. 'I will leave some men here to protect you, but under no circumstances leave the hotel. We know that Zetas have a hit-team here in Mexico City. Nine members, including one woman, have been linked to a killing of some of my people. They tortured and then beheaded them. You are their next target, and possibly me. If they catch you, you will suffer the same fate. We are trying to find them.' I could have lived without the details. Zetas are totally ruthless.

'Are they helping the Colombians?'

'No. But I have brought more of my men back into Mexico City to increase my personal security. This is my territory, so it is just a matter of time before we catch them.' He turns on his heel, his bodyguards following in his wake.

I call Claudia from the hotel lobby. She is thrilled to hear from me, but I sense immediately that something is not quite right. 'Keith?' She hesitates before continuing. 'About Paul.' Another elongated pause. 'He's putting in a lot of time with the children. It's nice that he's here. But he doesn't really want to return to Germany, and,' she is obviously trying to find the right words, 'he's asked if he can stay with us. There is a spare room here. Are you okay with that?'

'Of course,' I lie. 'No problem. Having a man in the house is good security for you.'

She sounds relieved. 'I was worried you would be angry. When are you joining us, Keith? It's been a week since I saw you.'

'Soon, I promise.' The words sound hollow and disingenuous. I don't tell her of the potential danger I am in but the chances of me getting out of Mexico alive are looking very slim. We talk for a further ten minutes before I hang up.

At seven o'clock that night a bodyguard taps me on the shoulder and hands me his radio. Santiago is on the line. There has been a change of plan, he says. The Colombians have moved the time to 8 pm. His men will now bring me to one of his warehouses, and we are to leave immediately. I know Santiago has a warehouse near the Plaza of the Three Cultures, where he stores a large amount of his drug shipments from Colombia.

The bodyguards lead me out of the hotel and into a waiting van. I feel like I am going to meet my maker. On the journey across the city, I think of what Al told me about Leonidas Vargas, a powerful Colombian drug trafficker who was being treated for a lung disease in Spain. A gunman entered his hospital room and fired four shots at the sleeping Vargas, using a pistol with a silencer. Vargas was head of the Caquetá cartel, which operates vast cocaine laboratories in Colombia, and was murdered by a rival drug-trafficking organisation. I am on my way to meet those rivals now.

My shirt is sticky with perspiration and beads of sweat dampen my top lip. The van comes to a stop outside the warehouse, a two-storey building with a large basement. An automatic door rolls up as we approach and we drive through into the bowels of the building. Three vans are already inside and at least twenty bodyguards. Santiago has stuck to his word, and marshalled his troops. A bodyguard opens the van door and points to the offices upstairs. I start to climb, willing my legs to keep walking. They are shaking and feel as though they will not carry me.

Santiago and three of his senior people are waiting at the top of the stairs. 'Come in,' he says, abruptly. 'The Colombians are on their way, Keith. They will be here in a few minutes and they have their own bodyguards. You need not be concerned. They are prepared to listen and get their money. But when they arrive, we will first give them some entertainment, okay?'

'Entertainment?' I don't get his drift. What I need is to get this deal done and get the hell out of here. I don't need any dancing girls.

The Colombians, when they arrive, look less than happy. Santiago greets them like Italian Mafioso, with hugs and pats on the back. He calls out for me to join them and I walk downstairs slowly, counting each step. *Twenty*. They don't offer a handshake. Santiago is doing all the talking, and they are listening to him. They nod in agreement and I stand there, like a naughty schoolboy, not understanding a word.

Santiago gestures for us all to follow him into the basement. It smells musty, the air fetid. Lights illuminate the far end of the basement like a stage show, but the rest of the basement is gloomy and dank. I can hear muffled voices. There are other people down here. A dozen body-guards follow me.

Boxes are stacked neatly along the side of the basement, obviously containing drugs. There doesn't appear to be another way in or out, other than the way we have just entered. Terror is overshadowing my awareness of anything else, except the people around me.

At the back of the basement, under the neon lights, nine people are on their knees, their hands and feet bound. One, a woman in her late twenties, is sobbing loudly. The eight men have frozen expressions, as though they are looking into the abyss. I recognise them as the hit-team from Los Zetas, the same people Santiago was talking about this morning. He has made good his promise, and found them. With horror, I realise they are going to be executed. This is the entertainment Santiago had mentioned.

He gives a command in Spanish, prompting one of his men, armed with a video camera, to move from one person to the next asking each to speak. Their voices are almost inaudible. My knees buckle when I realise they are being ordered to recite the last rites. The man with the camera returns to the first person in the line when he has finished recording them. A young man, no older than his early twenties, is jabbering in Spanish as another body-guard steps forward with his pistol and aims it at the side of his head, just centimetres away. The young man looks beseechingly at the shooter. '*Por favor, no lo hagas.*' He pulls the trigger. Fragments of skull and brain explode and he topples, face down. I turn away, vomiting.

The girl is screaming, jerking her head violently from side to side as the shooter slowly, methodically, works his way down the line. Six shots ring out, one after another, and then a chainsaw comes to life. I am riveted by the horror. A bodyguard saws off the victims' heads, their executioner calmly watching. He is through the first body in seconds, and moves to the next. The blood covers everything, and everyone.

The shooter stops at the young woman. They have probably already raped her numerous times. She has passed out, and they are throwing water on her face to wake her up. She has vomited and urine is trickling down her legs. She starts screaming again, looking at Santiago, begging for mercy. He ignores her, nodding to the shooter to move to the last man, whose head is down. He is muttering something in his native tongue, his lips moving, probably in prayer. The shooter yanks his head up by the hair, forcing him to stare into his eyes as he pulls the trigger. The growl of the chainsaw fills the basement again.

The woman is alone now in the line, the subterranean room filled with the stench of her excreta. Santiago gives the nod, and the shooter steps forward. He presses the gun against her forehead. She has stopped screaming and I notice, incongruously, her beautiful chocolate brown eyes and her long eyelashes, sticky with tears. '*Por favor, no lo hagas.*' Her voice is calm and soft now, almost lyrical. The shooter turns to Santiago again.

The woman has become composed and serene, focusing solely on her executioner, as though offering him forgiveness for what he is about to do. For a surreal moment, I think I see a smile on her lips before he squeezes the trigger and her head splatters with the impact of the bullet. I have wet myself again, piss running down the insides of my thighs. The chainsaw starts up, and I slump to the floor.

No words are exchanged as we walk back up the basement stairs and into Santiago's office. I am vaguely aware that I stink: my suit jacket is drenched with vomit and my trousers with pee and shit. We are all stained with blood. I no longer feel any fear. Instead, I am calm and devoid of emotion. I don't realise that I have sunk into a stunned stupor, deep shock protecting me from further distress.

Santiago takes us into a boardroom, where a laptop is set up on the table. He motions for us all to take a seat and I fall into mine, absently picking up a glass of water positioned on the desk in front of me. I can't coordinate my movements to bring it to my lips to drink.

Santiago is speaking, looking directly at me. 'Keith, those people had been sent to execute you. They would have skinned you alive, then murdered you and sliced off your head. It is what they do. Then they would try to get to me. They got what they deserved.' I don't reply. I know he is telling the truth, but this world of torture and murder is so foreign to me, I want no part of it.

Santiago can see that I am visibly upset. He orders me to snap out of it and put the recording on. I remove it from my briefcase and turn the volume up. The room falls silent as the Colombians listen to what Santiago has already heard five times.

They demand that I play the recording again, and give them a copy. They speak to Santiago, who is translating for them. 'They want their money,' he says. I am online with the bank in Paris in minutes and print out a copy of their financial statement: nine and a half million dollars. Santiago and the Colombians appear engaged in a heated discussion about the commission, which ends with a handshake.

'Transfer nine million to this account number,' Santiago instructs, handing me a folder with the details inside. The bank is in Spain. When the transaction is complete, Santiago gives me his account number to transfer the balance of five hundred thousand to a Dutch bank.

The Colombians have their money and Santiago has his commission. But I have no idea what they intend to do with me. Am I going to suffer the same fate as the nine victims in the basement, or will I walk out alive?

The Colombians rise, hug Santiago and leave. They don't acknowledge me. I can't move, glued to my chair as I hear their vans drive out of the warehouse and Santiago re-enter the room. If he feels any emotion about the executions he has just ordered, it does not show.

'You stink, Keith!' he says in a jocular voice. 'Go back to my house and change your clothes. Tomorrow, we will move you to La Paz to live for a while. You have had a lucky escape. The Colombians are not going to pursue you. The contract on your life has been terminated, and everyone will be notified.' He pats me on the shoulder.

'You are a lucky man,' he repeats. 'They have only agreed to this because you delivered the cash. They believe that if you worked for the DEA then you wouldn't be here, and the cash would have been frozen.' That cold smile again.

'They say their intelligence in America was misleading, that there is no evidence that you are a DEA undercover agent. Usually, they would have murdered you anyway, but I persuaded them to let you live. But understand this: if you fuck up again with the Colombians, they will kill me and my family, you and your family, and Daniel Gómez and his family. We are to meet in the morning at 9 am, the same place as this morning. If the transfer is confirmed by their bank, your life is secure.'

He hasn't drawn breath yet. 'In La Paz, you will be protected by the Arellano Félix family. I have spoken already with Eduardo, and he will protect you subject to you looking after his banking needs. He hates the other cartel families that are all looking for you. You are too hot for me here, but they will not risk going to Baja, because Eduardo has a strong hold on his territory. You will be safer with him.' He has finally finished. 'So, tomorrow we meet, okay?'

I muster a dry, 'Yes.'

Outside, before I climb into the van, a bodyguard orders me to undress. He has a hose in his hand. I turn to see Santiago yelling out to me, 'You are not going to leave a stink in my van! Take your clothes off, and we will hose you down!'

I strip, welcoming the cool water. I can hear Santiago and his bodyguards laughing at me, and I suddenly want to weep with humiliation and pity for the victims whose deaths I have just witnessed. This is such a far cry from the life I had before I was imprisoned. I doubt my sanity can hold out much longer.

42

Neither conscience nor guilt troubles Santiago, judging by his well-rested demeanour the following morning. In comparison, I am a jangled mass of nerves. I was unable to sleep all night. Every time I closed my eyes I saw the face of the executed woman, how she pleaded for her life and then her calm as death approached, the carnage of the bullet wound and the haunting growl of the chainsaw that finished her assassin's terrible work. His boot on her chest as he carved through her neck. Her body twitching, even after death.

'I have spoken to a group who own a new shopping mall in La Paz,' Santiago starts. 'They need new restaurants. So here is the plan. You will be sent to La Paz tomorrow and Eduardo has found you an apartment. Tell me, what do you know about restaurants?'

'Not a lot!' I answer, truthfully. I have no idea what he is thinking about getting me to do. I know nothing about setting up restaurants. Granted, my parents owned a hotel which had a coffee shop and a grill, and I helped out there during my school holidays. But this hardly qualifies me as a restaurateur.

'Do some research and come up with a plan,' Santiago continues. 'We are meeting my friends tonight and if you impress them, they will put up the money for the restaurant.' I refrain from shaking my head in amazement. Clearly anything goes around here. 'Eduardo's people will pick you up at the airport and then take you to one of their hotels. They will provide security for you. You haven't met Eduardo, but he knows you did the right thing by his family. You met and spoke with his brothers in the past, haven't you?'

'Yes, I have.'

'That is a good sign. They trust you and the Colombians, also. They phoned this morning, and the money is in their account. You won't have any further trouble with them, and the word is out that you are their friend. All is good.'

Thank Christ for that, I want to say. Instead, I nod my head and keep my response brief. 'Thank you.'

La Paz, in the south of Baja California, is a popular destination for American tourists. The resort town is situated on the tip of the peninsula and has a number of hotels and golf courses. The Gulf of California attracts abundant tuna, marlin and other game fish, making the ports on the southern tip a prime centre for sport fishing. It is also strategically important for the DEA, being one of two points of entry for cartel shipments of drugs into Mexico for transhipment to the States through Tijuana.

At the Mexico City hotel business centre, I check out the newly opened shopping mall on the internet. There are a number of restaurants, but none that serve seafood. The idea comes to me in an instant: why not open an upmarket fish and chip takeaway restaurant, selling fries out of a paper cone? I call some friends in Australia, who give me approximate costings of a fit-out and advice on machinery to use. By the end of the day, I have put together a plan which includes prices of the finished product, projected income and an expenditure statement. Finally, I download photos of similar establishments selling fries in cones.

I'm ready to make a presentation to the owners of the shopping mall. I am running on autopilot now and can't stop, even if I wanted to. The only way I can keep the nightmares at bay during my waking hours is when I can focus on something challenging, something positive. When I fall into sleep, the faces of the dead haunt me.

Santiago introduces me warmly. 'This is Keith, an Australian friend of mine,' he says, after vigorously slapping me on the back. 'He has a suggestion to open a restaurant in your new mall in La Paz. Tell them about it, Keith.'

I explain my idea, handing them print-outs of the proposal. No one looks at it and no questions are asked. Instead, the owner's son, Emilio, grins at me. 'When can you start?' he asks. The penny drops. The proposal is not important, all that matters is that I have come with a recommendation from Santiago. They will not dare turn down any suggestion he offers. *This is Keith, an Australian friend. Se puede confiar en él.*

I smile in return, playing their game. 'Next week.'

'Good. Then we agree to build this restaurant and we shall invest. It will only be a small takeaway, right?'

'Yes. Small. The cost is approximately a quarter of a million dollars.'

'Excellent. We will draw up a simple contract and give you twenty per cent equity for the concept. If it is successful, which I am sure it will be, then we will put one of the restaurants in each shopping mall throughout Mexico. What would you like to call them?' he asks.

'Otago Bay Restaurants. It's near my home town and I want it to be in the style of the New Zealand fish and chip restaurants.'

'Great. We will also set you up an office at the shopping mall, in the administration section, and provide you with a vehicle.'

Santiago speaks again. 'What is my equity?'

'Thirty per cent, and we will hold the balance of fifty per cent.' Judging by their smiles, it appears to be a done deal. Emilio thanks Santiago for the introduction. 'I will personally ensure my people at the shopping mall look after your friend,' he says, pumping his hand.

'That is appreciated,' Santiago replies. 'Eduardo Arellano Félix will do the same.'

The blood drains from their faces and Emilio is suddenly speechless. There is an uncomfortable silence before he speaks again. 'You can count on my staff taking special care of Keith, and I can assure you the restaurant will be opened well before time.'

Santiago turns to me after they leave. 'I knew they would like the idea.' If he requires a response from me, he doesn't get one. 'If you have any problems, call me or Eduardo. I am sure any misunderstandings will be resolved immediately.'

'I'm sure you're right,' I murmur.

Santiago organises my airline ticket from Mexico City to La Paz and also gives me some cash: ten thousand American dollars and another ten thousand pesos. It is not money I expected, but it is very welcome. My own funds are drying up quickly, and it's comforting to have some ready cash in case I urgently need to disappear again.

I call Claudia before I leave Mexico City. She sounds stressed. 'Keith, I haven't heard from you for a few days. Are you okay?'

'Yes, I'm fine. And you?' She ignores the question.

'What is happening?' I fill her in on the events of the past few days, taking care to avoid any detail of the executions. 'Santiago has made a connection to the Colombians and they have accepted the deal as I proposed. The contract on my life has been lifted and they will leave me alone.'

'I don't believe it! Are you telling me it was that simple?'

'No, it wasn't that simple. There were a number of discussions and it was difficult. But my tapes helped and, without Santiago, God knows what would have happened. Protecting the two cartel families' assets and cash was the best insurance I could have, and the tape.'

I think she is crying. 'I am so relieved, Keith. This madness has to stop. Are you going back to Washington, DC, or coming here to Norway?'

'I will stay in Mexico for a while. I need to. If I am seen to be protected by certain cartel members here, and it is known that the Colombians have lifted their contract, then there is a strong possibility that the rest of the cartel families may accept that I had nothing to do with the seizure of their cash and assets. This would allow us a much better chance to survive, and not be looking over our shoulders all the time.'

'How long will it take, Keith?'

'Six months, maybe eight.'

'Six months! Where will you live, and what will you do?'

'Santiago has made arrangements for me to open a restaurant in a new shopping mall in La Paz.'

Claudia laughs, a throaty, sensuous laugh that makes me wish I could hold her, right now. 'What do you know about restaurants, Keith?'

'Nothing,' I admit, grinning. 'But I'm keen to learn. I fly to La Paz today.'

'You're kidding me!'

'No, I'm not. I leave in about twenty minutes.' We need to discuss personal matters. 'How is everything with you and the children?'

'Good. We have found a house, and the children have started school. I've also got a position at the university in the Medical school, which I start on Monday. Your friend Grete has been just wonderful. She has opened so many doors for us.'

'And Paul?'

'He has been so helpful, Keith, and has asked for some leave from the university in Germany. He wants to stay for another month. Is that okay with you?'

'Yes, of course.'

She pre-empts the question I don't want to ask. 'Paul is not sleeping with me, Keith. I am treating him as just a friend. He respects that.'

'Thanks, Claudia,' I say. My voice is trembling, and I don't want to upset her further. 'I love you. I'll be in touch.'

I shake hands with the four bodyguards and board the flight to La Paz. They have no problem getting through departures: Santiago controls the airport.

43

Three suited men greet me in La Paz. I recognise one of them, instantly. The Stew-maker.

The Mexicans have imaginative names for the heavy hitters in the drug cartels. This cocky, ruthless thug earned his moniker because of his penchant for murdering guests who he invites to his flash parties, later dissolving their corpses in acid. His henchmen provide Mexicans with grisly entertainment, hanging victims' bodies, like meat in an abattoir, from the city's overpasses. The Stew-maker is well known within the drug trade and by the DEA, who estimate he is responsible for more than twelve hundred corpses.

Stocky, in his late forties, his paunch is a giveaway to his overindulgence in the good life, but his face is as taut as a painter's canvas, indicating cosmetic surgery. He speaks impeccable English. 'Welcome to La Paz,' he says, unsmiling. 'We need to leave the airport, quickly. Please follow us.'

The usual entourage is waiting outside. 'We will drop you off at the hotel, and we have allocated four body-guards for you while you are here,' he says. 'They will keep their distance but will watch you closely. Eduardo will be here in two weeks, and when he arrives you will make yourself available.'

He doesn't make it sound like I have a choice. 'Certainly,' I say. 'Any time.'

'Go to the shopping mall tomorrow by 9.30. You can't miss it. It's on the waterfront with all the restaurants. Ask to see Simon Lawson, the general manager. He's expecting you. Our men will be in the background keeping an eye on things. We control this town, so the police, security people and government officials all know you are a good friend of the Arellano Félix family. You will be okay. We don't expect any trouble.'

I decide to take a stroll around the small township and easily locate the El Dorado shopping mall, a massive complex of cafés, stores, live entertainment, art galleries and a theatre. The vacant shop where the restaurant will be situated has wonderful views overlooking the marina. But I'm under no illusions about this resort town. In the past twelve months, two adults were killed when assailants riddled their pickup truck with bullets, the one-year-old girl riding with them hit by multiple rounds and hospitalised in a critical condition. In a nearby neighbourhood, nine people were shot dead with a bullet to the back of the head, another five assassinated at a veterinarian's office and two police officers shot in a sports utility vehicle.

Simon Lawson arrives on time the next morning. He treats me like an old school pal, patting me on the back. 'Australia is fantastic, no? You will return home there one day, no?' He is looking over my shoulder. 'Where is your security?' I know by his question that he is aware I have Arellano

Félix protection. He hands me the keys to the vehicle and explains that they have found me a luxurious apartment overlooking the Bay of La Paz. We discuss basic necessities for the restaurant: kitchen equipment, food supplies, chefs. 'Leave all that to me,' he says, guiding me out of his office. 'I will handle all that for you.'

In the distance, I can see Eduardo's men watching. I have noticed that there are public phones on all levels of the shopping centre. I excuse myself from Simon and buy a phone card, making my way to the third level, where security cameras don't monitor the hallway, to the toilets where the phones are located. Security would see me enter the main passageway, and come out again. They would assume that I had been to the toilet. Eduardo's men cover all entrances. I race upstairs and make a beeline for the phones, dialling Morgan's number.

'It's Greece,' I announce without preamble.

Morgan is not as polite. 'Where the fuck are you? You're in deep shit. The Colombians' money's gone and everyone knows you are responsible. The director is screaming, my boss is screaming and we want the money back!'

'They can't have the money back,' I reply, as calmly as possible. 'The Colombians have it, and I have my life back. Well, to an extent. Put simply, you couldn't protect me, so I bought my freedom for the nine and a half million.'

'You what?' Morgan is screaming now.

'You heard me. I paid the Colombians their cash, and they cancelled the contract to have me murdered. And that goes for Claudia and the children. They have cancelled the contract on our lives.'

'And how do you know that?'

'Because I arranged a meeting with them through a contact in Mexico City.'

'Tell me you're kidding, please.'

'No, I am not. If you settle down, I'll explain.' I know she will be recording the telephone conversation and that, by now, several agents will be listening to the story as well.

She hears me out. 'So what you are telling me, Greece, is that you are now under Eduardo's protection?'

'That's correct.'

She lets out a long, slow breath. 'Jesus Christ. Do you realise what you are doing? He is a very, very dangerous man. Hang on a moment, I've got to take another call.'

I know she is getting instructions from her boss. 'We need you to help us get some very important information,' she says when she returns to the phone. 'The Arellano Félix cartel uses a team of lawyers in San Diego and New York. We know the ones in San Diego, but we don't know their contacts in New York. We would like you to try and get those details for us: phone numbers, names, addresses, home addresses, anything you can.'

She keeps talking so I can't interrupt her. 'Also, the Colombians are flying their shipments into Baja California. We know several sites where they land, but we need more information about who's helping them, how they ship the drugs to Tijuana and who else is protecting them. Can you find out as much as you can, without taking a risk?'

'Without taking a risk? Are you having a lend of me, Morgan? Do you know what these bastards are capable of?' My voice has risen in anger and I look around to ensure no one has heard me. I'm suddenly fed up with being a pawn for everyone else, pushed around like a piece on a chessboard. I lower my voice and repeat what I have said. 'Have you seen what they do to people? Do you know what these bastards are capable of?'

'Only too well, Greece. Only too well.' Her attitude has softened. 'Try to remember why we do this job. We probably can't win the war on drugs, but we can at least give it a shot.'

Her lofty sentiments fail to move me. Instead, all I see are visions of desperate men begging for mercy and the young woman's head being blown off in that stinking concrete basement. 'Save the speeches, Morgan,' I tell her.

'Greece, we understand the danger you are in. We really do. And we appreciate your work. Our offer to protect you back here in the US, new identification papers, a house and job, it still stands. You've earned it.'

'Before I go, Morgan: did you ever find out who in the DEA is responsible for the leak?'

'Afraid not.'

'Enough said, then, don't you think? You lot can't even look after internal issues, let alone protect me. I'll do my best to try and get the information, but I'm not prepared to risk my life again. I didn't sign up for this. I want to live, not go home in a wooden box.'

I need to hear Claudia's voice. She answers the phone in a breezy tone. 'Hi, honey, how are you?' She sounds happier than I have heard her in a long while.

'I'm fine. And you?'

'Fine. We're all settled in. It's so nice to go to bed and sleep without worrying anymore.'

'I know.' I feel like adding I wish that I could do the same, but I refrain. Instead, I tell her about my accommodation, and paint a word picture of the apartment.

'It sounds like a big place?'

'It is. I may have guests.'

'Like who?'

'Like you, I hope? When everything settles down, you might come to visit with the children?'

'Keith, I've got to tell you something.' I know what she is going to say before it leaves her mouth. She is crying now, apologising for rekindling a relationship of sorts with Paul. 'I love you, Keith,' she says. 'It just happened. I'm not proud of myself.'

'You don't need to explain,' I say. I am stunned, but I was the one who engineered Paul's visit, knowing he still loved her. What did I expect? Claudia needs stability and I can't provide that. She needs to know that she and the children can sleep at night without fear of being attacked. I want to tell her all this, tell her it's okay, but I can't speak.

'Say something, Keith!' Claudia beseeches. 'Please!'

I can't. My shoulders are heaving from trying to suppress my sobs and I am helpless to stop the tears sliding down my cheeks. I can hear Claudia's voice and other voices now, crowding in: my brother telling me our father had died; the gunshots in the hotel room in Mexico City; the imploring chorus of the nine wretched souls praying for their lives to be spared; the bullies at boarding school, taunting me; the nurse at Arthur Gorrie, *You've sure got some problems*; police officer Don Granger's warning to me, *Stay here any longer, mate, and you'll go nuts*; and that incessant chant inside my own head, *Coward, gutless wonder, you get what you deserve.*

I have dropped the receiver and am on my knees. I feel torn apart, shattered, and I know with certainty that if I don't get back on my feet, that if I stay here a second longer, I will never again find any courage to fight back.

Claudia is sobbing, begging me to talk to her, and I

finally find my voice. 'Claudia, as tough as it is, it's for the best. You've got to believe that. I won't contact you again, you need space to get on with your life. Give the kids a hug from me. I love you, and wish you all the luck in the world.'

I drop the phone and force myself to my feet. I don't have the energy to walk, instead leaning against the telephone wall as jumbled images of Claudia invade my thoughts.

The deep self-loathing I have tried so hard to suppress now rises to the surface. I have allowed myself to be used as a stooge for the DEA. I have allowed myself to tread a fine line between betraying my friend, Daniel, in return for my own gains. I have risked Claudia's life by selfishly wanting her with me. Now I've lost her and I've no one to blame but myself. I'm not prepared to lose anymore.

44

Eduardo's bodyguards pick me up from the shopping mall. Their boss must be in town, judging by the swollen number of guards who surround my apartment and the dozen black Ford vans snaked along the roadway leading towards the entrance to the Cabo Bello. I am patted down and given the green light to go inside, where Eduardo is waiting for me.

Tall and muscular, with a thin beard encasing full lips, his benign looks belie his nickname, El Doctor. His calling card is the use of medical equipment on his enemies, experimenting with ingenious methods of getting them to talk. He is on his cellphone, and doesn't acknowledge me. Something has obviously gone horribly wrong, judging by his grimacing look. I hope to Christ it's got nothing to do with me.

'We are leaving in two minutes,' he suddenly barks at me. 'Be ready.' Police cars join the convoy of vehicles that speed out of Cabo Bello. Eduardo stays on his phone as we travel thirty minutes from town.

Police wave us through a roadblock and we continue

until we reach three large vans surrounded by police officers. Through the open doors, I can see the occupants of a van, covered in blood and gore. Dead. The driver and the guard in each have been shot several times, their faces rendered unrecognisable by bullet wounds.

Outside the vehicles, six men, their hands bound and ropes around their necks, have gaping bullet wounds to the backs of their heads. Their bodies lie in pools of blood, bullet casings littering the surrounding area. The familiar acrid bile rises in my throat, and I have to inhale deep breaths to stop myself from vomiting.

I recognise one of the dead men. He was a leader in Eduardo's cartel, identifiable by the large gold ring worn by a select few. The ring bears the icon of Saint Death, a ghoulish grim reaper figure that gang members believe protects them.

I can guess what has happened. A shipment of drugs arrived from Colombia, courtesy of the Arellano Félix cartel, and has been ambushed. Eduardo now has the army and police, as well as his own people, hunting the hitmen. Unless they have an aircraft or a boat on standby, they have no chance of escape. But if they can get off the peninsula, they will head for the mainland where they can muster their own forces.

Eduardo is shouting and issuing orders. His own men are removing the bodies and cleaning up the site. His cellphone shrills again, and he punches the air with his fist. By the sudden change in atmosphere, my guess is they have been caught. I don't want to be around to witness the revenge. We race along the road to La Paz, and eight kilometres from the city turn off the main road towards a small farmhouse.

Thirty police officers, sporting black bulletproof vests and helmets, are standing over sixteen men, kneeling on the ground in front of them. A police helicopter hovers above, and I can hear vans parking at the entrance. Eduardo steps out of the van like a general at war and starts speaking in rapid Spanish to the police chief. They gesticulate wildly with their hands before the police chief calls out to his men to pack up and leave. Eduardo's troops now surround the kneeling men and the chopper heads off in the direction of La Paz. The police chief has taken the silver.

The farm is a dismal affair, with a dilapidated house, broken-down vehicles and emaciated chickens scratching in the dirt. The owners, a paunchy middle-aged couple, appear to have little money. A bodyguard brandishes a semi-automatic weapon in their faces, making sure they do not avert their eyes from the men on the ground. They will be spared, but will be made to witness the executions.

A chainsaw grumbles to life. I can't watch this again. I walk a small distance from the scene and slump against the trunk of a tree. I can hear the screams of the victims, crying and begging for mercy, but this time there will be no quick bullet. These men will be tortured, their legs or arms sliced off with the chainsaw to make them talk. Eduardo will extract a full confession within seconds. The victims know to tell the truth in exchange for a quick death; if they don't, it will be prolonged and excruciating.

The tree provides welcome shade from the damp heat, and I try to distract myself from the nightmare by watching seagulls soar overhead. I have gone to another place in my mind, distancing myself from the atrocities taking place here. I am back in New Zealand, nine years old on my uncle's farm in central Otago. The family is gathered at the old kitchen table, my cousins and I making a racket, eyeing off the last biscuit and scuttling outside as soon as the adults let us go. 'Be back before dark!' Mum yells as we tear off over the property, in search of boyish mischief. The only crimes anyone ever talked about then were cattle rustling or sheep stealing. Life was peaceful, wholesome and safe. I huddle into myself, rocking back and forth, and close my eyes.

I must have sat there for hours. The screams have ceased and the vans are now heading back up the lane towards the main road. One stops and the door opens. 'Get in,' Eduardo orders. He does not utter a word on the drive back, but nods solemnly at me when I get out of the vehicle at the shopping mall. I am too stunned to respond.

I wander around aimlessly for hours, unable to form a clear thought. As dusk settles on the town, I find a public phone in a hotel and dial Morgan's cellphone, telling her what has happened in the dispassionate voice of a person in deep shock. 'Greece, where are you calling from?' she asks when I have finished.

'The Finisterra Hotel reception.'

'I am going to hang up now. Book a room in a hotel, stay there tonight and catch a flight to San Diego tomorrow. I don't want you in Mexico any longer. You have seen far too much. You must come back.'

'I can't. The only way I can survive is to stay here.'

She begs me to return. 'You are in shock, Greece, and are making fundamental mistakes. You have called my cellphone, which will be traced. It is registered in another name, a woman who has no connection to the DEA or me. We will ensure her safety, but never phone me again on a cell.' She hangs up.

I have seriously fucked up. Soon enough, Eduardo will know who it is I called and try and find out what we discussed. Morgan will clean the trail, but I've made a potentially fatal blunder. I've survived so far, but I'm petrified that I'll make further mistakes. I have to keep my head down, finish the restaurant, and get out of here.

Eduardo is at the apartment when I return, and gestures for me to join him at the table. '*Vino?*' he asks.

'Thank you, yes.'

He is looking intently at me. 'Santiago tells me you have always looked after him, and has also told me about the . . . misunderstanding with the Colombians.' I don't like the way he says 'misunderstanding', emphasising the syllables with a hint of sarcasm. 'It is true, no, that you are now in the clear with them?'

'Yes,' I say, 'that is how I understand it.'

'You still have the other Mexican cartels chasing you, and you know if they find you, you will be executed just like the men were today?' There is a sadistic glint in his eye that is impossible to ignore. The bastard is enjoying this.

'I am only too aware of that, yes.' I swallow hard and move slightly in the chair.

'Well, you are very lucky, because I don't like them either. They have been trying to kill me for years, so we are both in the same boat.' He throws his head back and laughs and I wonder, momentarily, if he is mad, on such a power trip and out of touch with reality that he believes he is invincible. I decide it's safer to join in the laughter.

'Who did you phone earlier?' He has verbally cornered me and his laughter has stopped.

Morgan had given me the name of the phone's owner and her details so that I could repeat them if cornered. 'I rang an old friend in San Diego. Rosalie Hill. I felt lonely and after yesterday, I needed to talk to someone.' I know Eduardo will have the same answers as I am giving him now.

'What is she like?' He is testing me.

'She's in her late thirties, divorced with one child, a girl about seven years old. About five feet five, blonde hair, blue eyes and works for the University of Southern California in the library. She loves soccer and plays at the university.'

'Is she nice?'

'Beautiful.'

His expression has changed, and he is smiling. 'Have you slept with her?'

Now it's my turn to smile. 'Not yet.'

He has bought my story, and now changes the subject. 'I will have some banking for you later in the month. You will need to come to Tijuana for a few days and we will spend some time going over my bank accounts.'

I freeze. The DEA has instructed me never to go near Tijuana because of the staggeringly high murder rate there. 'I don't think that is a good place for me,' I reply, hoping he doesn't notice my fear. 'The place is crawling with DEA agents. I would rather stay away.'

He has chosen not to hear me. 'I will arrange your flight and your accommodation, and I will expect to see you in my offices within two weeks. Your safety is guaranteed.' The meeting is over, and he signals for his bodyguards to bring his coat. 'Until then, goodbye.'

I extend my hand to shake his, but he gives me a hug instead. The significance is not lost: I have now been taken into his inner circle. His bodyguards have seen this, my status has increased. I now realise the importance of going to Tijuana. I am going to be exposed to their financial operations.

45

The APEC Summit is being held in nearby Los Cabos next week, attended by high-ranking officials from the Asia–Pacific region. In readiness, the Mexican government is moving thousands of troops into the area, as well as federal police and military. The drug cartels will lie low until they leave.

The number of bodyguards around my apartment has doubled and one approaches with a cellphone in his hand, indicating Eduardo wishes to speak to me. 'There was a hit last night. Did you hear of it?' he asks.

'Yes, it was all over the news.'

'It was the Gulf cartel. They killed the pilot who was supposed to fly them out of Cabo. My men are looking for them. We believe you are not at risk, but I have increased your security.'

APEC lasts three days, after which the region returns to normal. So does the drug trade, with Colombian shipments arriving and being transported to Tijuana for the United States. By the end of the first day, twenty-one people are killed in a drug ambush. It's business as usual.

Eduardo has made the arrangements for me to travel to Tijuana. His men will collect me from the airport and I will stay in a safe house.

First, I need to contact Morgan again, but from a payphone this time. 'I am in La Paz, but flying to Tijuana tonight on the 6 pm flight, arriving around 8 pm,' I tell her. 'I'm travelling with a bodyguard, and Eduardo's team is picking me up at the airport.'

She doesn't try to hide her exasperation. 'I don't like this at all, Greece. It's highly dangerous. People are murdered every day in Tijuana.'

'I'm well aware of that. But it's only for two days, and I should be able to get the information you are seeking. Besides, they didn't request I go. It was a demand.'

'That worries me more. Be careful, very careful. We have our people in Tijuana and we will look out for you. If you need to get hold of me urgently, go to a restaurant called Buenos Aires, diagonally across from the Tijuana Cultural Centre. Ask to see Ignacio and ask him what American football team he follows. If he says "Chicago Bears", you can give him an urgent message. He will know to make contact with me, and we will find you. Are you clear on that?'

'Yep, got it.'

'Get this done, Greece, and go home to Australia. You've done enough.'

'I can't think of anything better.'

'Greece, I have to be honest here. There is a big chance you will be taken away for interrogation. You could be walking into your own execution.'

'That's heartening.'

'If they grab your hands, you know what is going to happen next. Leave any taping devices behind and look out for weapons.'

'They all carry weapons!'

'You will have to talk. And then they will kill you. Look, if you change your mind about going, I'll support you.'

'I won't change my mind.'

'In that case, I will personally call your wife if anything goes wrong.'

The flight to Tijuana is only one hour and forty-five minutes and follows the beautiful coastline of Baja California. I am extremely nervous, my anxiety not helped by a story headlined in the *Los Angeles Times* outlining the pay rise for Tijuana's Secretary of Public Security, Alberto Capella Ibarra. Capella has been a marked man since November, when two dozen gunmen shot up his house, and he now travels everywhere with twenty bodyguards. His wife and three children live outside Tijuana and he is regularly forced to cross the border into San Diego for his own safety. A pay rise, too, for the head of police, Leyzaolo, who is rarely seen in public without an AR–15 rifle slung over his shoulder. He lives at the tightly secure Mexican army base and, unlike most cops in Tijuana, Leyzaolo is believed to be honest.

I'm quickly escorted to a waiting van at the airport, with the usual security riding shotgun. We pull up at a resort hotel on Pacific Beach. I am only thirty minutes by car to the CBD of San Diego, and to safety. The head bodyguard speaks English. 'You will stay here tonight,' he says. 'Tomorrow morning we shall collect you at 9 am. Be ready. You are not to leave the hotel.'

I pour a stiff Scotch and stare out at the reflection of the moon on the water from the penthouse on the seventeenth floor. Home and the life I led before going to prison seem a universe away. Tijuana is the prime drug trade route into the US, turning over in excess of five billion a year in profits. The other drug cartels fight for a share of that profit, losing thousands of their gang members a year. The Arellano Félix family has over two thousand men in Tijuana, a small army that can handle any attack. The city is totally under their control.

The van picks me up the next morning, moving from the city centre and out into the squalid suburbs, where children play in the dirty streets among the rubbish and the buildings are scrawled with graffiti. The van picks up speed as we race along a freeway and slows down again at a small laneway that leads to a warehouse.

Inside, five vans are parked side by side and at least fifty bodyguards stand sentinel at the entrance and exit. I am escorted to the office block at the rear of the warehouse and shown into a small boardroom with a row of TV screens, which display views of different areas of the building. The DEA has told me that there are tunnels under the warehouse that lead to houses nearby. Eduardo and his senior men use these tunnels if they are ambushed, slipping away while his men fight off the attackers and call in reinforcements.

The DEA once received a tip-off about one of these tunnels during an earlier briefing with me. Agents scrambled out of the office and within minutes, with choppers hovering overhead, they were dropped onto the roof of the house where the tunnel exited. The agents emptied their magazines into the house, over a thousand rounds.

I was left sitting in the office at DEA headquarters watching the whole thing unfold on television, waiting for Morgan and Jim to return.

This tunnel was used by the Arellano Félix cartel and was built to transport drugs and immigrants illegally across the border into the US. Police found information in the tunnel indicating certain Mexican police were involved in the racket and, as a result, the army arrested the Tijuana police chief and forty other police officers, all on the payroll of the drug cartel.

The Tijuana and Juárez cartels are known to use the Baja police forces as their private armies. In 1996, the then Mexican President, Ernesto Zedillo, fired seven hundred federal police officers in one fell swoop. The next year, all federal police officers assigned to Baja California were once again replaced after the vicious slaying of the State Prosecutor, Hodin Gutierrez Rico, in Tijuana.

Eduardo enters the boardroom with five of his men, all trusted lieutenants from his own village. He gives me a hug and gestures to the coffee and water on the table. 'Please,' he says, 'help yourself.'

We start with small talk. 'Your accommodation is suitable, I trust?'

'Beautiful, thank you.'

'How is the restaurant going?'

'Fine. I should be ready to open soon.'

'You never know, Keith, if it is successful you may have a chain of these in a few years.'

'I hope so,' I lie.

Now he gets down to business. 'I need your advice. I have several bank accounts in the Caribbean, as you know. I also have a fifty per cent share in an investment bank in the Cayman Islands with Santiago and Daniel Gómez, and I want to know whether I should keep them.'

I don't hesitate for a moment. 'Definitely not. Close them all and move your funds within the next three months. The Caribbean is now closely watched by the DEA, FBI and European officials. You need to get your funds into Europe, opening accounts in the British Channel Islands, Jersey and Guernsey, Holland, Germany and Switzerland. Close down the bank in the Cayman Islands but don't sell it. A sale may come back and hurt you.'

'You are sure of this?'

'Positive. Do it quickly, because I know from reports that the DEA and FBI are working their way through all bank accounts, and if they find yours, they will freeze them. Warn Daniel and Santiago as well. You know the Colombians are closing their accounts and are moving their funds to Europe. Do it.'

'Who do you know and trust who can help me?'

'Do you have lawyers in New York?'

'Yes. I have a team of lawyers who act for me, and I trust them.'

'They will have their contacts. If they don't, then I will provide you with some names you can use. But ring them now. We need to move today, not tomorrow.'

I can't believe the way this is progressing. Eduardo is talking about the legal team the DEA wants information on. This group of lawyers must be laundering monies on behalf of the drug cartels and criminal gangs in the US. Eduardo is rattling away in Spanish to someone on the telephone. I can't understand a word he says, as usual.

'I have instructed them to open some bank accounts immediately and to close the ones in the Caribbean,' he tells me. 'Once they have been opened, he wants me to transfer three million to his trust account. I will do this today.'

'Sorry, you have lost me. Who does?'

'His name is Ricardo and he works for my lawyers. The funds will come from my account in the Caymans.'

I shake my head. 'Don't transfer funds from the Caymans. Do you have funds in the US?'

'No. I don't trust anyone in the US.'

'Okay, what about Europe?'

'No, nothing. All my cash is either in Mexico or the Caribbean.'

'Well, we need to get cash to your lawyer in New York.'

'How?'

'By courier,' I suggest. 'Get one of your men to take the cash across the border and then drive to New York and hand the money directly to the lawyer.'

'That isn't easy, and there are only a few men I could trust to do this. It will take time.'

'But you don't have time. It has to be done this week.'

'Well, I don't have anyone. What about you?'

'Me?'

'Yes, you.'

'Well, I could, I suppose,' I hesitate, 'but there is a risk with the border crossing and then getting to New York.'

'So you will do it?'

'I guess I can. Let me think. If I can work something out, then I'll do it. But the cost will be five per cent, plus expenses.'

Eduardo laughs and pats my hand, 'I knew you would help. Five per cent? Accepted. Okay, my men will take you into the city. Find yourself a coffee, think it through, and then we will get the cash.'

'Eduardo, if I go ahead with this, it will be in the next few hours. So have the cash ready.'

'It will be.'

I ask the bodyguards to take me to the restaurant Morgan suggested. I know I'm taking a risk, but this is urgent. 'Do you speak English?' I ask the waiter at the door. He shakes his head. 'Is Ignacio here?'

He points to a small, thin man setting up tables by the window. 'Ignacio,' the waiter calls him over.

I can't afford to waste time. 'Hello,' I say, a tad awkwardly. 'I need someone who speaks English and this restaurant has been recommended to me. Tell me, what US football team do you support?' I am speaking low and fast.

'Chicago Bears.' He looks as nervous as I feel. I am the only person in the restaurant, other than my bodyguards. I tell him I am also a Bears supporter. 'Call Morgan for me,' I mutter, before asking for a table. 'Just coffee and a light lunch, thank you,' I say when he pulls out a pad to take my order.

I go back downstairs after lingering over three coffees and a squid salad. The bodyguards follow in my wake. They would already have phoned Eduardo and told him I had chosen this restaurant. I know he will interrogate me as to why I spoke to Ignacio.

A group of three American tourists is standing on the street. I recognise one of the girls, an attractive woman in her late twenties who works with Morgan at head office. All are wearing casual clothes, shorts and T-shirts, and have cameras slung around their necks. The guy is holding a map of Tijuana. The tourist area is blocked off on both sides of Avenue Revolution, and well protected, but tourists often stray in Tijuana, are robbed and lose their cars. These three look very lost.

The guy yells out to me. 'Hi, excuse me? Are you American?'

'No, Australian.'

'We're lost. Can you help us?'

'Perhaps. Where are you heading?' He points at the map and I move closer towards them. The bodyguards start to circle, but I wave them away. 'It is okay.' I am huddled close to the Americans, looking at the map.

The girl speaks softly. 'Greece, what's up?'

'I am crossing the border with three million in cash to take to the lawyers in New York. I need to cross without any problems in two hours.' I look around, pretending to get my bearings. 'I think you need to walk down there,' I say, pointing. 'About five blocks, then take a left and walk another three blocks. You should be right.'

As I walk away, they yell out, 'Thanks, mate!'

The bodyguard who speaks English eyeballs me. 'How did you know where to send them?' he asks, suspiciously.

'I didn't.'

He starts laughing and repeats the story in Spanish to the other guards.

The bodyguards have reported back to Eduardo about the restaurant and the American tourists. In the boardroom, Eduardo questions me. 'How was the coffee?'

'Very good,' I reply, holding his gaze. 'A friend in Chicago knows one of the waiters, Ignacio, who loves the

Chicago Bears. He suggested to me that if I was ever here in Tijuana to look him up. I wanted to try their grilled meats, which are famous, but I settled for squid.' I shrug. 'The food was fine, nothing spectacular, but I can recommend their coffee. Have you eaten there, Eduardo?'

'No,' he says, grim-faced. I wait to be interrogated about the tourists, but it doesn't come. 'Well, have you a plan?'

'Yes. It's now just after 1 pm. I will head to the border in one hour, and I want ten thousand for expenses. I will wait close to the border and look for a family who are fair-haired, and ask for a lift into San Diego. I will tell them my car has been stolen. The border guards only look for Mexicans. Anyone who looks American, they wave through.' I figure my plan should work: the Tijuana border crossing is the busiest in the world, with thirty-three million vehicles and seven million pedestrians going through a year. 'If I'm not comfortable when I get there, I will come back and think of another plan.'

'What happens when you get to San Diego?'

'I will catch the train to LA, and then get the train to New York.'

'Train?'

'Yes. Security at the airports is very strict after 9/11, and I will be caught with the cash. I will get a first-class cabin and be in New York by Monday morning, to hand over to the lawyer. I want the lawyer to phone you from his office, with me present, so he acknowledges he has received the cash. He must also fax a copy of a receipt to you and hand one to me. The train leaves tonight from LA to Chicago at 10 pm. It is a forty-three-hour trip. Then I catch a train from Chicago to New York, another twenty hours. I need to be in LA by 9 pm, so I have to be across the border by 5 pm at the latest.'

'Okay. I will have my men take you to the border, and we will wait till you are picked up, and watch you cross. I will have men in the USA, if you need help.'

'I appreciate the offer, Eduardo, but I must do this on my own. When I have delivered the cash in New York, I will catch a flight to La Paz, via Dallas, and finish the restaurant. After it is opened, I will stay a week, and then leave for Australia.' I afford myself a smile. 'I want to go home.'

He stands and pumps my hand. 'Home is important. Let's get you to the border.'

46

Thousands of cars are queued up to cross into the US. I dress conservatively in an open-neck shirt with a button-down collar, navy-blue trousers and black shoes, and carry a briefcase. I get out of the van and start walking towards the lines of cars. There are four rows, and I walk between rows one and two, looking for a family. After fifteen minutes, I spot a car from Washington State. Perfect. They look to be in their thirties, both have sandy hair and there are two children in the back seat.

I lean close to the open window. 'Did you enjoy Mexico?'

'Not really,' the driver says. 'Too squalid for our taste. How about you?'

'No, my rental car was stolen and the Mexican police said it would be heading further south by now. So I'm walking back to San Diego to file a formal complaint.'

His wife hollers from the passenger seat. 'You're kidding me! You're walking all the way?'

'Yes, unfortunately. I don't have much of a choice.' It's such an obvious hint I'm scared they won't fall for it.

'Hop in,' her husband says. 'We can give you a lift to San Diego. Is that any help?'

'Are you sure? That would be great! I'm staying in the city. Thanks so much.'

We introduce ourselves, and Larry starts to slowly inch forward in the queue. He doesn't have passports for his family: Americans can go either side of the border with their driver's licence. We are two cars from the crossing. The customs officer waves the first car through and stops the one in front of us, checking papers. Then it is our turn. He takes one look and waves us on. Within less than two minutes, I am inside the US and heading towards San Diego.

I don't know if the DEA team has seen me or not, but I'm certain that Eduardo's people will follow until I make the delivery in New York. Larry drops me at the train station and they bid me a safe journey, the kids waving from the back seat as they drive away. I'll be at LA Central Station by 8.30 pm, in time to catch the 10 pm to Chicago. I slump into a seat and ponder my surreal situation. I now have both the DEA and the Arellano Félix cartel protecting me. If anyone tries anything, they won't get far. They will be either arrested or shot.

All I am carrying is four shirts, two extra pairs of trousers, underwear, socks and a briefcase containing three million dollars. I've also got my laptop, wallet, expenses and passport in a small suitcase with wheels.

Morgan will know where I am by now. The DEA would have viewed the tapes of the border crossings and picked up on Larry dropping me at the station. An agent would have waited for the train at LA and followed me as I bought the ticket to Chicago. They will know that Eduardo's men are there too, and both the DEA agent and his men will swap teams before Chicago, so I won't recognise them. The agencies and the drug cartels always follow the same rule: change the people who are tailing a target. I can only pray that the DEA doesn't attempt any contact with me with Eduardo's men watching. I'll be executed before I reach New York if they do.

I put the briefcase with the money at the end of my bed and under the sheets, so if someone creeps in during the night to rob me they will have to take the bed apart to find it. The clickety-clack of the train's motion rocks me to sleep. It doesn't take much: I'm totally exhausted. When I pull back the blinds at first light, I see a vast expanse of arid cattle country. We are in Arizona, heading to the city of Albuquerque, New Mexico.

I shower and go to breakfast in the dining car. The tables, beautifully set with crisp white linen, are filling quickly. A couple in their late fifties ask if they can join me. I don't much fancy company but wave to the seats. 'Be my guests.'

They like to chat. 'My name is Jack and this is my wife, Eileen,' the man says. 'We're from Aurora, just south of Chicago. We have been visiting our daughter, who lives north of LA.' Jack is bald and round-faced, his loud yellow-checked shirt accentuating his paunch. They look an unlikely couple: she exudes class, in long cream pants, a soft green sweater and an expensive gold chain. She looks ten years younger than him.

'You on holidays?' Eileen smiles.

'Yes. I'm going to Chicago and then on to New York.'

'Australian?' Jack queries.

I nod. 'Kiwi originally, but I've lived in Australia for many years. In Melbourne.'

Eileen is staring out the window at the passing desert landscape. 'Did you enjoy your sleep, Greece?'

I look at her, blankly. 'I'm sorry, I didn't catch your question.'

'Morgan sends her regards, and asks if you had a good rest.'

'I have no idea what you are talking about.'

I'm starting to panic, and Eileen keeps talking. 'Morgan will be joining the train in Kansas City. We have sighted at least five of Eduardo's men on board. They are working in shifts. There is one group next door to your sleeper and some travelling in economy seats. Both Jack and I are in the sleeper car and we have another three agents on board. The DEA took ages to pick you up on the video at the border, and by the time they found you the train had arrived in LA. Jack and I are from the FBI. We will stay with you until Chicago.' She stands and stretches her legs. 'Train travel gives me cramps. We will meet you on the observation deck after we depart Albuquerque. Is there any message you wish to pass on?'

'I don't have any idea what you are talking about,' I reply, affecting a puzzled look. 'The only Morgan I know was the wife of a good friend who worked at the US embassy in Canberra. I think you have the wrong guy. However, I'm happy to have a drink with you on the deck later.' I can't play their game. I have no idea who they are, and they could be Eduardo's people. If it is a trap, and I go along with it, I won't make Chicago.

I am sitting on the deck for twenty minutes before Jack and Eileen call out to me. 'Hi, Keith, can we join you?'

Jack starts speaking. 'I've spoken to Morgan, and she said that Special Agent Kevin Takahashi, the DEA attaché at the US embassy, had a meeting with Justice Bernard Armstrong in Melbourne regarding your employment with the DEA. You have coached rugby at the University of Point Loma, and you were also the assistant coach in San Diego.' He is trying to prove his credentials and is right on both scores. 'Claudia and the children came to most of the games and you always stayed for the BBQ dinner with the team afterwards.' Right again. 'When you arrived in San Diego to work for the DEA, you stayed at the Holiday Inn, where you met Claudia and the children.'

Eileen has taken over the conversation now. 'You met Kevin Takahashi with Terry Houseman, a retired police commander in Australia who had worked for the FBI for fourteen years –'

I cut her off. 'Eileen, I believe you. Here is the message for Morgan. I have three million in the briefcase and I am delivering it to a law firm in New York. I have told Eduardo that I will only hand the cash to the partner he deals with personally. I know the DEA wants to nail this firm, but the agreement I have with Morgan is that they do not raid or arrest the partner until they have gathered a lot more information and I am safely back in Australia, so there is no link to me. There is no need for Morgan to get on the train. She should meet me in New York and witness me delivering the cash.'

'Thanks, Greece. We'll pass all this on. We won't be contacting you again but will continue to watch your back. Stay safe.'

Jack hands me his camera and asks if I would take some photos of Eileen and him together. 'Thank you,' he says, retrieving his camera. 'Best of luck to you.'

The train chugs into Chicago at five in the afternoon. By 10 pm, I am on the train to New York. I'm cursing myself for not taking the risk and flying. Even first-class train travel does not stop the nausea that continues for hours after I disembark.

I check into the Hilton Times Square Hotel, a few blocks from the law firm. Eduardo's men will have the area covered, as will the DEA and FBI. Morgan will be the team leader and will be waiting for me to leave the hotel. I recheck my instructions from Eduardo and drift into an uneasy sleep.

The law firm is Reynolds and Able. I have no appointment, but understand that Eduardo's people will have notified the lawyer, Christopher Gable, of my expected arrival. I take the elevator to reception on the twenty-first floor, greeted by an attractive girl in her early twenties who bids me a cheery good morning. 'May I help you, sir?'

'Yes, I am here to see Christopher Gable.'

'Do you have an appointment?'

'No, I'm afraid not.'

'Well, that is difficult. Mr Gable is one of the senior partners and he has a very busy schedule.'

'I understand, but I would appreciate it if you could advise him that I am here.' I hand over a typed note, giving the name Keith Wilson and the company Otago Bay Restaurants, La Paz, Mexico.

She looks at the piece of paper, and back at me. 'I will phone his assistant. May I tell her what this is about?'

'I'd prefer to discuss that with Mr Gable, if you don't mind.'

Her cheery demeanour is starting to fade. 'Take a seat.'

His personal assistant, a middle-aged woman with an officious air, emerges from her office. 'Mr Gable does not take unsolicited appointments,' she says, pursing lips stained with cherry-coloured lipstick at odds with her terse personality. 'I can make an appointment for you to see him, either later in the week, or next week. He is exceptionally busy.'

'Please check with him. He will see me.'

She sighs but does as I ask and goes to Gable's office. Less than a minute later, she is back, her cheeks now matching the colour of her lips. 'Please follow me, Mr Wilson. I am sorry, there seems to have been a lack of communication about this. I do apologise.'

'Accepted,' I answer. 'These things happen.'

Gable is standing by the window, which offers a picture-perfect view of the dramatic New York skyline. An antique desk has pride of place in the room and cedar bookshelves laden with law books line the walls. A photo of a much younger woman and two young children sits on his desk in an ornate silver frame. The office reeks of old money and high fees.

Gable, tall and slightly overweight, wears a pinstriped suit with a white shirt and red bowtie. He is clearly uncomfortable. He paces up and down, discourteously waving an arm for me to take a seat. His assistant offers coffee and he snaps in response. 'No. I do not wish to be disturbed. Please leave us.'

He launches into a tirade as soon as the door is closed. 'I have no fucking idea why you brought cash. The money should have been wired! Where the fuck do you suppose I bank three million dollars in New York?' I say nothing and he continues his verbal diatribe. 'I am feeling sick over this! Eduardo phoned me last night at home and announced that the cash was being delivered this morning. He was adamant I must accept it. Before I could say anything, he put the phone down. I couldn't call him back, he had switched his fucking phone off.' He is running his fingers nervously through his hair. 'I can't bank three million in cash! If my partners find out, I'm fucked! Working for these Mexican pricks gives me sleepless nights. I'm not charging enough, fuck them!'

I wait until he runs out of steam. This corrupt, greedy bastard has none of my sympathy.

'Let's do the following,' I order. 'Lock the door to this office, and then we will count the cash. You will phone Eduardo and tell him you have received it, and I'll speak to him as well. I will then bank the cash into your account, for a fee of a hundred thousand dollars, which you will pay me yourself. This will not come out of Eduardo's money. I want a receipt for the three million now, from your accounts department, and the cash will be banked into your account before lunch today. But I have to make some calls to arrange it. Do you understand me?'

'Yes.' He looks as though he is about to start crying.

'Pull yourself together,' I bark. 'Ring Eduardo now.'

He tells Eduardo that I have arrived and that we are about to start counting the cash. 'Put your cell on speaker, so Eduardo can hear us count it together,' I demand. I open the briefcase. It is stuffed with hundred–dollar notes sorted into bundles of one thousand each. At every ten thousand, we call out the figure. It takes fifteen minutes to get to the bottom of the pile. 'All counted,' I tell Eduardo. 'But we have a problem.'

'What problem? I don't like problems.'

'Gable is shitting himself over the cash. He doesn't know what to do. I've offered to bank it for him today in New York, and am charging him a hundred thousand dollars for the exercise. This fee isn't to be deducted from your money, nor is he to charge you the fee. I should bank it this morning.'

'Can you do it?'

'Yes, but it will take me a couple of hours to make some contacts. This is a one-off transaction, Eduardo, and the fees charged for this deal will be another thirty thousand to the banker I know. No one else will touch it. Gable can pay that as well.' I look up as he gives me a withering look. 'I don't think he's too happy about this.'

'That is his concern,' Eduardo laughs. 'I'll make sure he pays, Keith. Well done.'

'Thank me when I have completed the transaction. I want the hundred and thirty thousand dollars in cash from Gable within the hour, as I need to make calls and get the job done.'

Gable hangs up when I am finished. His fat cheeks have turned a nasty shade of grey. 'I am going to the accounts department,' he says. 'Wait here.'

I have no idea how I am going to bank the cash, but Morgan will make it happen. I need her recording device to tape the whole conversation. This is the evidence the DEA wants, but I will need to have their assurances that they will not arrest Gable until several months down the track. And I can't be linked to the tape in any way. I have to somehow make contact with Morgan without Eduardo's men seeing me.

47

Gable returns with the hundred and thirty thousand in cash. He is sweating and furious. A lot of awkward questions have been asked by the accounts department and he was ill-prepared. He gives me the cash and demands a receipt. I laugh at him. 'You are kidding. Give me the cash. I will be back in an hour for the briefcase.'

I head to a Starbucks coffee shop near the law firm and hunch into a rear booth. I don't know how to contact Morgan. I can't safely ring her from anywhere and I also know that Eduardo's men will have followed me. They will see I am not carrying a briefcase, so they will think I have made the drop-off.

I am deep in thought when I hear Morgan's voice. 'Good job, Greece.' She is sporting a Starbucks apron, looking like a staff member as she leans in and cleans my table. 'Our people followed you and Eduardo's boys are outside. The one we think is tailing you is buying a coffee now.'

'Morgan, listen. We haven't banked the cash. It is still upstairs in Gable's office and he is terrified. I am charging him to bank the cash this morning. Get me a recording device so I can tape the conversation of him handing over the three million.'

She doesn't stop cleaning the table. 'How the hell are you going to bank three million in cash here in New York?'

'You're going to arrange it, Morgan. We have an hour. Let me know which bank I can deposit it with and who to see. You've got to keep your hands off Gable and his law partners for at least six months, or I am a dead man. You have what your boss wants and more.'

I take my time after she leaves, dawdling over a coffee and using the public phone in the shop to make bogus phone calls. I return to my table and an hour later, a guy taps me on the shoulder. 'You finished with that newspaper?'

'Yep. Feel free.'

He reaches down to pick up the paper and drops a small package into my lap. 'Thanks,' he says.

'No problem.'

I pick up the package and head back to Gable's office. Inside are detailed instructions for the banking. I am to go to JP Morgan Chase Bank on Park Avenue and ask for Jason Bates, who will be expecting me. They have also supplied the recording device that looks like electronic car keys.

Gable looks even more unwell now than he did earlier, his bowtie removed and his top three shirt buttons undone. 'Okay, Mr Gable, I can bank the cash for you. Where is it?' He bends down and pulls the briefcase out from under his desk.

'I need to check it again, to be sure that we have the three million dollars in the case.'

'Are you suggesting I have taken some?'

'I'm not suggesting anything, Mr Gable. But we are banking Eduardo's cash to your trust account, and I want to make sure that the whole lot is there, otherwise it's my cock on the block. Let's check it again.'

When I am satisfied he hasn't touched the money, he hands me the firm's account details on a slip of paper. 'Can you read them to me again so I can double-check?' I need his voice for the tape, his instructions of the account number and confirmation of the cash. He doesn't twig to what I am doing. 'I will bank this within the next hour and come back with a receipt,' I tell him. 'Once we have confirmation from the bank that the money is in your account, we'll fax a copy to Eduardo and I'll be gone.'

'Thank Christ for that,' he says.

Jason Bates is unprepossessing: short, rotund and with cold eyes behind his bifocal glasses. 'Please follow me,' he says, turning on his heels.

Morgan and five other agents are waiting in his office. She is back in her normal clothing, and I recognise the guy who dropped the package. 'You're in the wrong game, Greece,' she says, taking my hand. 'Have you got the tape?'

'Yes. It's still recording.' She takes it and orders the money be counted and the receipt made ready. Bates opens the briefcase and feeds the cash through a counting machine.

Morgan turns to me. 'This is beautiful work, Greece. The director is going to be so happy. We have them in the bag! Let's bank the cash.'

I hand the account details over to Bates and he disappears through the doorway.

'Where is the hundred and thirty thousand?' Morgan asks me.

'Here.' She takes the cash, counts it and hands me back twenty thousand. 'Greece, this is for your efforts. The rest is DEA property now. You know that, don't you?' I figure I'm lucky to get twenty. It would be classified as proceeds of crime.

Bates reappears with three copies of the bank's confirmation that the money has been credited to the law firm's trust account.

'Well done, Greece, well done,' Morgan says. 'You are a credit to the agency. Now head back to La Paz, open the restaurant and go home.'

Gable is back to business as usual when I return to his office, the buttons on his shirt done up and his bowtie back in place. 'You want a coffee?' he asks.

'No, thank you. What I want is to get this finished.' I hand him the bank's confirmation of the three million and another copy for his records. 'We need to ring Eduardo again with the confirmation.'

His face hardens as his smarmy lawyer's attitude returns. 'After I check it myself.' He phones his office manager and waits while she checks the money is there. 'Accounted for,' he tells me.

Gable talks fast to Eduardo. 'The funds are in our account. We will get the ball rolling for you today and I will scan and email you the bank's confirmation.' There's a pause.

'He wants to talk to you.' Gable hands me the phone, scowling. He doesn't like to play second fiddle.

'Good work, Keith. Where did you bank the funds?'

'JP Morgan Chase Bank, 270 Park Avenue.'

'Can we use the source again?'

'No.'

'Pity. So you are leaving now for La Paz?'

'Yes. I will fly to Dallas and stay the night there. I'll be back in Mexico tomorrow.'

'I will be in touch.' He hangs up.

When the DEA closes down the firm in New York, the Arellano Félix cartel may link the bust to me. The DEA will advise the firm that they have been under surveillance for months and that several other people will be arrested as well, including me. Whether they buy the story, who knows? But right at the moment, all I want to do is sleep, and I ache to see Claudia. She has sent me at least fifty emails telling me she misses me, and that Paul is not important. I've ignored them all. Going to Norway isn't an option: I have got to stay away from her, as hard as that is.

I hail a taxi and head to the airport. This time tomorrow, I'll be back in La Paz, and on the downhill run for home.

48

The impact of violent Mexican criminals stretches far beyond Mexico's borders. There have been assassinations in Argentina, Peru and Guatemala, the killers arrested as far away as Italy and Spain. I am only too aware of the implications of this for me: I am at risk with other cartels, and even back in Australia I have to be alert. My only hope is my insurance package that will force the DEA to keep me safe.

The DEA is concerned about the increasingly complex strategies of cartel families. Historically, they had been content to transport South American narcotics through Mexico and then hand them over to US street gangs and other organisations for distribution inside the States. But in recent years, the Mexican groups have grown in power and have begun to take greater control of the entire narcotics-trafficking supply chain. With greater control over distribution and the reduction of middlemen comes greater profitability, and the cartels are looking for expanding markets like Europe. And expansion equals risk and escalating casualties.

I ponder an analogy for the roles I have played for the US Department of Justice, both for the DEA and FBI. It is like joining the French Foreign Legion, but the difference is when you serve with the French you are given citizenship, respect, honour, free medical benefits, a bonus payment and the right to call yourself a former legionnaire. With the US and Australian government agencies, you get a handshake, broken promises, lies and a blank denial that you ever worked for them. They say, 'We are protecting your security', and when you ask them for a letter, then the threats begin. Now I am back in the inner circle of the Arellano Félix cartel, I could be pressured to do another transaction in Mexico. I've got to get out, as fast as possible.

I wonder what the agency would do if I were to be attacked when I return home to Melbourne? Would they come to my aid? I doubt it. They would leave the situation to the local police to sort out, and that would bring with it its own dramas and nightmares. 'You worked for the DEA? Can we see some proof? You haven't got any?' Chances are, I would be locked up for lying to police or for being delusional. None of it is a cheerful prospect.

Staying here is worse. I don't want to become a drug war refugee. I don't want to end up like people who fall foul of the cartels, who are kidnapped, beaten and held captive in a death house, a tiny room no bigger than a gaol cell, with little ventilation. Those who miraculously survive their ordeal speak of their eyes being bandaged and being constantly beaten into unconsciousness. They can hear nothing but the screams of other captives being tortured and assaulted, and occasionally the desperate moan of a man, *Oh, my God!*, before a shot rings out, followed by an eerie silence.

After each torture or murder, the captors delight in gloating: 'You're next. Don't fall asleep – you have a long sleep coming!' Sometimes they remove the bandages from the prisoners' eyes and force them to witness an execution, the slitting of a victim's throat or a man burning to death, ramming a sock in their mouths so they will not cry out. 'This is how you are going to die,' they warn. 'This is how your end will come.' Some are spared execution and are instead put on the payroll to work for the cartels. Most flee to the States and seek the extradition of their enemies.

I send Claudia an email when I get back to La Paz. Mostly I lie, telling her I am happy that she and Paul are back together as a family unit. The truth is harder to tell: our time together was incredibly special and I still love her.

The restaurant opening is only days away. It normally takes months to complete a project in Mexico. They work on the principle of *mañana* (we will do it tomorrow). Protection from the cartels offers corrupt expedition of the work. It promises to be an interesting crowd at the unveiling: undercover DEA agents working the room, drug cartel members, owners of the shopping mall and government officials who would go to a stranger's funeral if they thought they might get some publicity.

The day before opening, Eduardo comes to see the restaurant with Santiago. 'It is a credit to you,' he says, looking around at the decor, admiringly. 'We should franchise the concept. I will speak to the owners. And I will make sure you get a percentage of the company.' He gets to the point of his visit. 'Well done in New York. It went very well. Santiago would like to do the same.'

My immediate thought is: fuck, I'm not doing that again.

'When are you planning to leave for Australia?'

'A week today. Why?'

'I would like you to travel via New York and London. I want you to nurse these pricks in New York and then go to London and close a couple of accounts for me. Nothing more, nothing less. You will not be compromised. I will buy your airline ticket home and cover your expenses.'

'Is this the last job?'

'Yes, it is.' Oh God, I want to believe him.

'And Santiago is hooking into the same system?' I don't wait for him to answer. 'I don't think that is a good idea. He should use other lawyers in New York and have funds sent from your account at the law firm to the new law firm. If one lawyer fucks up and gets caught, you need to be separate, so you can protect each other. And I would fire the lawyers once you have the accounts opened, because they are out of their depth and they will turn on you as soon as someone from the US government comes knocking on their door.'

'What do you suggest?'

'As soon as you have the accounts opened in Europe, send someone to another law firm in Switzerland to open new accounts, close the old ones and start covering your tracks. I am worried about the lawyers in New York coming clean if something blows up.'

'What are you telling us, that they are about to be raided by the US government?'

I realise I have said too much and quickly backtrack. 'No, I'm not saying that. What you should do is transfer the funds to an investment bank in Austria, and then I can collect the funds in cash and deposit them into another account for you. If you do this, then there is no record of the money after it has been transferred. The trail ends, and your cash is protected. But I will only do it for you, Eduardo. When I have completed the transaction, Santiago can manage himself. I am not confident about the lawyers in New York. They were shit-scared when I arrived with the cash.'

I outline the money trail. 'I'll open an account with the Austrian National Bank in New York and then have the law firm transfer the funds to them. I will then wire the funds to the Austrian National Bank in Salzburg, fly to Austria and take the funds out in cash. I'll catch a train to Switzerland and bank the money into an investment bank, Julius Baer, under a trust for you in Zurich. The money trail will end in Salzburg. No one will find your cash, and then you can transfer funds from the Caribbean to your new account in Switzerland.' Now I use a bargaining tool. 'You must protect my interests in Otago Bay Restaurants. I think it has a fantastic future in franchising, and I would like the twenty per cent equity I was originally offered. I will charge a fee for my services.'

'I will arrange everything for you,' Eduardo says, standing. 'You should work for us full-time.'

I manage a weak smile. 'Lovely offer,' I say. 'Thank you, anyway, but no.'

The restaurant opening is a huge success, with the usual suspects — officials, two-bit celebrities and politicians — vying for attention. Eduardo and Santiago do not attend, but they send some of their henchmen to make their presence felt. They stand languidly in the corner, too interested in the free tequila, beer and wine to care much about the other guests. The idea of fish and chips eaten from a paper cone has proved instantly successful. I give a speech, translated by an interpreter, thanking everyone whose name I can remember. When the last guest leaves, I sit alone in the restaurant, looking out at the dark waters of La Paz and sipping a chilled white wine. I miss my old life so badly.

I update Morgan by telephone about Eduardo's request. 'We will give you the green light and will raid the lawyer's office in New York within three months, not twelve,' she says. 'When does this all happen?'

'In four days. I'll tape the conversations, of course, and Eduardo will have me followed.'

'That's fine. We'll be tailing you as well.' I sense she wants to say more. 'Greece, we need your tapes, director's instructions. You will have to hand them over.' I know she is recording this conversation, as required by the director.

'What tapes?'

'Don't be foolish,' she says. 'You know what tapes.'

'The agency will never honour any agreement. I simply won't exist.'

'Greece, the tapes. If you do happen to find them, make sure they never reach the hands of the Mexican government, otherwise we are all in the shit. The cartels will have copies of them within hours of them being delivered to the government, and they will come for you.'

I land at New York Airport, with the car-locking device ready to record. This time, I am shown to Gable's office without any preamble. He looks even more nervous than he did last time. There is no small talk. 'Okay, what is the plan with the funds?'

I run him through the plan, quickly. 'Once we have opened the account, you will wire two million into that account. You keep the three hundred thousand in your trust, less your fees. Your involvement with the transactions will cease from today. I need written instructions that I have sole discretion over the account in Salzburg. You will write that instruction now. Do you understand?'

'Yes. Eduardo has made it clear that I should follow your instructions.'

The transaction goes smoothly at the bank. 'The funds will be wired into the account this morning,' I explain to the manager. 'I also want you to open a Euro account with your branch in Salzburg and wire the fees there.'

He nods. 'I can arrange all of that.' He takes a copy of my passport and has me sign an authority form giving me complete access to the money in Salzburg.

I am stopped by security as I enter the first-class lounge at the airport. 'Could we check your hand luggage, please, sir?' they ask. I don't think I have a choice. They usher me into a small room and close the door as one takes a cellphone from his pocket. He dials a number and hands the phone to me. It's Morgan. 'Hi, Greece.' The ingenuity of the DEA never ceases to amaze me. 'Well done. Give the recording to the guy who gave you the phone. Has the transfer been successful?'

'Yep. All the details of the accounts are on the tape. I will be able to collect the funds tomorrow.'

'Have a safe journey. We will have people in Switzerland and Salzburg to protect your back.'

UNDERCOVER

By late afternoon, I am in a plane climbing above New York City, heading to Europe. I close my eyes. Soon, all going to plan, I will be on a flight to Australia.

49

The bank manager is expecting me. I phoned ahead to make an appointment and he greets me formally. 'I trust you enjoyed your flight? How may I be of assistance?'

'I would like to withdraw some cash from my account, thank you.' I hand him the account details and my authority letter from the Austrian National Bank in New York.

He reads the details and asks for proof of identity, logging on to the computer. 'I am sorry, sir, but we cannot release the funds until tomorrow,' he says. 'They have to stay in our account for twenty-four hours, and we only received them this morning.'

I am furious. 'I requested immediate access from New York.'

'Yes, but we cannot release them until this time tomorrow.'

Any delay will cause immeasurable problems, particularly with Eduardo, but I can see by the bank manager's stance that he won't change his mind. Right about now, I'd like to scruff him by his pinstriped shirt.

'How much do you wish to withdraw?'

'Two million.'

I don't change expression but he does, his eyes bulging. 'Two million. In cash?'

'Yes.'

'I can't do that. We couldn't, sorry.' Now he is tripping over his words, clearly harried.

'Can't?' I repeat.

'Yes, can't. Perhaps we can arrange a few hundred thousand dollars, but the amount you require would need at least two weeks. Even then I would require head office and government approval, and the Austrian authorities would be all over this.'

'How much can you give me in cash tomorrow, without head office approval?'

He thinks for a moment. 'Two hundred thousand dollars.'

'I will need two hundred thousand tomorrow and the same amount the following day. I also need eight hundred thousand in American Express traveller's cheques tomorrow and the following day.' Traveller's cheques are as good as cash and there is no trace once they have been issued by the bank because the largest denomination they come in is one hundred dollars. That's a lot of cheques I'm going to have to sign to make up the eight hundred thousand.

He jerks his neck inside his shirt collar. 'It will take me a day to arrange this, but it will be ready for you by tomorrow.'

My first contact is with Eduardo. I explain the hold-up but am pleasantly surprised by his understanding. 'Take your time, do it right. I appreciate your call. Ring me when you are finished at the bank and you have the cash and cheques.'

My second call is to Morgan. 'The bank manager may contact the Austrian authorities,' I warn her. 'You need to make sure I am covered.'

'I will ensure the Austrian authorities seize the account and send it to us, and destroy any other records,' she assures me. 'I will close the door on any investigation.'

I prepare for the marathon signing ahead of me. That number of traveller's cheques is going to take me three days.

I am at the bank as soon as it opens the next morning and am immediately shown into the manager's office. He smiles, always a good sign. 'This will be a long day, so if we can start?' I say, wanting to move past the pleasantries. He waves me to a chair and produces the traveller's cheques. I psyche myself up for the task ahead and start signing my name, taking fifty minutes to get through the first one thousand cheques. I finish my first day just after 5 pm, and head back to the hotel with two hundred thousand in cash and a further eight hundred thousand in cheques.

The next day, I pay the hotel account in cash and call for a taxi. I return to the bank, and go through the same tedious routine. By the time I finish at 2 pm, I have cheques and cash totalling two million – minus the balance spent on bank fees – and a hand that aches from signing.

I have a bad feeling that my friendly bank manager has notified the Austrian authorities. 'Where are you off to now?' he asks, as I prepare to leave.

There is no way I am going to tell him the truth. 'The railway station,' I reply.

'May I call a taxi for you?'

'Thank you, please do. I would like to catch the train to Berlin, which leaves before 5 pm. I will wait outside.'

I know his phone call is going to be to the authorities, that there is no taxi being organised. I walk outside, flag down a cab and jump in. I have to leave the country without being taken in by the Austrians for questioning.

Salzburg is very close to the German border, around one hundred and forty kilometres, and the taxi driver is happy to take me there. There is no checkpoint on the German border and we arrive at Munich Railway Station just after 7 pm. There is a train leaving for Zurich within the hour.

A phone call to Morgan confirms that the US Department of Justice will take care of the Austrian authorities and I will no longer be on their radar. Morgan will also ensure that the Austrian National Bank won't take the issue any further.

I am at the investment bank by 8.30 am the following morning. I know the manager, Carl, from my days at Essex Finance when he worked at Barclays Bank in London. 'Go on through,' the receptionist smiles.

'Good to see you, Keith. It's been a long time,' Carl greets me warmly. 'Come on in.'

'Carl, I need you to look after this bag for me for the next two days. I shall need access to it daily.'

'Certainly. I'll have it placed in our main safety deposit box.'

'I also need to open a US nominee account for a client of mine. He wants to deposit one million today, and over the next two days a further million.'

'That's easy.' He switches on the computer and passes me an account number. He asks for a name of the nominee company holding the account. 'La Paz/Claudia/Cabo Bello,' I tell him.

I hand over two cards with a signature and a photo and thumbprint of the account holder. He takes them and gives me a password. The information I have provided all belongs to Eduardo. 'The account holder reserves the right to change the authority,' I tell Carl. Eduardo will now be able to access the account number online and use his password to transfer the funds anywhere in the world.

I open the briefcase and take out two hundred thousand dollars in cash and the traveller's cheques. I'm not looking forward to more signing, but when I finish, the deposit of two million will be in the account. On the final day I practically pound on the bank's door to be let in. I sign the cheques with a practised flourish and am so elated when I finish that I want to hug the starchy personal assistant who has popped in every hour, presumably to ensure I have not knocked off the crown jewels.

I look at my watch. 3.27 pm. British Airways leaves Zurich at 5 pm to London. From there, I'm booked with Qantas, right through to Melbourne.

50

I have two last things to do. From the airport, I dial
Eduardo's cellphone number, giving him his password and
account details. I ask him to access his account to verify the
amount that is in there, less the bank fees. Seven minutes
later, his voice comes back on the line. 'All here, Keith.'
There is an awkward silence for a few seconds, which he
fills. 'Thank you. If you ever want to work for me, full-
time, you have my number.'

'Thank you,' I reply, uncomfortably. 'I will keep that in
mind.'

My next call is to Morgan. She sounds as relieved as
I am that the transaction has been successful. 'We are all
extremely happy with the work you've done, Greece. We
will move on the law firm in the next few months.'

'Morgan, the DEA did not pay me what was promised.'

Another silence. 'I'm sorry, Greece. What can I say? It's
all out of my hands.'

'I figured that.'

She wants to change the subject. 'What are your plans,
now?'

'Plans? My only plan is to get this aircraft off the ground and get a stiff drink. I reckon I've earned one, Morgan.'

'I reckon you're right,' she laughs. 'Have one for me.' Her voice is serious again. 'Thanks again, Greece. You've done a remarkable job. You really have. Take care of yourself.' She is gone.

I am tempted to make one last call to Claudia, to hear her voice and tell her I am safe. But I think better of it. It is not the time. I should leave well enough alone. But I am sad beyond belief to lose her.

I settle into the Qantas flight from London and order a glass of champagne. The flight attendants' smiles are as big as the Australian outback and their accents music to my ears. 'Good evening, ladies and gentlemen. It is a pleasure to have you on board today's Qantas flight to Singapore and Melbourne. We aim to make your flight as pleasant as possible, but first we must demonstrate the safety features of this aircraft . . .' I switch off and close my eyes as the flying kangaroo roars down the runway and climbs over London.

I'm going home.

Aftermath

Russet autumn leaves skitter down Melbourne streets and there is a damp chill in the air, presaging winter. I have been back in the city three months, and revel in the safe familiarity of home with Susan.

But I am not the same man. Something has died in me.

My friends ask me to explain what I did in America and what Mexico was like. I lie, telling them I worked for the Department of Justice as a specialist in tracking money. And as I speak, their faces come to me again: the bleeding, wounded Colombian mumbling in his native Spanish in the hotel room, surrounded by his dead associates; the voice of the man in the basement, begging for mercy, *Por favor, no lo hagas*; and the girl, calm and surreal in the final seconds before her execution.

Most nights, I reach for a glass of red to soothe my nerves so I can sleep. Most nights, I drink more than one glass. Nothing helps. Solid, restful sleep evades me. During the day, my stupor sometimes lasts for hours, before I snap back to reality. I am sixty-three years old and walk the streets like a ghost.

The deceit and broken promises haunt me, too. I am still waiting on the outcome of the pardon petition. The move to Maribyrnong Immigration Detention Centre stalled the decision, despite recommendations by the Victorian parole board and the Immigration Department that working for the US government as a DEA agent in Mexico would significantly help.

In addition, they promised the matter with Pearce would be resolved and I would have an excellent chance of seeking gainful employment back in Australia. I do some work, casual mostly, but I will never again stride amongst the bankers and mortgage brokers in their immaculate suits as they hurry down Collins Street in Melbourne. After what I have seen, I no longer wish to.

I know that I was an expendable item, a pawn of the DEA. Worse, I cannot shake the feeling that the whole exercise was a set-up from start to finish.

Was I placed in that hellhole, Sirius East, not for my own protection but for the sole purpose of meeting Daniel Gómez?

Was a deal done between the United States and Victoria's Department of Justice?

Sometimes I wonder if Claudia, that spirited woman who gave me back my sense of worth, who made me remember the beauty of love, was a set-up too. She never panicked, hardly asked any questions. Was that because she already knew the answers? I hear nothing from her. Her emails, beseeching me to change my mind and move to Oslo, remained unanswered for so long she gave up writing. It doesn't stop me missing her.

Pearce has mounting police evidence against him, including proof that he deals illegal steroids and had a close associate who dealt cocaine. The associate's contact in the cocaine trade operated out of Mexico with the Arellano Félix cartel. He travelled to the US and entered Mexico as a tourist, arranging a transhipment of cocaine to Australia and was arrested on his return. He died in prison. Rumour has it that Pearce has taken over this role in the Australian arm of the sugar industry, another nasty player in the Melbourne underworld. Police are also looking into his suspicious tax history and claims that he committed fraud in order to acquire properties. Pearce has bigger problems than me to worry about now.

Our children have made Susan and I proud: Mark and Kate both completed university degrees and have top jobs, and Sam is a pilot. He doesn't dwell on the past. *What's done is done*, he shrugs, and neither Kate nor Mark will discuss what they endured while I was in prison: the car bombings, death threats and intimidation. They turn away, and I am impotent with shame. Susan and I still share a house, but she can't forgive what has happened, and I avoid the accusatory look in her eyes whenever the past is mentioned. We are locked in a holding pattern, a strange dance from which we feel we cannot escape. I have let her down and need to make amends.

The DEA has moved on the law firm in New York, arresting Gable and others implicated in the sting. So far it has not been traced back to me, but I live in fear of the cartels tracking me down and have a phobia about closed rooms.

I need to be able to see some light. Swimming, walking and running help, but they don't stop the nightmares, don't stop my terror and don't stop my night sweats. My life in America and Mexico seems like an eternity ago.

I hear from no one there, except one brief phone call from Morgan, two months after I arrive home, telling me she is retiring. 'My work is done, Greece,' she said. 'How about you? How are you getting on?'

I tell her the truth. 'It's a struggle, Morgan. I feel like I'm looking over my shoulder all the time.'

'Greece, you know what?' she says. 'You are right to look over your shoulder. You always should. Take care of yourself.'

I devour any news of Mexico and the DEA. Arrests of cartel leaders continue, as does the shocking death toll. But if authorities hope that another murder spells the death knell of the cartels, they are wrong. New breeds inevitably step up to fill the power vacuum, hungry for fame and with inherited, corrupt links to law enforcement officers. The unbreakable hierarchy of the past may be gone, replaced by a splintering of criminal cells, but Mexican authorities have not seen the last of the major cartel families.

David Shirk, Director of the Trans-Border Institute at the University of San Diego, gives this blunt warning: 'Old cartels don't seem to go away. They just seem to morph into new variants over time. There's strong continuity for these organisations, dating back multiple generations of smugglers.'

Far from reducing the violence, Mexican authorities have witnessed unprecedented bloodshed in clashes between cartels. Worse, amalgamation between some groups has created an unholy alliance that strikes fear into officials. Mangled and mutilated bodies are left like human garbage around Tijuana, their tongues cut out and heads chainsawed off. Human remains are left to disintegrate in barrels of acid, strewn conspicuously on busy streets.

'The problem,' a DEA agent once confided to me, 'is that Mexico and Colombia can furnish supply, and the United States can furnish demand. It's a filthy, filthy marriage.' So the violence and corruption continue. Every night, city streets across Mexico are rent with the wails of grieving mothers, the screams of victims begging for mercy and the piercing sirens of police and ambulance vehicles racing towards yet another murder scene. Every night, city streets across Mexico are a war zone. And every night, I thank God I'm out of there.

As winter closes in, a package arrives from an unmarked sender. I open it in the lounge room when no one else is around. Inside are DEA tapes of conversations I had with cartels in Mexico City. I play one and suddenly I am no longer in Melbourne but back in Mexico, in that stinking hotel room surrounded by dead bodies.

Inside the package I also find a highly confidential DEA report of the shoot-out in Mexico City.

The actual positions of the bodies and bloodstains appear to be the main corroboration of the investigation and construction of the event methodology as captured on cellphone camera by Greece and emailed to the DEA San Diego field office. There are no (known) witnesses to this event in the hotel suite, although there was a hotel employee – a housemaid – apparently working in the corridor close to the entrance door to the suite, vacuuming the carpet. She did not report the incident. The housemaid's failure to report the gunshots may be attributed to any number of factors: the noise of the vacuum cleaner drowned out the sound; the solid oak door to the suite may have deadened the sound; the housemaid may have been wearing and listening to an iPod; a combination of the above or simply that she heard the gunshots, but did not want to become involved by reporting the matter.

I often wonder how I managed to escape a bullet. The best I can come up with is that I was not armed. Violence breeds violence so, by not being aggressive, I was able to escape with my life. Or I was just lucky.

The tapes and report are US government property, highly sensitive. I take copies and send them to Canada, Asia, New Zealand and Europe, while ensuring the originals are in safekeeping. I don't know who has sent me this gift, but I can guess. There is one last item in the package, smaller than the rest, and I chuckle as I turn it over. A Starbucks coffee card. I quietly thank my anonymous sender.

Acknowledgements

I would like to thank my agents Lauren Miller Cilento and Therasa Jazowy from the Harry M Miller Group for their wisdom, patience and help in securing a publisher.

I am indebted to Debi Marshall, her husband and her mother for endless hours of guidance, support and editing.

I also would like to thank Geoffrey Hossack for his feedback and encouragement.

Alison Urquhart and all the staff at Random House have been wonderful in their support and especially their judicious editor, Maisie Dubosarsky, who has helped me unlock so many doors in my story.

I don't know how to thank my family, both in Australia and New Zealand, for their encouragement, patience and understanding.

Finally, to my fellow early morning swimmers, the Dendy Icebergers – thank you for your good humour and honest opinions.

Keith Bulfin is a New Zealander, born in 1946. He grad-
uated with a Bachelor of Arts from the University of
Queensland with a double major in Economics in 1983.
He has worked in the finance industry in South Africa
and the UK, and for the University of Papua New Guinea
as an administrator and lecturer in Accounting. Working
in the Australian investment banking industry as a share
and mortgage broker in the 1980s, he pleaded guilty to

a conspiracy to defraud over the valuations of Lasseters Casino and Dreamworld.

Keith spent three years in a Supermax prison, where he was introduced by prison authorities to two Mexican fugitives. It was his friendship with them that led to his recruitment by the US Department of Justice to operate a covert banking operation in Mexico for the Mexican drug cartels. He was then reassigned to Washington, DC and the FBI to operate a covert bank, targeting Middle Eastern countries and terrorist organisations. He has worked as an expert advisor on money laundering with the National Security Council in Mexico, various foreign governments, policing agencies and multinational companies.